the dream of the stone

the dream of the stone

Christina Askounis

Simon Pulse
New York • London • Toronto • Sydney

SIMON PULSE

An imprint of Simon & Schuster Children's Publishing Division

1230 Avenue of the Americas, New York, New York 10020

Copyright © 1993 by Christina Askounis

All rights reserved, including the right of
reproduction in whole or in part in any form.

SIMON PULSE and colophon are registered
trademarks of Simon & Schuster, Inc.

Book design by Steve Kennedy

The text of this book was set in Hiroshige Book.

Manufactured in the United States of America

First Simon Pulse edition April 2007

2 4 6 8 10 9 7 5 3 1

Library of Congress Cataloging-in-Publication Data

Askounis, Christina.

The dream of the stone / Christina Askounis

p. cm.

Summary: Fifteen-year-old Sarah discovers that her brilliant older brother's top-secret research for the Institute involves interstellar travel and a threat to a planet millions of light-years away.

ISBN-13: 978-1-4169-3568-1 (hc.)

ISBN-10: 1-4169-3568-1 (hc.)

ISBN-13: 978-1-4169-1187-6 (pbk.)

ISBN-10: 1-4169-1187-1 (pbk.)

[1. Fantasy] I. Title.

PZ7.A8374Dr 2007

[Fic]—dc22

2006005201

The author would like to thank Dr. John A. Wheeler of Princeton University, for permission to quote from an article by him.

"Running to Paradise," by William Butler Yeats, was published in
The Collected Poems of W. B. Yeats, The Macmillan Company, 1956.

This book is for
the Elizabeths in my life—
my daughter and my mother,
here and There—
and for Laurel,
wise teacher, kind friend,
sine qua non.

Author's Note
to the New Edition

Much time has passed since the original publication of *The Dream of the Stone*. One of my very first readers, a boy who gladdened my heart by pronouncing *Dream*, "the best book I've ever read," will soon earn his PhD. My children, who played make-believe games in the hallway outside my study while I wrote early drafts, have now grown up and are living their own lives—one around the corner and one across the Atlantic.

I think it was Isabel Allende who said that once a book is finished, it's like a child who moves out and gets his own apartment. The book has a new life out in the world, with those fascinating strangers, its readers. The author, too, moves on, takes up new projects, does something with the now empty space that the writing of the book once occupied.

When I received the news that Simon & Schuster wanted to introduce *The Dream of the Stone* to a new generation of readers, I was of course delighted. Because of the resurgence of interest in fantasy in recent years, I had hoped to see it back in print, and my agent at International Creative Management, Lisa Bankoff, along with her enterprising assistant Tina Dubois Wexler, had taken up the cause. But I confess that I also felt a bit of trepidation. Books are mysterious things; they change as we change, because we bring a different self to the page when we return to any book. Sometimes it seems almost unrecognizable. What would I find?

Like Sarah who hides out in the library, seeking solace in the books she loved as a child, I sat down to read. And again like Sarah, I found that the characters—Sarah herself, Angel, Sam, Miladras—greeted me like old friends and drew me back into their world, a world that sprang once more to life. As happens in the best of friendships, we simply picked up where we had left off. With the aid of my wonderful new editor, Susan Burke, I went over *Dream* line by line to prepare it for its encore, smoothing a cowlick here, tying a loose shoelace there, all the while growing more excited, more hopeful as I thought of its venturing out upon a new life in a new century, a time when courage and love surely matter more than ever, when we must all brave the darkness and seek the Light.

Christina Askounis
Durham, North Carolina
Easter 2006

I keep saying to myself, "What is it? What is it?" It's something. It can't be nothing! I don't know its name so I call it Magic. . . . Sometimes since I've been in the garden I've looked up through the trees at the sky and I have had a strange feeling of being happy as if something were pushing and drawing in my chest. . . . Magic is always pushing and drawing and making things out of nothing. Everything is made out of Magic, leaves and trees, flowers and birds, badgers and foxes and squirrels and people. So it must be all around us. In this garden—in all the places.
    —FRANCES HODGSON BURNETT, *The Secret Garden*

There may be no such thing as the "glittering central mechanism of the universe" to be seen behind a glass wall at the end of the trail. Not machinery but magic may be a better description of the treasure that is waiting.
    —ASTROPHYSICIST JOHN A. WHEELER

You must do the thing you think you cannot do.
    —ELEANOR ROOSEVELT

one

Thursday's Child

Outside the March sky was gray and overcast, threatening snow, but in Sarah Lucas's room a fire blazed in the blue-tiled fireplace, and the lamp beside her canopy bed cast a cheerful light. Balancing *Wuthering Heights* on her knees, she poured a second cup of tea from the small brown teapot on the bedside table, took a bite of toast, and licked the honey from her fingers. There was homework to be done, but it could wait.

Now and then she glanced at her watch. Her parents were flying all the way across the country from California in a small plane they had rented. If there was a snowstorm coming, she hoped they would arrive before it did. Both her mother and her father were good pilots, and Sarah knew it was possible to fly above a storm, but sooner or later you had to come down.

This morning, walking the quarter mile down the gravel lane to wait for the school bus, she had thought she smelled snow in the air. But not a single flake had fallen all day. There was only the dull, looming sky, the color of smoke, the same sky every time she looked out the classroom windows, and again when she got off the bus that afternoon and started up the lane. It weighed on her like a heavy coat. She'd been glad to get out from under it, to get home and make tea and carry the tray up to her room.

She heard the doors to the kitchen cupboards downstairs being opened and shut, opened and shut. Mrs. Woodley, the woman who stayed with Sarah whenever her parents were gone, could never seem to find things in their kitchen.

The smell of bay leaves and onions simmering in a beef stew drifted up the stairs, and mingled with it, the dark, seductive scent of a chocolate cake in the oven. Mrs. Woodley always baked her blue-ribbon fudge cake the night Sarah's parents came home. Her father had a weakness for chocolate and pretended to swoon whenever he slid the first bite into his mouth.

Sarah got up to poke the fire, staring into the flames for a long moment, then hopped back into bed and leaned against the pillows, surveying her room. It was just what she'd always wanted, her blue and white bedroom, with its forget-me-not wallpaper and window seat and braided rug. Sarah was eight years old before her parents—freelance journalists who traveled around the world covering news stories—decided it was time for the family to stop living out of suitcases and settle down at Sycamore Farm. Now she was fourteen, but she still felt a kind of wonder that this was *her* house, *her* room. It had been a dream for so long, the one thing Sarah wished for at night when she saw the first star through the windows of hotels or rented houses. The view from the windows changed—pagoda roofs, a market square, spires and golden domes, or nothing but an air shaft and a brick wall so near she might have touched it if she had dared to lean out the window—but if there was a patch of sky and a star, she made the wish, and it was always the same.

Not that it hadn't been fun, in a way, all the moving around. It could have been a lonely life, but it wasn't. Even though her parents had been gone a lot, Sam was always there. Her brother was four years older, but they were friends. They'd had to be; for years neither of them had anyone else to play with. But they would have been friends anyway. Different as they were, they shared everything, even the same birthday in May.

She dipped the last triangle of toast into her cold tea, careful not to drip on her book, and wondered if Sam would be coming home too. Her parents had flown to California to try to persuade him to leave the Institute, where he'd been working since he finished graduate school. When Sam was offered the job, they were excited for him. But then Daddy started asking questions: Who was behind the Institute? Where did it get its money? Sam came home one weekend, and his first night back they argued all through dinner.

He didn't come home again after that. Sarah wasn't sure why; maybe he was busy, or maybe he didn't want to face Daddy's and Mother's questions. So last week they'd gone to him.

A newspaper photo of Sam, tacked on the bulletin board over the rolltop desk, grinned at her from across the room.

His picture had been in papers all over the country when he got his doctorate. "Boy Wonder," the headlines had called him, because he was the youngest PhD—barely eighteen—in Caltech's history.

It hadn't seemed so remarkable to anyone who knew him. Their parents liked to tell the story of how, when Sam was two, they went to check on him in the middle of the night and found him wide awake in his crib, staring into the dark. When they asked him what he was doing, he answered, "Watching the numbers." He had to watch them in his head, he explained, because he couldn't write yet. "Shall we write them down for you?" they offered. "Yes, please," Sam said.

The numbers turned out to be algebraic equations.

The story found its way into the newspaper articles, along with other Sam stories: how he had taught himself multi-variable calculus at eight, won a full scholarship to study physics at Oxford when he was twelve. "Your brother must be weird," a girl at school had said to Sarah when the news of Sam's PhD appeared.

"He is not!" Sarah had snapped back.

And he wasn't, she thought, pulling her quilt up over her knees. Not in the way the girl had meant. Sam was just Sam. He talked to himself when he was thinking hard. And he did look like a mad scientist when his cowlick stuck straight up and his glasses were crooked. But his glasses weren't the awful, thick kind—they were gold wire and tortoiseshell, and they matched the reddish brown of his hair; they made him look old-fashioned in an interesting way, like a poet in a tin-type. Sam liked baseball and old cars, and twice, for about a month each time, he'd had a girlfriend. What made Sam different hardly showed on the outside. He was . . . Sarah nibbled on a crust, thinking. Intense, that was the word. The way certain colors were intense. Like the blue of the king-fisher. They'd seen one on the river Isis, in Oxford. They were gliding along in a punt, and Daddy was explaining how Lewis Carroll had told the story of Wonderland to the real Alice on this very same river, when suddenly there was a flash of brilliant blue high in the trees and a kingfisher flew across the water. The last time Sam was home, he'd stretched out on the rug by the fire while Sarah did her homework. He was so quiet she'd almost forgotten he was there, when suddenly he said, "Remember the kingfisher?" The urgency in his voice made it seem like the most important thing in the world.

And maybe it was. For the memory had lifted her out of the gray wasteland of her civics textbook into a dazzling green world where anything might happen.

Come home, Sam. Sarah sighed and put her empty cup on the bedside table. But Mother didn't seem to have much hope that Sam would change his mind and leave the Institute.

"Obstinate child!" her mother had said the night before she and Daddy left for California. "Can't think where he gets it from." She said the last with a wry smile. It was a family joke that Sam's mulishness was matched only by Mother's. Beneath the smile, though, Sarah sensed her mother's anxiety about Sam. But there wasn't any point in trying to talk about it; she would only say that Sarah "wasn't to worry."

Sarah had sat on the bed in her parents' room, watching her mother stuff socks into the corners of her suitcase. "I don't think you're going to need wool socks in California, Mother."

"No?" Her mother ran her hands through her fluff of light brown hair. She had grown up in northern England and spent her childhood in a country house. On winter mornings she'd had to break a crust of ice on the water jug before she could wash her face. It went against her grain to go anywhere without warm socks.

Sarah liked to imagine her mother as a little girl in Yorkshire, riding her pony out on the moors like Cathy Earnshaw in *Wuthering Heights*. There was still something of the country girl in her mother's pretty face, all cream and roses, like a china teacup, and in her candid blue eyes. Sarah's own eyes were greeny brown, like the water in the pond in summer. Her hair ("It's not just plain brown, sweetie," her mother always said, "it's a lovely chestnut") was heavy and thick and stick straight, just like Sam's, only long. Sarah wore it in a single braid down her back. She thought it made her look a little like the artist she wanted to be one day.

"The desert can be quite cold at night, you know," Mother went on, searching her pockets. Sarah spotted her mother's glasses on the dresser and reached for them. "Oh, thanks, darling. Where was I? Oh yes, the cold in the desert. You probably don't remember that time in Egypt—no, you wouldn't, you were only eighteen months old . . ." She stopped in midsentence and looked around the room, her hands on her hips. "I'm forgetting something, I just know it."

"Cameras? Film?" Sarah suggested, although they were the last things her photographer mother would forget. She might be hopelessly disorganized when it came to housework or remembering dates—more than one guest had shown up for dinner only to be greeted by Margaret Lucas with a blank *What on earth are you doing here?* look on her face—but where photography was concerned, she was methodical.

"The equipment's all packed, though I imagine most of

the Institute is no-go to photographers. Secretive bunch, those people. Aha!" She held up a finger. "Shower cap!"

Sarah followed her into the bathroom and sat on the edge of the tub. "Who *are* 'those people,' Mother?"

"Well . . ." Sarah knew her mother was weighing how much to tell her as she studied the contents of the medicine cabinet. "That's just it, darling—we hardly know anything about them, and no one else seems to, either. Your father's been poking around for months trying to turn up information, and you know how persistent he is."

"But Sam must know. He works for them."

Her mother looked away. "He knows what they choose to tell him. And he doesn't appear to *want* to know anything else. That's what bothers us." She leaned down, patted Sarah's cheek, and brushed the hair from her eyes. "Anyway, pet, you're not to worry. Don't you want me to trim your fringe before I go? I don't know how you can see with all that hair in your eyes. You look like a terrier."

"I can see perfectly well. And they're called *bangs*, Mother. This is America." Even after twenty-five years of marriage to an American from Brooklyn, Sarah's mother had never quite shed her peculiar British vocabulary.

"So it is." Her mother headed back into the bedroom empty-handed and preoccupied. Sarah gazed at her. How small her shoulders looked; they made her seem fragile somehow, in need of protection, as if she were the child and Sarah the mother. Sarah plucked the shower cap from its hook on the back of the bathroom door and went to help her mother finish packing.

❁

A muffled cry at the window interrupted her thoughts. Ozymandias, their honey-colored tomcat, glared at her through the glass. Snow was falling.

"All right, all right." Sarah threw back the quilt and got out of bed. Ozzie liked to climb the sycamore tree outside the window and jump onto the sill. He was yowling, scolding her for being so slow, though she could hardly hear him. She knelt on the window seat and raised the sash, the screen, and finally the storm window, letting in Ozzie and a gust of frigid air that sent her homework papers sailing off the bed.

"Forgive me for tarrying, O King of Kings," she said as he darted past.

Already a drift of white had collected on the windowsill and along the pale arms of the sycamore. She leaned out and peered into the gathering dusk, feeling the snow's tiny stings on her face. The pond's surface was tarnished pewter, the stand of pines on the other side no more than a dark smudge, like the suggestion of trees in a charcoal drawing. Beyond them the empty fields stretched, white earth meeting white sky along an invisible horizon.

The room was growing cold; she closed the window. For a moment the light seemed to dim, as if a shadow had fallen over the house. The flames in the fireplace wavered and shrank. The snow was falling faster now, sticking to the glass. Soon it would be impossible to see out.

Because of the snow she did not hear the crunch of tires on gravel as a car came up the lane, turned into the drive, and stopped. But Ozymandias did. He stretched and yawned, revealing sharp white teeth and the pink, ridged roof of his mouth, then leaped off the bed and trotted downstairs as the doorbell rang.

Sarah slipped her moccasins over her socks, padded down the hall, and looked out the front window. Through a small patch of glass not yet covered by snow, she could see a black-and-white state police car.

There were voices in the dining room. They stopped when she was halfway down the stairs.

The state trooper was a large man; standing in front of the china cabinet, he blocked it almost completely. He held a wide-brimmed hat. There was an indentation in his glossy cropped hair where the hat had been.

Mrs. Woodley sat at the dining-room table, her hand over her mouth. She looked stricken. "Oh, Sarah, honey." Mrs. Woodley reached for her clumsily. Sarah's hip bone pressed painfully against the arm of the chair.

"What's wrong?" Sarah asked, looking at the trooper. "What's the matter?"

Ozymandias leaped onto the mantel above the fireplace, where he wasn't allowed to be, and threaded his way among the photographs.

"There's been an accident." The state trooper ran his fingers along the brim of his hat.

Sarah felt suddenly cold, clammy, the way she had a few weeks ago when she was coming down with the flu. The stripes on the wallpaper shifted and jumped out at her.

"We just received a call from the state police in California. Your parents' plane went down in the Sierra Nevada. I'm very sorry."

"Down? You mean it crashed?"

"We're not sure exactly what happened—the engine appears to have failed. They were evidently trying to land when they ran into some heavy fog. The plane hit the side of a mountain and just"—he looked down—"disintegrated."

"But they're all right, aren't they? They're okay?"

The trooper shook his head.

"Are you saying they're dead? My parents?"

"I'm terribly sorry."

"And Sam? Sam, too?"

"Your brother wasn't with them. He's been notified. He's on his way."

Sarah couldn't breathe, couldn't think. In the fireplace a solitary ember glowed, blinked, and went out. She turned and walked to the front door and opened it, staring blankly into the small enclosed area they called the mudroom, where the firewood was stacked.

Mrs. Woodley's chair scraped across the floor. "Sarah, honey, where are you going?"

"Outside."

"But you haven't even got a coat—wait!" She turned and rummaged through the hall closet.

Sarah stood with her arms out, like a child being dressed, as Mrs. Woodley drew the coat up over her shoulders. The coat was her mother's. It smelled of her favorite perfume.

"You can't go out in your moccasins! It's snowing!" Mrs. Woodley cried. "Put on your boots!"

But Sarah was already out the front door, walking down the narrow flagstone walk, past the bare dogwood and crab apple trees, between the cars parked in the drive, up the lane, and into the woods, while all around her the snow kept falling.

❉

The year they moved to the farm, just before Sam went off to Oxford, he and Sarah built a tree house in the woods. It had been a long time since they'd played there together, but Sarah still went to the tree house whenever she wanted to be alone, scaling the short, makeshift ladder. On summer afternoons she climbed up to the roof and lay dreaming in the leaf-light.

Now she stumbled along the path, feet aching with cold. Color drained from the world as the light left it; the trees looked black; the smell of smoke hung in the air. She reached the solitary oak and threw her arms around its massive trunk and hung on as the world slipped from its axis and spun crazily into space.

Mother. Daddy. She dug her fingernails into the rough bark and pressed her forehead against it until the pain sent flares shooting through her head. *Oh, God, please let it not be true, let it be a nightmare and let me wake up now, God. . . .*

There was a noise over her head, the creak of a board. She looked up. Through the cracks in the tree house floor she saw a flame. For a second she wondered wildly if the tree house was on fire.

No. There was someone up there. A vagrant probably, one of the homeless men who wandered into the nearby town now and then, following the little-used railroad tracks that ran through a corner of their property.

She picked up a dead branch and hurled it at the tree house.

"Get out of here! Can't you read?" She swiped at her tears, her streaming nose. "It says 'No Trespassing'! 'No Trespassing'!" She threw a rock this time, knocking snow from the boards.

The door to the tree house swung open. Sarah stepped back.

An old woman crouched in the doorway, peering down at her. With the toe of an enormous black rubber boot she nudged something toward the opening. It was a coffee can full of burning sticks. The smoky fire cast undulating shadows on a face crisscrossed with thousands of tiny lines, like the glaze on ancient porcelain. But her eyes were anything but old. They were gray and clear and fathomless, like a little child's.

"Your house," she said. Her stained duffle coat was fastened at the collar with a pink plastic diaper pin.

"Yes." Sarah felt her face redden. Her mother had always been kind to the homeless people who came to the door, sending them away with a sandwich and sometimes a few dollars. "You . . . you can stay here if you want."

Black ashes, light as butterflies, floated out the door and up into the sky.

The woman looked at Sarah's moccasins, then at her face. "You need real shoes. Traveling shoes. 'Thursday's child has far to go.'"

She's crazy. And then, with a tiny electrical jolt, Sarah remembered sitting on her mother's lap in the rocking chair:

"'Monday's child is fair of face,'" her mother had recited, "'Tuesday's child is full of grace, Wednesday's child is full of woe, . . .'"

Sarah had been disappointed when her mother said she was Thursday's child. She would much rather have been fair of face, like Monday's, or better yet, "bonny and blithe, good and gay," like Sunday's.

Mother. Sarah brought her hand to her mouth, rocking to and fro.

The woman was watching her, motionless.

She knows, Sarah thought. *She knows about Mother and Daddy. No—that's wrong, she can't know, she's just a poor old woman. . . .*

Sarah pulled three crumpled dollar bills from the pocket of her jeans, the change from a five she had used to pay for her school lunch that day. That day? A thousand years ago, in another world. The door to that world had closed behind her, never to be opened again.

"Here . . ." She stepped on the first rung of the ladder and reached up with the money. The old woman bent to take it. For an instant Sarah thought she smelled roses. The woman spread the bills out, one by one, examining them in the firelight as if she'd never seen money before.

"Thank you," she said.

Sarah walked away. Behind her the old lady called out something she couldn't understand, something crazy, about being waylaid. Before Sarah had gone far, she saw the beam of a flashlight bobbing through the trees and heard the state trooper calling her name.

Orphans

That night in the empty airport terminal Sarah sat on a hard orange plastic chair and waited for Sam. Father Griffiths waited with her. He was the rector of the small Episcopal church in town and an old friend of the family. He'd come the moment he heard the news, leaving his houseful of children, and stayed all evening to field calls and answer the door. Sarah hadn't wanted to see anyone. Father Griffiths turned people away, brought tea to her room, and kept the fire going until it was time to leave for the airport.

In the small waiting area the clock on the wall registered each passing minute with a click. There was a coffee stain like a starburst on the speckled tile at her feet. Beside her Father Griffiths leafed through a newspaper someone had left behind. She was grateful for his silence. He'd sat on the edge of the bed in her room and held her while she cried, as though she were one of his own children. But kind as he was, she'd felt awkward in his embrace. She needed Sam. She ached for him.

It was after midnight when the drone of an approaching engine broke the silence, and she stepped outside into the cold, under the icy, glittering stars. She could see her breath.

The last time Sam had come home, she and her parents had stood waiting as the Institute's private jet appeared out of the clouds. They had teased Sam about having a jet plane all to himself, like a millionaire. Sam hadn't liked it, Sarah remembered. He'd gotten all prickly.

The same sleek white jet landed smoothly and taxied to a halt, lights blinking. A man rolled a set of metal steps up to the door of the plane, and after a moment Sam appeared, carrying a small suitcase. He wore the old, beat-up leather bomber jacket he always wore and the Brooklyn Dodgers baseball cap their father had surrendered to him years ago. He saw her, started down the stairs.

"Sam!" Sarah ran the last few yards across the runway.

At the bottom he staggered off the last step, caught his balance, carefully put his suitcase on the concrete, and opened his arms to her. He'd been crying.

They stood embracing for a long time, holding each other so tightly she could hardly breathe.

"Sam, I keep thinking I'm going to wake up."

"I know," he said. "I know."

They walked to Father Griffiths's station wagon, arms around each other's waist. Sarah got in the middle and took Sam's hand as he slid in next to her.

They pulled out onto the highway. The radio was on. News. Hope for renewed negotiations in the Middle East, an earthquake in Central America, and then: "Charles and Margaret Lucas, the well-known husband-and-wife photojournalist team, were killed today when their small rented plane crashed in a wilderness area in the . . ."

Father Griffiths lifted a hand from the steering wheel and was about to turn off the radio.

"No," Sam said. Sarah felt him brace himself against the seat. His eyes were closed.

"The couple," the news cast continued, "who co-authored numerous books and won the Pulitzer Prize for their coverage of the fall of Saigon, were returning from a visit to their son in California. . . ."

Sam was squeezing her hand, hard. The light from the arc lamps along the highway streamed over them.

"They left freelance journalism six years ago when Charles Lucas took over as editor of the *Westminster Dispatch*. Under his leadership the paper has received national recognition for investigative reporting. No reason has been given for the crash. Next up: sports."

Father Griffiths reached for the knob and silenced the voice.

When they arrived home, Mrs. Woodley had beef stew warming on the stove and a loaf of fresh bread on the kitchen table. She offered to spend the night. Sam politely but firmly sent her away. Tomorrow morning Uncle Bernard and Aunt Helena would arrive. In the meantime, Sam said, they would be fine on their own.

He closed the door behind Mrs. Woodley and let out a long breath. Then he went to the liquor cabinet in the dining room, took out a bottle, and carried it into the kitchen. Sarah followed him from room to room, not meaning to, just wanting to be where he was. He took a glass from the kitchen cupboard and filled it halfway.

She stood watching with her hands in her coat pockets as

Sam sat down at the kitchen table, took a big swallow, and made a face.

"What are you drinking?" Sarah asked.

He turned the bottle around and looked at the label. "Bourbon." They were silent. "Sarah," Sam said, "have you ever seen me drunk?"

"I've never seen you drink."

"That's what I mean. Don't worry, okay? Why don't you sit down, have some of that soup or whatever it is?" He waved at the stove.

Sarah hung her coat on the back of a chair, turned the flame off under the pot of stew, poured some ginger ale into a glass, and sat down. The ginger ale was flat. Her mother had bought it for her two weeks ago when she had the flu, bringing it to her on a tray with a glass of crushed ice.

Sam picked at the label on the bottle of bourbon. His face was blotchy, and his eyes behind his round glasses were red and swollen. He looked as if he'd been in a fight. The glass in front of him was empty now. She couldn't remember seeing him take a second swallow.

"If I had come home like they wanted me to," he said, "they'd still be alive."

She didn't understand. "But then you would have been on the plane! You would've been killed too!"

"No . . ." His face twisted, as if her failure to grasp his meaning caused him physical pain. "I mean if I had come home *before*, when they wanted me to. If I had left the Institute. Damn it!" He hit the table with both fists, making the glasses jump.

"That doesn't mean it's your fault!" She circled the table

and put her arms around him. He was still wearing his jacket; the leather was stiff with cold and creaked as she hugged him. "It's not your fault."

He hid his face against her, his shoulders shaking. A momentary panic rose in her. His crying was so unlike hers; his harsh sobs frightened and embarrassed her. She held him closer, rocking back and forth, feeling her own tears slide down her cheeks into the corners of her mouth, tasting salt. She stroked his hair as their mother would have done.

"I'm sorry," Sam was saying over and over, his words muffled. "I'm sorry, I'm sorry."

She had brushed her teeth and put on her flannel nightgown when Sam knocked on the door; he was wearing one of Daddy's bathrobes. He'd showered, and his brown hair stood up in spikes. "You want the top or the bottom bunk?"

When she was little and woke from a bad dream, Sarah had always gone to Sam's room and slept in the other bunk. It was something she used to do even before they moved to the farmhouse, because their parents were so often away. Even the sitters she liked best were not the comfort she wanted in the middle of the night.

"I was just going to ask you the same question," Sarah answered, and they both smiled for the first time since Sam had come home.

Father Griffiths led a memorial service at Saint Julian's, the little stone church on the town square. Sam and Sarah sat in the front pew holding hands. People who had known their parents through their work, but who were strangers to Sarah and Sam, kept coming up and introducing themselves. Sarah's friends from school filled the back of the church.

Afterward everyone came to the house for a luncheon arranged by Mrs. Woodley. The table was crowded with platters of ham and roast beef, salads and rolls and cakes prepared by neighbors. Sarah's friends crowded around the table, eating all the desserts. The adults stood around talking, with drinks in their hands. As though it were a party, Sarah thought.

She wore a navy blue dress with a white lace collar and cuffs. Aunt Helena had picked out the dress. She seemed anxious that Sarah should "look nice, with all these people coming," and went through Sarah's closet looking for something suitable, while Sarah sat on the bed watching. Aunt Helena also suggested that Sarah put her hair up, instead of wearing a braid down her back. In the end they compromised, and Sarah wrapped her braid around her head like a coronet. She had seen a picture of her mother, at seventeen, with her hair worn just this way. As she stood in front of the oval cheval mirror in her bedroom, Sarah saw for the first time a resemblance between the girl in the old photograph and the one in the mirror.

At the luncheon Sarah did her best to make polite conversation with the people who came up to her murmuring words of sympathy. Sam, looking uncomfortable in a suit and tie, stood in a corner talking in a low voice to Uncle Bernard. Before church Sam had slicked down his cowlick with water, but now it was standing up again. He made a point of telling her the glass in his hand contained nothing but Coke; Sarah was relieved.

From time to time she glanced up to find him looking back. In the middle of a conversation with a reporter who said she had known their parents in Beirut, Sarah felt a tap on her shoulder. It was Sam.

"Will you excuse us?" he said to the woman.

"What is it?" Sarah asked as he steered her into the laundry room off the kitchen. His face looked grim.

"Let's go for a walk."

"What about all those people?"

"What about them?"

Most of the snow had melted, leaving the ground spongy and soft. In the flower beds along the front walk a scattering of gold and purple crocuses had appeared. Her mother's crocuses. But her mother would never see them.

The air was mild, the sky a pale, uncertain blue. They walked along in silence until they reached the woods.

"Why do you keep looking around like that?" Sarah asked.

"Keep your voice down," Sam whispered.

"Why?"

He glanced over his shoulder at the way they had come. "How much did Dad and Mother tell you about what I was doing at the Institute?"

"Not much."

Sam broke a twig off a pine branch and began pulling off the needles one by one, tossing them to the ground. "I'm working on a project I started thinking about a long time ago, back at Oxford. When I finished up at Caltech, I was hoping to get a grant so I could see if my theory worked. But

I couldn't get anybody to listen. Who's going to hand over five million to an eighteen-year-old, even if he is a certifiable boy wonder—"

"Five million *dollars*? What is this project?"

"I can't tell you, Sarah. I'm sorry, I can't. Anyway, I couldn't make much headway without funding, but I kept plugging along. And then one day"—Sam took a deep breath—"this fellow in a three-piece suit shows up and wants to take me to lunch, says he's read some of my articles. Over the shrimp cocktails he tells me he represents an organization called the Cultural Institute for the Propagation of Humanistic and Exploratory Research—CIPHER. We had a laugh over the name. Then he tells me the organization is prepared to fund my experiments. In full."

Sarah stopped walking. "All that money?"

"A blank check. No waiting around for some committee, no time limits. I thought I was dreaming. But it was real. And for the last six months I've been going at it full tilt. I'm on the verge of something so . . . stupendous I can hardly believe it." His cheeks flushed. "You think I'm some sort of unfeeling weirdo, getting excited about this now?"

"No," Sarah said too quickly.

"Maybe I am," Sam said, looking into the distance. "Maybe I should . . ." He didn't finish the sentence.

Sarah chipped a piece of bark off a pine tree with the tip of her shoe. "Daddy said the Institute smelled wrong to him."

"I know. He said the same thing to me."

"What did he mean?"

"He meant he couldn't find out where their money comes from."

"Do you know?"

"I could find out if I wanted to. It's all in a computer file somewhere."

"Why haven't you?"

He shot her a surprised look. "Well, for starters, I'd have to break in. If I got caught . . ."

"But why is it such a big secret? Doesn't that make you think they must be hiding something?"

"There could be perfectly legitimate reasons for maintaining secrecy about the funding. They say the donors wish to remain anonymous. Maybe they're rich people who don't want their names on mailing lists, I don't know. . . ." He flung the stripped twig he'd been holding to the ground. "How did we get into this, anyway?"

You brought it up, Sarah thought.

"I've gone over it a dozen times," Sam was saying, "with . . . with Mother and Dad."

They walked on in silence. The woods were very still. Melting snow slid from pine boughs and fell softly to the ground.

"Sam, don't you want to know why they're giving you all this money?"

"Of course! But why should I assume there's something underhanded about it? They were farsighted enough to recognize I'm on to something that could alter the course of human history. If I'm successful, the whole world will know it, and CIPHER can take the credit for backing me when everyone else thought I was a lunatic dreamer."

Sarah studied him out of the corner of her eye. Sam never exaggerated; it was unscientific. If he claimed this project could change history, then it probably would. But what sort of discovery could do that?

"What will the Institute *do* with this . . . this whatever it is?"

"Use it! For 'humanistic and exploratory research.' That's what they say they're about, and at this point I have no reason to doubt them."

"What if they give you a reason?"

"Then I'll . . . I'll do something! I may be obsessed, but I'm not depraved." He seized both her arms. "Sarah, don't you see? This is my chance—probably my only chance—to do something . . . something glorious! I can't let it go by. I can't!"

"Yes, but . . ." *But Mother and Daddy wanted you to leave the Institute,* she started to say, but couldn't.

The sun went behind a cloud. Sarah had been wearing her coat open, but now she drew it around her and belted it.

"I know they wanted me to leave," Sam said, reading her thought. "But I can't leave now. It's more important than ever now. If I quit, it would mean I'd have lost Dad and Mother and everything I've worked for, too—everything I've dreamed of—"

Sarah stroked his coat sleeve. "I guess we're going to be living in California for a while, then. Will we have to rent out the house while we're away?"

He looked at her and then looked down. "You can't live with me at the Institute. It's in the middle of the desert, Sar—there's no school or anything."

"I'll do homeschooling, like we did when we were traveling all the time. You can tutor me. Or somebody else can if you're too busy."

Sam shook his head. "It wouldn't work, Sarah. Besides"—he drew himself up with a breath—"it's all arranged. You're going to live with Bernard and Helena."

Sarah took a step backward, teetering as the heels of her pumps sank into the soft loam beside the path. "*Helena and Bernard?* You must be crazy!"

"Sar—"

"I hardly know them! We're not even really related! Bernard is—was—Daddy's stepbrother!"

"It's what Dad and Mother wanted. It's all in the will."

"What?" Sarah stared in disbelief.

"Bernard showed it to me this morning before the funeral."

"I don't believe it! I don't believe Mother and Daddy would want me to go live with strangers in New York City. It's all so you can keep working on your precious project! I won't do it!" She turned and stalked away, back toward the house. It was difficult to walk fast in her pumps—she nearly turned her ankle.

"Sarah . . ."

She kept going. How could he? Daddy and Mother had wanted him to give up the project, to come home, and now they were dead and even that wasn't enough to make him stop. She wanted to say it out loud, to hurt him the way he was hurting her.

Sam caught up with her. "It won't be for long, I promise. As soon as I'm certain I'm on the right track, I'll publish my findings. Once I do that, I can get a job anywhere, and we can be together." He touched her shoulder. "Please, Sarah, try to understand."

"I want to stay here! We could get someone to live in, someone like Mrs. Woodley—"

"You're only fourteen. You need to be with family."

"Family! Then what about the aunts? Why can't I go stay with the great-aunts, in Oxford? You lived with them your first year!"

Sam shrugged. "Maybe Mother and Dad thought the aunts were too old now to take care of a teenager. And they're in England."

"There must be somebody else!"

"Helena and Bernard are *it*. Mother and Dad never dreamed we'd lose both of them . . ." He took her hand and held it tight.

"It's not fair!"

"Nothing about this is fair."

They had reached the top of a rise. From here the house was visible, nestled in its hollow. A plume of smoke rose from the chimney. Through the bare trees she could see a gleaming crescent of the pond behind the house. All around it stretched the fields, where patches of snow still lay, like scattered pieces of a puzzle.

The first time Sarah ever saw the house, she recognized it like the face of an old friend, for she had drawn it with her crayons a hundred times: the box with a triangle for a roof, a chimney with smoke curling out of it; windows with curtains drawn back and her own face, surrounded by a halo of scribbled hair, smiling out.

The reality was better than anything she could have drawn or even imagined. She hadn't thought of ivy climbing up the side of the house, covering two of her bedroom windows, filling the room with a green, underwater light in high summer, nor had she dreamed of a tiny stone cottage next to the house—a springhouse, her parents said, but she knew it was enchanted.

"Why?" she said aloud. "Why would they want me to go live with . . . with those people?"

How could she leave behind the barn swallows darting and swooping in the dusk, and the little spiders in the hedges, their webs starred with dew? Or the yellow violets in the springtime woods, or the fires in autumn, or drowsy summer afternoons in the old wooden rowboat, drifting beneath the sycamores?

Sarah's eyes welled with tears. How could it be that one moment your life was beautiful and happy and safe, and the next it had collapsed and left you in howling darkness?

"I won't go," she said. "This is my home. You can't make me leave it."

Sam put his arms around her. "Sarah, I promise, as soon as I can arrange it, we'll get a place together. We'll be room-mates, just like we used to pretend in the tree house, remember? You ever go up there anymore?"

"Sometimes." They drew apart. He was trying to make her feel better by talking about the tree house. As if she were a toddler who had dropped her ice cream cone and needed to be distracted.

"Come on—can you manage the ladder with those high heels on?"

"They're not high heels," Sarah said, letting him pull her along by the hand.

When they reached the tree house, Sam went first, testing each board of the ladder. He unlatched the door. It swung open, loose on its hinges. He poked his head through the doorway. "You been camping out up here?"

"It was a tramp." Sarah saw the old lady in her mind's eye: the lined face, the clear gray eyes.

She stared up at the hem of Sam's overcoat, waiting for him to put his knee on the floor and hoist himself the rest of the way through the door. But he just stood there, half in and half out.

"What's the matter?" She had a sudden, dreadful picture in her mind of the old lady lying dead on the floor of the tree house. "Sam, what is it?"

All at once he scrambled up the ladder and into the house. She followed and found him hunched over, peering at the back wall, his eyes inches from the wooden boards.

"Close the door," he ordered when he heard her behind him. "Close it, quick."

three

The Tree House Equations

"**Sam, what is going on?**"

"Who was up here?"

"An old, raggedy lady. A hobo. I told her she could spend the night here, and I gave her some money. It was after . . . after I found out about Mother and Daddy."

"Look." He pointed at the wall. With the door closed the only light fell through cracks between the boards and the one small window, covered with cloudy plastic. Gradually Sarah's eyes became accustomed to the dimness, and she saw that a sheet of plywood that had been used to patch the back wall was completely covered with doodles: arrows, numbers, Greek letters, and here and there a word or phrase—"charge conjugation" and "violated" and "probability density function." Above it, like an inscription, were the words *Sic itur ad astra*. Lying at the base of the wall was a charred stick—from the old lady's fire?—that evidently had been used as a pencil. The sooty coffee can stood in a corner.

"What does it mean?"

Sam was still staring at the wall with his mouth open. "I

could be wrong—oh, Lord, please don't let me be wrong—but I think it's the set of equations I've been looking for. It's the key."

"That's impossible! How did they get here?"

Sam didn't hear her; he was frantically searching his pockets. "My notebook! Sarah, please . . ." He grabbed her arm. "Go back to the house, get my notebook—oh, jeez, where is it?" He drummed his fist on the floor. "It's either in my suitcase, in the pocket, or on my desk. A small black three-ring binder. If you can't find it, just grab some paper. And a flashlight and a pencil."

"Okay, okay!"

"Don't say anything to anybody, understand? Not one word!"

"*Okay.*"

"And hurry!"

Some things, at least, haven't changed, she thought as she descended the ladder. When they were growing up, they had spent hours working on Sam's experiments, and she had always been the one to go ask the hotel desk clerk for a pair of scissors, or run down to the corner for a giant lemonade when the Brain grew thirsty from his mental exertions. It wasn't that she minded, really—it had been fun, most of the time. But she wasn't a little kid any longer. She deserved to know more.

As she reached the edge of the woods and started down the lane toward the house, a man appeared from behind the barn. He had his hands in the pockets of his overcoat and looked as if he were out for a stroll. That in itself wasn't unusual; visitors to the house often took walks, enjoying the scenery and the quiet. But there was something odd about him, about the way he was pretending he hadn't seen her. Had she met him at the memorial service? She couldn't be sure. There had been so many people.

"Hello," she said as they passed each other.

He nodded without speaking and walked on, up toward the woods.

First the old lady, Sarah thought, *then the writing on the wall, and now him. What is going on around here?* She looked over her shoulder, but he had disappeared among the trees.

In the house she was caught for fifteen minutes in a round of good-byes but finally escaped up the stairs and gathered the items Sam wanted. She was on her way out the back door when a hand fell on her shoulder. It was Uncle Bernard.

"Going for another walk?" he asked, staring at her over the tops of his half-glasses. His balding forehead was corrugated with wrinkles.

"I . . . I need some time alone." The lie came easily to her lips, surprising her. There was an uncomfortable pause while he continued staring. Then he let her go without another word. She had the feeling he had wanted to say something else, maybe something about its not being good manners to leave guests on their own.

She walked toward the pasture gate and swung it open, hurriedly threading her way around the patches of snow as she took the shortcut to the woods. Anybody could see her in the open field, but she couldn't afford to lose any more time. Sam would be crazy with impatience.

❁

Sarah knelt next to Sam, her hose snagging on the rough wood floor, and held the flashlight while he copied the scribbles into his notebook and recited them under his breath. "It's elegant," he said over and over. "It's absolutely beautiful."

She studied the crude charcoal jottings. Maybe if she looked at them long enough, they would reveal their secret.

"Point the flashlight over here," Sam said.

She moved the light. Her knees hurt. She shifted her weight and looked around. The tree house was spacious, as tree houses went; the spreading branches of the white oak supported a floor wide enough for four or five kids to put down their sleeping bags, provided you didn't mind an elbow or two in your ribs. A small shelf still held prizes she and Sam had found in the woods: the near-perfect skeleton of a baby owl, a collection of stones worn smooth by the brook. In a corner lay a deck of cards, a pair of old binoculars, and two paperback books, swollen and warped from having been left out in the rain.

Except for the coffee can, which still held a few half-burned pieces of wood, there was no sign the old lady had been there. Unless, of course, the mysterious doodles were hers. But how could she have known the equations? It made no sense.

Sam stopped writing and stared at the wall.

"Finished?" Sarah asked. "My knees are sore."

"What? Oh, yeah. Yeah, I'm finished." He pointed to the words *Sic itur ad astra*. "Know what this means?" he asked. "You took Latin, didn't you? The literal translation is 'Thus one goes to the stars,' but it can also mean 'This is the path to immortality.'"

"Latin?" A memory rushed at Sarah: the old lady calling to her from the tree house as Sarah walked away. "She was speaking Latin! I thought it was just gibberish."

"The old woman? What did she say?"

"It was crazy—it sounded like 'temples, ammonia, Ray waylaid' or something."

"Temples . . . ammonia . . ." Sam slapped his thighs. "*Tempus omnia revelat*! Was that it?"

"I guess so."

"'Time reveals all things'! 'Time reveals all things'! What else did she say? Start from the beginning. Every word."

He listened to the whole story without interrupting. "There's one more thing," Sarah added. "I hadn't really thought about it until now. Her smell. She smelled like rose petals."

Sam chuckled.

"But Sam, don't you see how strange that is? Her clothes were filthy and her hair—"

"I guess even hobo ladies like perfume."

"But it wasn't perfumy. She smelled like petals. Like that rose petal potpourri the aunts used to have out in those Chinese bowls around their house, remember?"

"How could I forget? They sent me a little lace bag full of it for Christmas one year."

They smiled at the memory. Great-aunt Elspeth had mixed up the tags on their presents, so that Sam had opened the potpourri sachet intended for Sarah, and Sarah had received a pair of large, hand-knit black wool socks.

Their eyes met, and Sarah saw the flash of sorrow cross Sam's face. She knew he was thinking what she was: There would be no more merry Christmases for them.

"I love you, Tadpole," Sam said. "Just remember that."

"I love you, too, Sam." She turned and looked at the wall. "Is it really what you hoped—the key?"

"It sure looks like it."

"But how could the old woman have known what you were working on?"

"I don't know," Sam said, shaking his head. "I do not know. It's a riddle wrapped in a mystery inside an enigma. Winston Churchill said that," he added. "In another context, of course."

"Does this mean you'll be able to finish sooner?" she asked wistfully.

He patted her shoulder. "A lot sooner, though I can't say exactly when."

"Sam, you have to tell me what this is all about. I won't tell anyone, I promise!"

He frowned. "I don't think I should, Sar. I've already told you more than I intended to, but I had to make you understand why I've got to go back. They made me sign a contract saying I wouldn't discuss the project with anyone outside the Institute."

"Not even your family?" Sarah said, realizing as she spoke that she was his entire family now, and he was hers.

"No one. Anyway, it's hard to explain. And they definitely wouldn't like it if they knew."

They, Sarah thought. *Who are "they"?* "Sam, tell me. I promise I'll keep it a secret."

He hesitated, studying her for what seemed like minutes. "Have I ever told you about wormholes?" he asked at last.

"As in earthworms?"

He shook his head. "As in quantum foam. The entire universe is permeated by a sea of wormholes—incredibly tiny tunnels, ten to the minus thirtieth centimeter—that lead from one part of the space-time continuum to another. Look"—he raised his hand—"let's say my fist is an apple. A fly comes along and lands on it. The only way the fly can get to the other side of the apple is to crawl over the surface. But a worm could tunnel its way through the apple to the other side. A wormhole is like a shortcut through the universe."

"Are there little tiny quantum worms that go through these tunnels?"

Very funny, his look said. "There's nothing in the tunnels. Not even time. No past, present, or future. So if you could travel through one—"

"You'd get to another part of the universe in no time at all?"

"You catch on fast. The trouble is, you'd first have to find a way to extract one of these wormholes from the quantum foam, and then generate an energy field powerful enough to enlarge the wormhole and keep it stable and open so somebody could travel through it. But I think I have."

"You have? How?"

"Antimatter. When a particle meets up with its antiparticle, they annihilate each other—*boom!* Cancel each other out. The only result is energy. I figured out a way to use that energy to create a very powerful force field. I call it the Looking Glass, like the one in the Alice story."

"You can step through it? Into another part of the universe?"

Sam smiled a long, slow smile. "Not yet. But I'm getting close."

"Sam, that sounds really dangerous! What if something goes wrong?"

"Everything's dangerous."

Sarah swallowed; her mouth had gone dry. "Where will you go?"

"Somewhere with great beaches, I hope."

"Be serious!"

"I'm searching for a planet with an atmosphere as much like Earth's as I can find. I'll send probes first, to gather samples—"

They heard the sound of twigs snapping underfoot. Sarah looked through a crack and saw a figure in a gray overcoat swiftly retreating through the trees among the deepening shadows.

"Him again!" She scrambled for the binoculars before she remembered they were broken. When she looked again, he was gone.

"Guy in a gray overcoat?" Sam asked.

Sarah turned around. "How did you know?"

"He's been hanging around most of the afternoon. He's a Guardian. From the Institute. They've got their own security police."

"Why is a policeman following you around?"

"Protecting their investment. I suppose they want to make sure I don't crack up and go babbling secrets to the competition or something. And speaking of secrets . . ."

He drew his shirtsleeve down over the inside of his palm and held it in place with the tips of his fingers. "I hate to do this," he said, and began to use his sleeve as an eraser, making small, slow circles on the wall. One by one the figures disappeared into charcoal clouds. "It really ought to be taken down and hung in the Smithsonian next to Einstein's blackboard."

"So why are you—is it because of him? The Guardian? But won't the Institute know all about these equations eventually?"

"There's no reason they need to know anything before I'm ready to tell them. They have their little secrets and I have mine. Besides, whoever put these equations here must've had a good reason for making sure no one would be likely to find them except you or me."

"But why?"

"That's the question, isn't it?" He wiped his hands on his trousers and winked at her.

Exile

Aunt Helena and Uncle Bernard lived on the tenth floor of an ugly yellow brick building. The apartment was always too hot; it made Sarah sleepy and gave her headaches, but Aunt Helena complained of drafts and wore a sweater over her shoulders.

Sarah's room was a long, narrow space like a shoe box, with a single window overlooking an intersection. It had been Uncle Bernard's study, hastily cleared out to accommodate her. The sweetish odor of pipe tobacco still clung to the drapes. On the wall there was a rectangular patch of wallpaper lighter than the rest, where Uncle Bernard's law school diploma had hung.

They had refused to let her bring Ozymandias. She pleaded and promised and cried and slammed doors, but Aunt Helena said she was allergic to cat dander, and Sam had taken Ozzie with him. Then, a week after Sarah moved in, Aunt Helena took her to visit a friend down the hall. The friend had a fat, boring tabby who lay in Sarah's lap like a sandbag. Beside her on the sofa, Aunt Helena hadn't so much as sneezed. "She just doesn't want a cat," Sarah told Sam on the phone. Sam told her that was a pretty cynical attitude for someone who was only fourteen ("Almost fifteen," she reminded him). After they'd hung up, she looked up "cynical" in Uncle Bernard's dictionary, just to make sure she knew precisely what it meant: "contemptuously distrustful of human nature and motives." *I'm not,* Sarah thought, letting the heavy pages fall shut. *She said she was allergic, and she isn't. She lied.*

It was probably a good thing Ozymandias had gone with Sam. At least at the Institute he could run around outside. Sam said the cat liked chasing tumbleweeds and horned toads. One morning Sam had awakened to find a dead lizard on his pillow, compliments of Ozzie.

Less than a month after her arrival in the city Uncle Bernard paused during dinner and, wiping a shiny smear of grease from his chin, announced with an air of satisfaction that Sycamore Farm had been sold.

Sarah rose from the table, pain knifing her insides. She went to her room and locked the door and buried her face in the pillow so Helena and Bernard would not hear her sobs.

Most of their belongings had been put in storage. Sarah had been allowed to bring a few of her own things—her starry quilt, a white china cat with blue eyes her father had given her, the cheval mirror—but they seemed sadly out of place in their new surroundings. In bed at night, waiting for the darkness that never really came, listening to the whine of sirens and the rattle and wheeze of the radiators, Sarah lay with her hands under her cheek and gazed at the pale shape of the china cat on the bureau. She couldn't see its unblinking blue eyes, but she could feel them looking back at her, reproachful, questioning: *Why did you bring us here? Where is my mantelpiece? And where is the fire?*

Sam promised to write and call, and he did, though not as often as Sarah needed. His letters were short and funny, meant to cheer her up. When she found one waiting for her after school, she took it to her room and read it over and over, searching for anything that might give her reason to hope.

Just before they parted, Sam had said, "I wouldn't put it past the Guardians to read my mail, coming and going. And they may listen in on my phone calls too. So never let on that I told you about the Looking Glass."

That was no problem. Sarah wanted to know only one thing: when he would be finished.

She dragged herself through the routine of school and life in the apartment, her grief always with her, weighing her down, making her feel strangely afraid. Again and again she found herself thinking of her mother or father as though they were still alive. Sitting in biology one afternoon, she was looking out the window and glimpsed an old man on the corner. Without really thinking about it, she drew a sketch of him in her notebook and, when she'd finished, was surprised by how good it was. *I have to show this to Mother,* she thought, and a full second passed before she realized the truth: She would never show anything to her mother again.

Maybe Aunt Helena and Uncle Bernard aren't really bad people, Sarah thought, looking up from a dinner of over-cooked roast beef, mushy green beans, and watery potatoes; it was just that everything they did was wrong. They said the

wrong things when she was sad, they laughed at jokes that
weren't funny, they ate the wrong food, and they even hung
their towels in the bathroom the wrong way.

*Of course, they probably think that I do everything the
wrong way. But they're wrong.* She looked at her plate to hide
the faint smile that came to her lips. But not quickly enough.

"Is something funny?" Uncle Bernard asked. "How about
letting us in on the joke?"

That was another thing; they *pried*. She had the feeling
they were always watching her, always looking for a way to
slip their tentacles into her mind, to expose what she was
thinking and feeling. Her parents had never done that.

When she didn't answer, Bernard persisted: "Come on,
now—we saw you smiling. Didn't we, Helena?"

"It was nothing, really."

"How is school?" Aunt Helena asked, sawing her roast
beef into tiny triangles one at a time.

Terrible, Sarah wanted to say, but of course she couldn't
say that, they would just end up acting concerned and making useless suggestions, so she said: "Okay."

The high school had guards at the front door and cast-
iron bars on all the street-level windows. Everyone had to
pass through a metal detector. The stairwells were covered
with spray-painted graffiti. There were two thousand students, and most of them looked as if they'd rather be anywhere else.

She prayed to be invisible, left alone. It was the best she
could hope for. People wanted to be your friend only when
they could tell you didn't really need one.

But worse even than the loneliness was something else,

something Sarah had no name for. It happened for the first time a few weeks after her arrival in the city. She had decided to take the subway to Greenwich Village after school. She'd been there once with Aunt Helena, on an errand, and had seen an art supply store. As usual, Aunt Helena had been in a hurry and they had not done much more than glance in the window. Sarah was sure she knew where the shop was from the subway stop, though she couldn't remember its name or the street it was on. But when she had walked the three blocks to where she thought the shop would be, it wasn't there. She kept walking, thinking perhaps it was farther away than she remembered.

It was beginning to get dark. She started back, her shoe rubbing uncomfortably against her heel, went down a side street that looked vaguely familiar, made another turn, and tried to find the first street. But instead of boutiques with vintage clothing in the windows, there were dimly lit grocery stores where the smell of roach spray drifted out the open doors, shops with windows crammed full of dusty second-hand furniture, and one window displaying nothing but the hands of a mannequin with painted red fingernails.

Ahead of her on the crowded sidewalk a bottle shattered, spraying glass. Someone cursed. She crossed to the other side of the street. A shopkeeper came out of his store and locked the door. The window was crowded with religious statues. One of them was a naked man, his pale flesh pierced with arrows. The shopkeeper undid the bolts that held up a steel curtain, and it fell to the sidewalk with a crash.

Stop and ask someone for directions, she thought. *No, keep walking. Don't speak, don't touch, and you will be invisible, you will be safe.*

The back of her heel was raw. She winced with every step, curling up her toes. She longed to take off her shoe, but the sidewalk was littered and filthy.

Behind her someone was making loud kissing noises. She walked faster, trying to ignore the pain. A man's voice called to her. The words were foreign, but their meaning could not have been clearer.

She had no thought now but to get away. The crowd of faces streaming toward her in the yellow glare of the street-lamps looked brutish and frightening, not like human beings at all. Then it came to her: *This is the way it really is, I've just never seen it before. . . .*

Then, up at the next corner, she saw her father. It was his coat, his walk. She limped after him as fast as she could, her shoe flapping against the sidewalk. *It can't be,* she told herself. *But it is, it is, there's been a mistake, it was all a terrible mistake.* He must have gone home, looking for her, and they told him she was in the city.

"Daddy!" He didn't turn around. "Daddy!" At last she reached him, touched the sleeve of his coat. The man turned, and Sarah saw his face, jowly, creased with deep furrows that ran from his nose to the edges of his mouth. Nothing like her father's face.

"I thought . . . I'm sorry . . ."

The man looked down at her hand on his sleeve and drew his arm away.

"Wait, please!" Sarah cried. "There's a man following me—he was making noises. . . ."

She looked around. The sidewalk, which moments before had been crowded with people, was empty except for a woman carrying a baby in one arm and a bag of groceries in the other.

❉

It happened again and again after that. Sitting on a bus, or in the cafeteria at school, or walking down the street. Without warning, a layer peeled off the surface of things, and she saw the ugliness underneath. But the ugliness wasn't the worst of it; it was the feeling that none of it meant anything at all. At those times she tried to think of home, but it seemed unreal and distant, like a movie she'd seen a long time ago and had almost forgotten.

She would not let herself forget. She took an art class the last nine weeks of school and slowly, painstakingly, painted a view of the farmhouse from memory. In May, for their birthday, she sent the painting to Sam. His present to her was a map of the universe that glowed in the dark; she attached it to the ceiling above her bed.

The city spring passed almost invisibly into summer. At home her mother's peonies would have bloomed, pink and ivory, the crab apple tree would be a cloud of deep rose, and the bullfrogs on the pond would sing down the night. Here there were only tulips in the divider, and sidewalk trees budding inside wire cages, and temperatures that slowly climbed until the windows of the tenements were flung open and the sounds of life inside spilled out onto the street: arguments, radios blaring lively Spanish songs, babies crying.

Then school was out, and Aunt Helena began a relentless campaign of suggestions: "Why don't you advertise as a babysitter, put a card up in the lobby?" "Wouldn't you like to take a summer course?" "Why don't you invite the little Markham girl in 10D over?"

Sarah fled. She took her sketchbook to Central Park and

filled it with drawings of ornate iron lampposts and trees
and sleeping dogs. When she tired of being outside, she
went to the neighborhood branch of the public library. The
grimy stone building was old and dark and cool, smelling
of books no one had read in years. It was crowded, mostly
with people who probably didn't have air-conditioning at
home. They sat around the scarred wooden tables, flipping
through magazines under the green-shaded lamps and
slowly revolving ceiling fans. Sarah roamed the stacks,
searching the shelves for the books she had loved when
she was little: *Treasure Island* and *Little Women* and The
Chronicles of Narnia; Dr. Dolittle and Nancy Drew; *The
Wind in the Willows*; the Oz books. She sat reading by the
hour with one leg tucked under her, the skin of her bare
calf sticking to the chair seat, twisting around her finger a
strand of hair that had come loose from her braid, reading
and reading. Some of the books were falling apart, their
pages held together with tape that was brittle with age. But
they were better than any new book could have been;
turning one of the thick, deckle-edged pages and dis-
covering an illustration of Ozma or Ratty or even Long
John Silver was like coming across the face of an old,
beloved friend in a strange place. The books welcomed her
and drew her into their worlds, where nothing had
changed, inviting her to leave behind her loneliness, at
least for a little while.

One day in late August, when the library's air-conditioning
had broken down, Sarah stepped outside to cool off and
found it was even hotter on the street. When she returned to

her chair, she noticed a folded square of paper on top of her stack of books. It was pink library scrap paper. There were small stacks of it on the tables by the card catalogs.

She unfolded it. Written in elegant, looping script were the words "May I recommend *Through the Looking-Glass*? With the original Tenniel illustrations, of course. Page 105 is particularly enlightening."

Sarah pushed her chair back, scraping the legs against the wood floor, and, frowning, read the note again. Was somebody playing a game? Somebody who had been watching her, keeping track of what she'd been reading? She scanned the room, nearly deserted now because of the heat, to see if anyone was glancing at her from behind a newspaper. No one was.

Aunt Helena had warned her about the "strange types" who hung out at the library. "Don't get into conversations with them," she had said. "They'll just ask you for money or make lewd remarks." Aunt Helena hadn't said what you were supposed to do if they wrote you a note suggesting a book.

She went over to the card catalog, found the drawer marked CAR-CARTEL, and set it on top of one of the high tables. There were half a dozen editions of *Through the Looking-Glass*—but only one with illustrations by John Tenniel. It was shelved on the second floor, up a curving staircase with an iron banister. She started up the stairs, hurrying now, her sandals slapping the wood. A man at the top of the stairs stood aside to let her pass. She hurried through the stacks, scanning the numbers, and finally found the right shelf.

But where the book should have been there was an empty space, like a missing tooth.

five

Six Impossible Things
Before Breakfast

"Looking for something?"

Sarah jumped. Two dark eyes peered at her over the row of books. Then they vanished. A moment later a boy stood at the end of the row of shelves, blocking the way out. He held a book against his chest: *Through the Looking-Glass*.

She looked from the book to his face. For a moment she could do nothing but stare. It was a striking face. If she had spotted him in a crowd, she would have studied him in secret, would, if she'd had the chance, have tried to capture him on paper. There was something noble in that face, in the fine, strong bones and in the way he held his head: as if he belonged not in torn blue jeans and an old T-shirt, but in the robes of a warrior prince.

He returned her stare, a hint of mischief behind his dark, intelligent eyes.

A pencil sketch would never do, she thought a little wildly. *Not for skin like that. Like honey with the sun shining through it.*

Her gaze was first to falter. When she looked down, he leaned against the shelves, pretending to study the cover of the book. A lock of hair fell over his forehead. He had a crown of loose brown curls, coaxed toward gold by the sun.

"I was looking for that book," she said.

"I know. What'll you give me for it?"

"You mean money?"

"Money?" He considered this, toying with the ends of a faded red bandanna tied around his neck.

She tried to push past him, but he used one arm to make a barricade.

"Here, take it." He nudged her arm with the book. "Go on. I was teasing."

"Thank you," she said as haughtily as she could manage.

He made a little bow and with a graceful sweep of his arm directed her to pass.

She walked away and looked back. He was watching. "How did you know I wanted this book?"

"I know lots of things . . . Sarah Lucas. Aren't you going to see what's at page 105?"

"How do you know my—did *you* send me that note?"

He shook his head.

"But you read it," she said.

"Yes," he admitted, "I read it."

"Did you see who left it?"

"Yes."

"Well?" Sarah demanded.

"Well what?"

He was teasing again, but this time she could tell. "Please, I need to know."

"An old lady. White hair, tall. Never seen her around here before. You know her?"

"No." She stared at the book as if the words on the cover could somehow explain everything.

"That seems to be a popular book," the boy said. "Somebody else was looking for it too. He was very disappointed when he saw it wasn't on the shelf."

"He?"

The boy shrugged. "You must've passed him on the stairs."

Her mind flashed back to the man at the top of the stairs, stepping aside to let her pass. A white shirt, cold pale eyes . . . she had barely glanced at him.

"Actually, I don't think it was the book he wanted. I think it was the letter."

"What letter?"

"The one at page 105."

She opened the book, shook it. There was nothing there.

He slipped his hand under his shirt and handed her an envelope, warm from the heat of his body. She stared at it in confusion: The envelope was addressed to her in Sam's handwriting, and it bore a stamp, but it hadn't been postmarked.

"Did you read this, too?" she asked.

"Didn't have time." He grinned, and suddenly she was aware of how she must look, red faced from the heat, her wrinkled blouse half in and half out of her shorts. She wiped the perspiration from her upper lip and tucked a loose strand of hair behind her ear.

"Hot in here," he said.

"Yes. Well, thank you."

"Anytime."

She listened for his footsteps as she started downstairs, half hoping he might follow her, but heard nothing. Midway she paused and scanned the reading area. None of the men around the tables looked like the man she had seen on the stairs, and there were no old ladies of any description.

She started to tear open the envelope, then hesitated. No, not here. Someone might be watching, someone she couldn't see. She handed the book to the librarian, who checked it through and gave it back without looking at her.

Outside the sky was white, the air heavy and humid as the inside of a Laundromat. She headed east toward the park, waiting for the light at a corner where a man stood with his cart under an umbrella. There was a glistening block of ice on the cart, covered with a striped dish towel, and four bottles of syrup in candy colors.

The man caught her looking. "What flavor you want?" he asked, already removing the dish towel from the ice. He smiled, revealing a gold tooth. "S'good," he assured her. "All natural."

Sarah hesitated, not knowing how to refuse.

"Lime," she said, fishing for change in her pocket. The man scraped the ice with a metal scraper, scooped the shavings into a paper cone, doused it with green syrup—no lime was ever that green, Sarah thought—and handed it to her.

It *was* good. She nibbled at it, letting the ice slide down her throat, as she crossed the street into Central Park. It was cooler there, but only a little; there was no breeze, and even the trees looked droopy. At the playground dozens of little kids ran in and out of the spray from the sprinkler, screeching, holding their plastic buckets over the jet of water and then uncovering it.

Sarah found a space on a bench in the shade, next to two women. They were speaking rapidly in French while they jiggled the handles of two enormous, shiny, baby carriages. They glanced at her as she sat down, and then ignored her. She put the book down on the bench and tried to open the letter with one hand while she ate the snowball with the other, but it was too awkward, so she took one last bite and tossed the paper cone in the trash. Then she licked her fingers and tore open the envelope.

Tadpole—
Smuggling this out with one of the cleaning ladies who's going on vacation—she's scatterbrained, but I'm pretty sure she's not one of them.
There are thousands of them, Sarah, and they're <u>everywhere</u>. Had this dream about Dad—can't go into it now—anyway, I broke into their files through my terminal & found their membership lists. Names, addresses, occupations, incomes, when they joined, etc., all in code. Looks like they turn over all their money & then get some back, like an allowance. So that's where the Institute gets its millions—from these drones out there. Substantially bizweird, wouldn't you say? Why the drones should want to turn over their earthly goods is another question.
Thought I'd nose around a little more and see what else I can find out.
Everything is falling into place with the Looking

Glass. About to do some secret tests—don't worry if you don't hear from me for a while.

Ozzie sends greetings to the Royal Head Scratcher.

Love,
Sam

PS: Letter from Great-aunt Daisy: All 3 aunts distressed to hear you're living with H. & B. Elspeth says she and Mother had a conversation not long ago—M. "quite clear and emphatic" should anything happen to her and Dad, you were to come live with them (???). Maybe D. & M. changed their minds—aunts are fairly ancient—and just didn't want to say anything. Thought I'd let you know in case you hear from them. DO NOT mention this to H. & B.

PPS: Burn this letter.

Despite the muggy heat, Sarah felt a sudden chill. Suppose Aunt Helena and Uncle Bernard had lied? But they couldn't have—it was in the will. The will that *Uncle Bernard* had shown to Sam.

"You get all your mail that way?" a voice asked. "Kind of complicated, isn't it?"

It was the boy from the library. He stood in front of her, his hands in his pockets.

"Are you following me?"

"I was following him"—he shifted his eyes, indicating someone behind him—"and he was following you."

"Who?" Sarah craned her neck to see around him.

"Guy in a white shirt. Don't look, stupid. Do you want him to see you?"

"I don't believe you," Sarah said. "You're making it up."

He took his hands from his pockets. "You calling me a liar?"

"You called me stupid."

The women on the bench stopped talking.

"How old are you?" Sarah asked abruptly.

He looked surprised. "Seventeen."

"Then, you're old enough to know when you're being a nuisance."

"I don't need this," he said to the sky. "I should just walk away, I know it."

"Why don't you, then?"

He stared at her for a moment, and then he was gone.

Sarah looked down at her sandals, biting her lip, feeling angry, foolish, and disappointed all at once. One of the babies, hot and bored with staring at a string of plastic elephants, began to fret.

She got up, rubbing the indentations on the backs of her bare legs made by the park bench slats. There was no man in a white shirt in the playground—not that she could see, anyway.

She walked to the coffee shop on the corner of the avenue—the ice man nodded, smiling, as she passed—and ate a grilled cheese sandwich. The waitress brought her a second glass of iced tea, and Sarah sipped it slowly. She shouldn't have been so rude to that boy. He had made sure she got the letter, after all. She saw him in her mind, his dark eyes that seemed to take in everything about her at once. The girls at home would say he was cute, but "cute" was entirely the wrong word for someone with a face that could have appeared in mosaic on the wall of a palace.

She'd been scared, that was all, scared and confused. She tore a paper napkin into ragged squares and arranged them on the table like pieces of a puzzle: the boy, the man in the white shirt, the will, Sam's letter, the old lady who had delivered it.

Could she and the hobo lady from the tree house be the same person? Sarah twirled the plastic straw around in the glass. A cleaning lady, Sam had called her. Surely he would have noticed something about her that would make him wonder. But maybe not. When he was absorbed in his work . . . unless she started to spout Latin while she was mopping the floor, he might not make the connection.

But how could she have made it to California and gotten a job at the Institute? How would she even have known about the Institute? Of course, that was no more impossible than her knowing Sam's missing equations.

No more impossible than Uncle Bernard coming up with a phony will.

But why? Why would Aunt Helena and Uncle Bernard want her? They certainly didn't seem to like having her around. Money? There were trust funds—one for Sam, one for her—and Uncle Bernard was in charge of the money until their twenty-third birthdays. In the meantime he doled out her allowance, a few dollars more than she had received at home because living in the city was more expensive.

But there wasn't enough money for her to go to a private school. When they first explained this, solemn faced, she was surprised but not suspicious. She had attended public school at home anyway, and she had no idea how much money there might be in the trust fund. But that was before the farm had been sold. Surely there would be enough money now? She would have to ask Sam the next time they talked—whenever that might be.

Her parents had never discussed money with her. Sarah knew they weren't rich, but they weren't poor, either. They could have bought her a horse—they'd told her so—but they had wanted her to save a third of the money to pay for it. Sarah had been sure that by the time she saved enough from her sporadic babysitting jobs and Christmas and birthday presents, it would be too late: The horse she really wanted would no longer be for sale, or she'd be in college. She'd never have a horse of her own. A memory of an angry scene flashed through her mind, a dinner-table argument that had ended with her screaming hateful things at them, pounding up the stairs to her room, and slamming the door. She had been so angry she had never apologized.

I didn't mean those things I said. I'm sorry. She felt her throat constrict, her eyes begin to fill. *Not here,* she told herself. *You can't cry here.* In fact, she had cried in the coffee shop before, more than once. A memory would come out of nowhere, without warning, like now, and she would be unable to hold back the tears. No one, not here in the coffee shop, nor in the subway, nor in the library, had seemed to notice, although they must have seen her. Maybe people saw other people crying all the time in the city, and everyone knew you were just supposed to look away. It was like being alone, which was all right. If anyone had sympathized, if anyone had put a consoling hand on her shoulder or given her a hug, she would never have stopped crying. Besides, Sarah thought, pulling a napkin from the stubborn dispenser and blowing her nose, being ignored by strangers was infinitely better than suffering through Aunt Helena's attempts to comfort her.

In the beginning Sarah thought her tears made Helena uncomfortable, so uncomfortable that she didn't know what to do. But it was more than that—it was clear Helena felt she had a role to play as the kindly aunt. She did a passable job as long as nothing much was asked of her, but when the role called for something more, she became flustered. She delivered her lines, but they were clumsy and flat, lacking any true feeling. And both of them knew it. After the first few times Sarah had tried hard not to cry in front of her anymore.

It was getting late. She drank the last of her iced tea, went into the restroom, and washed her face with cold water. Then she unfastened her braid, brushed her hair out, and rebraided it, watching herself in the small, cracked mirror over the sink.

Her parents had never mentioned the argument about the horse after it was over. They hadn't acted hurt or withdrawn; they had just gone on as though it had never happened. From time to time—when they were in an especially good mood—she would bring up the subject of a horse again, but they stood their ground. Once her father had said that maybe a long-lost rich uncle would die and remember her in his will.

"Have I got one?" she had asked hopefully.

He had laughed and said, "Well, there's Bernard—he's loaded to the gills, with no heirs, but I'm afraid he's in the pink of health, kiddo. Better not count on it."

She put her brush back into her purse and returned to the table. She supposed she'd have to go soon or order something else. She gazed out the window and tried to look as if she were waiting for someone.

Loaded to the gills: It meant rich. But Uncle Bernard didn't seem rich. In fact, he and Helena seemed to have less money than her parents.

Sarah felt a knot tighten in her stomach.

Looks like they turn over all their money & then get some back, like an allowance.

There are thousands of them, Sarah, and they're every-where.

No. Aunt Helena and Uncle Bernard were too . . . too ordinary.

Through the Looking-Glass lay on the table in front of her. She flipped through it, glancing at the pictures of the Jabberwock and the Red Queen dragging Alice along by the hand. She turned to page 105, wondering if she'd been meant to look for more than the letter there, and found a conversation between Alice and the White Queen:

"I can't believe *that*!" said Alice.

"Can't you?" the Queen said in a pitying tone. "Try again: draw a long breath, and shut your eyes."

Alice laughed. "There's no use trying," she said: "One *can't* believe impossible things."

"I daresay you haven't had much practice," said the Queen. "When I was your age, I always did it for half-an-hour a day. Why, sometimes I've believed as many as six impossible things before breakfast!"

When Sarah returned to the apartment, Aunt Helena and Uncle Bernard met her at the door. Aunt Helena had her purse over her arm. Was it her imagination, Sarah wondered, or did the two of them seem nervous?

"Goodness, you're late," Helena said. "We've already eaten, and we have to go out now. There's a plate for you in the oven."

"I stopped by the library on the way home from the office," Uncle Bernard said. "You weren't there."

"I was." Sarah held up *Through the Looking-Glass* as evidence. "Then it got too hot, so I went to the park."

"Maybe you should spend more time at home," Bernard said.

"Why?"

They looked at each other.

"We just like to know where we can find you, dear," Aunt Helena said smoothly, patting her stiff pearly blond hair. "Hadn't we better go, Bernard?"

When the door had closed behind them, Sarah ran to the window in the living room and waited until she saw them emerge from beneath the awning in front of the building and start walking quickly down the street. Then she went to the front door and slipped the chain lock into place.

Their bedroom was dark, the shades pulled down, the curtains drawn. Now that Uncle Bernard's desk and chair had been moved in, the room was crowded with furniture. Sarah went over to the desk, switched on the brass lamp, and laid the book down next to it. One by one she opened the drawers and went through them, her heart racing. She had to be careful about putting everything back exactly the way she found it; unlike her father, whose desk had always been piled with books and slips of paper and stubby pencils, Uncle Bernard had a place for everything. There wasn't so much as a stray paper clip.

Nor was there a copy of the will. There was nothing out of the ordinary at all, just bills and records and warranties.

She turned off the lamp and sat back in the chair, feeling a mixture of relief and disappointment. Maybe her imagination had run away with her.

Still, it was odd about Great-aunt Daisy's letter. And the money business too. Both things might have perfectly logical explanations. Maybe she ought to write the aunts herself. But what could she say?

She got up and went into the kitchen and punched Sam's number on the telephone. It rang twice, and she thought he was answering, but it was his machine.

"Sam, it's Sarah," she said after the beep. "Call me when you can, okay? I need to talk to you. Bye."

She opened the oven door and sniffed, then peeked under the tent of foil. A dry piece of chicken huddled next to some shriveled peas and a boiled potato. She stuffed everything in an empty cereal box she found in the trash and put the plate in the dishwasher.

Standing in the middle of the kitchen floor, she was nagged by the sense that she had forgotten something. The book! What had she done with it?

She found it, finally, lying next to the lamp on Uncle Bernard's desk.

"Some spy you'd make," she said aloud. Her hands had gone cold and clammy. Suppose he had found it there? He would know she'd been in their bedroom, at his desk. She was going to have to be more careful, just in case. . . .

There are thousands of them, Sarah, and they're everywhere.

I was following him, and he was following you.

Sometimes I've believed as many as six impossible things before breakfast!

Burn this letter.

She took Sam's letter from her pocket, smoothed it out, and read it once more. Then she unlocked the front door and stepped out into the hallway in her bare feet, leaving the door open behind her. At the end of the hall there was a small square door in the wall that opened like a mailbox into the incinerator shaft. She tore Sam's letter into strips and then into tiny squares, holding them in one hand and opening the door with the other. A blast of heat rose from the darkness. She thought she could hear, ten floors below, the faraway roar of the furnace. She thrust her hand into the shaft and let the pieces fall.

"Hello there!" a voice behind her called.

Sarah jumped, her hand flying to her chest.

"Oh, did I startle you, dear? I'm so sorry." It was Mrs. Gillespie, the one with the fat tabby. She held a brown paper bag full of trash.

"You shouldn't leave the door open like that when you go out, you know," the woman said, blinking, her eyes magnified enormously by the thick glasses she wore. "Anyone could get in. You never know. I'm sure you watch the news."

"Yes. I was just . . ."

"Burning a letter?" Mrs. Gillespie smiled. "Very wise. I burn all mine. You never know. Not that I get very many anymore.

People are just too busy. They'd rather call, don't you think?"

"I . . . I guess so. Well, good night." Sarah started for the apartment door.

"Good night, dear. Stop by and pet Fritz whenever you like. He took a real liking to you. It's not everyone he'll go to, you know."

Sarah forced a smile and quickly closed the door, leaning against it with her hand over her pounding heart.

Was Mrs. Gillespie one of them too?

Stop it. You're getting paranoid.

The apartment suddenly seemed quiet. Sarah heard the refrigerator switch on. She left the chain unfastened so she could make a quick escape if she needed to, then took a deep breath and walked through the rooms, turning on lights, peeking around doors, even checking the closets and under the beds, wondering what she would do if she discovered someone.

Have a heart attack.

Girl, 15, Found Dead of Cardiac Arrest in Empty Apartment; Police Look for Clues in Mystery Death of Teen

She threw back the shower curtain.

But there wasn't anyone. She turned on the TV in the little room off the kitchen just to have the sound of human voices, went into her room, and sat on the edge of the bed. *Call me, Sam,* she thought, beaming the command toward him. The two of them had tried to communicate this way many times before; they even had a name for it: mental radio. For a moment she believed it was going to work. She imagined the telephone ringing, Sam's voice on the other end. She stared at the china cat on the bureau. Minutes passed.

A siren wailed, grew louder, then began to fade. She went to the window, knelt on the carpet, and rested her elbows on the sill. From this height, if she squinted, the people on the sidewalks looked more like ants than humans. They all carried little bits of matter, the way ants did; except that instead of bread crumbs they carried babies and shopping bags and newspapers. They moved like ants too, purposefully, as if they had a destination in mind. She followed a few of them, one at a time, like a god observing from on high.

Absently she traced "Sam" on the glass with a fingernail, over and over.

That was when she noticed one small figure far below who wasn't moving, a man standing against the wall of a building across the street. At this distance his face was a small, pale blur, but she could tell from the angle of his head that he was looking up. Looking up at her window. He wore a white shirt.

It's summer, she told herself. *Lots of people wear white when it's hot.*

But half an hour later, after she had tried in vain to read herself to sleep and went to the window once more, he was still there.

six

Angel Muldoon

Summer came to an end with no word from Sam.

Sarah never saw the man in the white shirt again, or if she did, she didn't recognize him. But sometimes, walking through Central Park or sitting in the library, she felt as if someone was watching her.

She wrote Sam, called and left messages on his answering machine. "Don't worry if you don't hear from me for a while," he had said in his letter. But how long was "a while"? And how could she possibly not worry?

School began again, the streets and sidewalks gradually gave up their heat, and the sky cleared into a hard, bright blue. One afternoon in October she was doing her homework at a picnic table in the park when she heard the sound of horses' hooves and looked up to see two riders cantering toward her on the bridle path. In the dying light of the afternoon, against the backdrop of the city's towers, the horses seemed magical, creatures out of a forgotten world.

The girl on the high-stepping bay wore a riding helmet

and jodhpurs and gleaming black boots. Her blond hair was pinned in a bun at the nape of her neck.

The boy on her far side rode bareback on a big dappled gray, completely at ease, his long legs dangling. They were about to pass out of sight when, as if feeling Sarah's gaze, the boy turned and looked back. They stared at each other in surprise. It was the boy from the library. He reined in the gray.

"Hey!" the girl slowed her horse, circled around. "What are we waiting for?" Her eyes swept over Sarah. Sarah was almost disappointed to see that she was not as beautiful as she had seemed from a distance; her pointy face spoiled the picture.

The boy looked at Sarah as though he wanted to speak. Instead he lifted one hand in greeting and nudged the big gray into a canter, leaving the girl to follow.

That night Sarah found "Riding Academies" in the yellow pages. One of the listings was for stables just a few blocks away. She couldn't believe that for six months she had been living that close to horses and didn't even know it.

The bell rang, the last bell of the day. Sarah waited until the classroom had emptied, and walked down the corridor to her locker. It smelled like banana peel inside, even though she had never once kept a banana there.

She threw her Latin book into the locker—she hadn't wanted to take Latin at all, but French II had been full—and took out math.

"Carry your books?" a voice asked. She whirled around and found herself face-to-face with the boy she had seen in the park. She was too surprised to speak.

"Come on," he said, starting down the hall, "let's get out of here before they lock me up and try to teach me something useless."

"Don't you go to school?" she managed to ask as they hurried out the front door past the security guard.

He laughed. "Not me."

So how had he managed to track her down? Why would he want to—she'd been so rude to him that afternoon at the playground. . . .

He seemed not to notice her embarrassment. "I went to first grade for a few weeks," he said. "I remember a lady with long red fingernails, like a witch. She grabbed me by the shoulders and shook me. I ran out the door and never went back."

They were on the street now, walking fast. The boy had pulled her books from her arms in a mock tug-of-war and was carrying them on his hip. His Batman T-shirt was so old she could barely see the faded picture on the front. He wore a bandanna around his forehead.

"Don't your parents mind?"

"What is this? An interrogation?" He stopped. "Recite the Ten Commandments," he said abruptly. "You can't, can you? Know how to tie sailors' knots? Read clouds? What about this?" He closed his eyes.

She was a child and I was a child,
    In this kingdom by the sea,
But we loved with a love that was more than love—
    I and my Annabel Lee.

"Edgar Allan Poe," Sarah said. "I love that poem."

"I can recite dozens of poems. I can box, too. Real boxing, according to Queensberry rules. And fence"—he brandished an imaginary sword—"they don't teach *that* in school. And I can dance and swim and read Morse code and ride. You like horses, don't you?"

"How did you know?"

"I could just tell. Anyway, most girls like horses. Horses and poetry."

"How much does it cost to ride at that stable?" Sarah asked.

"Doesn't cost me anything. I work there."

"You do?" They were standing on the corner waiting for the light. "Lucky."

"You muck out twenty stalls a day and tell me how lucky you feel."

"I wouldn't mind."

"I'll remember you said that."

They crossed the street, making their way around the nose of a taxi. The boy thumped his fist on the taxi's hood. "Hey, this is a pedestrian walkway, okay?" The taxi driver rolled down his window and spit. "Nice," the boy said.

They walked in silence past the hot-dog vendor outside the playground gates and turned down a path under a canopy of trees. All the newspaper reports of girls attacked by strangers in the park flickered through Sarah's mind. She glanced sideways at him. He was ambling along with her books in one arm, his back very straight, whistling.

She had to trust someone.

They emerged from the trees on a grassy knoll overlooking

a large pond. A rowboat with a man and a woman sitting in
the bow drifted along under the falling leaves.

"Ever been on the lake?" the boy asked.

"That's not a lake," Sarah said, sounding more scornful
than she meant to. "It's more like a pond. We had one almost
that big in back of our house where I used to live."

"Did you fish in it?"

Sarah nodded. "There were some smallmouth bass, but I
never caught anything except sunnies."

"When she was a little girl, my mother used to catch fish
with her bare hands. Once she found a ring inside a fish. She
gave it to me." The boy held up his hand, displaying a wreath
of golden leaves, exquisitely detailed. The edges of some of
the leaves had worn away a little, but the delicate, branching
veins were still clearly visible.

"It's beautiful," Sarah said. "It looks very old."

"My mother said it was part of a treasure, a tribute to a
king, and that it came from somewhere very far away. There
are some markings inside—words, I think—but I've never
found anyone who could read them." He slipped off the ring
and handed it to her.

She studied the odd symbols engraved on the flat inner surface. "They don't look like any letters I've ever seen," she said,
returning it. "How did your mother know that about the ring?"

"She has the Sight. You know—if you give her something
to hold, she can tell you who it belonged to or where it came
from. She's a Gypsy."

"Does she tell fortunes?"

"She used to." He turned and began walking along the
bank.

"A Gypsy told my fortune at the state fair last year," Sarah said, catching up with him. "But I don't think she was a real Gypsy. She just said stuff like I was going to marry a handsome man and have five children and be very happy."

He held back an overgrown branch so she could get past. "Maybe you will."

"No, I won't. I'm going to be an artist and live in the countryside in Italy. In a villa." She had not thought of the Italian part until now, but it sounded wonderful.

"Then, I'll come and visit you," he said. "In my *vardo*. It's like a camper, only much better. Look . . ." He took his wallet out of his pocket and removed a piece of paper, old and creased from having been folded and unfolded many times. It was a black-and-white photo that looked as if it had been cut out of a magazine or a book. A dark man sat proudly on the driver's bench of a horse-drawn wagon, staring into the camera. Sarah peered at the grainy photograph. The wagon had high wooden sides and a roof and a door, all covered with carved designs of birds and flowers.

"It's beautiful," Sarah said. Then she remembered she had said the ring was beautiful too. She tried to think of something else to say, something to equal his offering of the picture.

He studied the photograph a moment before replacing it in his wallet. "My *vardo* will be even more beautiful. I'm going to travel all over Spain and Portugal. And Italy," he added with a wink.

They came out of the park and stood on the sidewalk as the traffic rumbled past them, then crossed the avenue to stand in front of the American Museum of Natural History.

Sarah stared up at the banners flapping in the wind over the entrance.

"Want to go in and see the dinosaur skeletons?" the boy asked. "We can get in for free—I know all the guards."

"No, thanks. I probably ought to be going."

"Not yet," he said. "I haven't even introduced myself." He held out his hand. "Angel Muldoon."

"Angel? Is that your real name?"

"I don't know my real name," he said, sitting down on the museum steps with her books. "My mother hasn't told me what it is. When a Gypsy baby's born, his mother whispers his true name in his ear, but it's kept secret until the child grows up."

"But you're seventeen."

He laughed and leaned back carelessly against the steps, stretching out his long legs. "Old enough to know when I'm being a nuisance, right?"

Sarah flushed. "I'm sorry—I didn't mean to be rude. I think I was a little scared of you."

"I figured it was something like that. It's okay."

Sarah toyed with her shoelace. "Is Angel a Gypsy name?"

"It's Cornish. You know, Cornwall, in England?" She could tell he thought she might never have heard of it. "King Arthur's castle is supposed to be there," he added.

"I know." She and her family had stayed in a small cottage in Cornwall once, on a cliff overlooking the ocean. In her mind she saw the wild gray sea, heard the cries of the gulls. She and her father had taken a long walk one windy afternoon, and he had told her the story of Merlin and Arthur, of Lancelot and Guinevere.

It was getting harder to recall her father's face. Would a time come when she couldn't remember what he looked like at all?

Angel was staring intently at her, as if he sensed her thoughts.

"My parents happened to be in Cornwall when I came along. My father's Irish—he used to be in an acting troupe. They traveled a lot."

She liked it that Angel had been born in Cornwall and that she had been there. It seemed like a bond between them. She was wondering whether to tell him about the cottage on the cliff when he said, "You ask a lot of questions, you know that?"

"I guess I get it from my dad. He's . . . he was a journalist." Sarah stared at her sneakers. "He and my mother were killed in a plane crash in March." She hated telling people. No one ever knew what to say—what was there to say? Or else they said too much.

Angel lifted his hand and, after a second's hesitation, put it on her shoulder. "Now I understand," he said, "why you always look so sad."

Always? What could he mean?

He let his hand fall. "Have you seen that guy again? The one who was following you?"

"I think I did," Sarah said, startled into recollection. "Once. That night. A man in a white shirt was down in the street, looking up at my window. I never saw him again, but sometimes I feel like someone's watching me. . . ."

"It was probably just me." He looked almost shy for a moment. "I've been—you know—sort of keeping an eye on you. I know you told me to get lost and all, but . . ." He paused. "Why'd he want that letter, anyhow?"

"I don't know," she said, hugging herself. In the shadow of the building the air was chilly.

He studied her. "You're not scared of me anymore, are you?"

"No."

"What are you afraid of, then?"

"I don't know exactly. That's what makes it scary."

He leaned toward her, very close but not touching.

"I won't let anyone hurt you," he said, so softly that at first she wasn't sure she had heard him correctly.

"Nobody can promise that."

"Angel Muldoon can."

Sarah saw Angel every day after that. He was there mornings when she came out of the building, and was waiting on the school steps every afternoon. She kept a pair of jeans and a flannel shirt and her old boots at the riding stable. After she changed clothes, she helped him saddle the horses and lead them from their stalls on the second floor down to the ring, where their riders waited.

She told Helena and Bernard she had to stay after school to work on the school paper. She didn't want them to know anything about Angel and the stable. The time she spent there was her one joy, and she wanted to keep it safe from their poking and prying. Every evening before she left for the apartment, she stood in the stable's restroom and washed the smell of horses from her skin.

Sometimes, if a horse needed exercising, she got to ride.

Angel, who preferred riding bareback, taught her how (he told her that Alexander the Great and his cavalry had conquered the world riding bareback—stirrups hadn't been invented yet). For days her thigh muscles ached from holding on, and she sported purple bruises from two bad falls. But Angel was a good teacher, and she kept trying until she could stay on at a gallop, though she never quite lost her fear of falling.

She had never seen anyone better with horses than Angel.

He seemed to read their minds. He had horses in his blood, he said. His grandfather had been a Lowari Gypsy from Romania, in eastern Europe. The Lowaris had trained and traded horses for generations.

"Angel has a way with horses, all right," said Pam, who, with Jody, ran the office and gave lessons.

"Horses aren't all," Jody said, and the two women laughed in a way that made Sarah uncomfortable.

Sarah noticed that the girls and women who came to ride were always asking Angel to help them mount their horses, to raise or lower their stirrups, to check the girth when he had checked it only moments before. Sometimes when this happened, he would catch Sarah's eye and wink as if the two of them shared a secret.

Sitting in school or lying in bed late at night, she wondered what it would be like to kiss him. She had been kissed before, by boys she knew in school back home, but most of them had been either shy and nervous or clumsy and insistent. Angel would be none of those things; she could tell by the way he touched the horses, stroking them, talking softly to them. But he had never tried to kiss her. He seemed careful not to touch her even, so that when they did touch accidentally, his fingers grazing hers as he handed her a currycomb, their bodies brushing against each other in a stall, she felt the contact like a mild shock.

One rainy afternoon in late October, when he had finished mucking out the stalls, they sat in the hayloft with their legs dangling over the edge, sharing a thermos of the strong and sweet black coffee he liked.

"Do all Gypsies like their coffee this strong?" Sarah asked.

Angel nodded. "Black as the devil, hot as hell, and sweet as love—that's what they say."

Sarah managed a smile.

He put the plastic cup down on the straw between them. "Is there anything wrong? You seem worried."

"It's Sam." Sarah split a piece of straw with her fingernail. "It's been almost two months since that letter. I've called and left messages on his answering machine, but he never calls back." Little by little, as they worked together in the stable, Sarah had told Angel everything except what she had promised Sam to keep secret about the Looking Glass. "I even called the Institute's main number," she went on, "and asked the operator to page him, but he didn't answer the page. The third time I tried, the operator transferred me to one of Sam's assistants. He said Sam was in the testing chamber and couldn't be reached by phone. He said he'd tell Sam I called, but I still haven't heard anything."

Neither of them spoke. Rain lashed the windows. The horse in the stall below snorted and tossed his head.

"Something's wrong, Angel! I just know it. I have to go out there."

"To California?" He poured the last of the coffee. "It's a long way."

"I know. And I haven't got the money to fly. I haven't even got bus fare."

"You're not thinking about hitching, are you?"

"What else can I do?"

"I'll go with you."

"You will?" She hadn't allowed herself to hope for this, but here it was. She threw her arms around him. "You're the best friend anybody could have."

"It will be an adventure," he said, gently freeing himself.

"I'll have to put everything in the pack I take to school, so Helena and Bernard won't suspect anything," Sarah said, thinking aloud. "But what about you? What will you tell your parents?"

"Oh, I've gone on the road before. My father won't say no. He roamed all over the world when he was my age. 'Home-keeping youth have ever homely wits,' he always says. That's Shakespeare."

Sarah tried to imagine what her own father would've said if she—or Sam, for that matter—had announced plans to hitchhike across the country. How different Angel's life was. She realized suddenly that apart from what he had told her on the museum steps, he had said very little about his family. She didn't even know his telephone number or where he lived.

"Besides," Angel was saying, "Da knows I can take care of myself. He ought to—he's the one who taught me how."

For the rest of the afternoon they made plans. Angel would ask for his paycheck on Thursday afternoon rather than Friday; they would meet Friday morning in front of her building. That way they'd be a whole day's distance from the city before Helena and Bernard found out Sarah was missing.

"'Last night you slept on a goose-feather bed,'" Angel sang to her as he worked, "'With the sheet turned down so bravely, O! And to-night you'll sleep in a cold open field, along with the wraggle-taggle Gypsies, O!'"

She was late for Latin. A pipe had burst in the girls' dressing room during PE and they'd had to get dressed under the bleachers.

She kept her head down as she entered the room and went to her seat at the end of the third row.

There was a substitute teacher, a white-haired woman in an old-fashioned suit, wearing dark glasses. *Good*, Sarah thought as she slid into her seat. Last night she'd been too keyed up to do her homework; maybe the substitute would simply give them some busywork to do in class. Sarah slumped down, trying to hide behind the football player in front of her.

"Let us now take up the perfect indicative tense of the verb of the first conjugation," the teacher was saying. Sarah opened her notebook.

Chalk went *tap-tap-tap* across the blackboard. "*Amavi*: 'I have loved.' ''Tis better to have loved and lost than never to have loved at all,' according to Tennyson. Would you agree?" she asked the class. No one answered. "You have no thoughts on the matter? You have no thoughts at all, perhaps?"

She toyed with the chalk. "One could say 'I did love' rather than 'I have loved,'" she went on, pacing the room. Her slip was showing beneath the hem of her skirt, a half inch of lace. "Or with Catullus, who no longer respects his lover but cannot stop desiring her, *'Odi et amo.'* 'I hate, yet I love.' *'Excrucior,'* says Catullus. 'I am being tortured.' Ah, human love." She gazed at the ceiling. "How mysterious, how paradoxical it is."

The sound of pencils scurrying across notebook paper died away. Everyone was looking at the teacher, who continued to stare at the ceiling. Could she even see anything through those glasses? The round black lenses looked completely opaque.

The trace of a lovely, flowery smell drifted past Sarah. She sniffed the air, smelled her hands. Not soap.

"Tedious business, conjugation. *'Dabit deus his quoque finem.'* Translation?" The teacher looked hopefully around the room. "From Virgil's *Aeneid*: 'God will grant an end even to these troubles.'" A ripple of laughter ran through the room as she turned and began writing on the board in large, looping letters.

Sarah copied the Virgil quote into her notebook and sat back, gazing at the board and twisting a strand of hair around her pencil. Something stirred in her memory, tantalizing, just out of reach. That handwriting. Someone else had handwriting like that; one of the aunts?

A moment later the memory rushed to the surface, and Sarah sat bolt upright, dropping her pencil. It rolled crazily across her desk and fell on the floor, bouncing on its eraser.

It can't be, Sarah thought. The football player, grunting, stretched to retrieve her pencil and handed it to her with a grin. He was missing one of his front teeth.

Sometimes I've believed as many as six impossible things before breakfast!

But—if . . . if she was the old lady who had written the note about *Through the Looking-Glass*, then she also must be—she had to be . . .

Sarah tried to imagine the teacher in a shabby coat and knitted cap, her hair long and stringy instead of woven into a neat figure eight.

While the rest of the students relaxed into their seats— the substitute had left conjugation behind and was reciting a limerick in Latin about a woman named Chloë who buried seven husbands—Sarah stared, her mind seesawing crazily. It was her. No, it wasn't. It couldn't be. It wasn't just that she looked different, cleaned up and neatly dressed; there was more to it than that. There was something changeable about her very appearance, something that made her look a little different from one moment to the next, like a cloud or a reflection on water. A quivery aura of light outlined her against the blackboard. No one else seemed to notice; they were all exchanging amused glances, enjoying the novelty of being entertained in Latin class.

Sarah looked back. The light was still there. *It must be because I've been staring at her for so long,* Sarah thought, try- ing to blink it away.

"As I shall not be seeing most of you again," she was say- ing, "I should like to leave you with this piece of advice: *Semper ubi sub ubi.* Translation?"

"'Always . . . ,'" a girl in the front of the class began. "'Always'—is *ubi* 'when' or 'where'?"

"'Where,' in this instance."

"'Always where . . . under where'?"

"Quite right."

The class exploded into laughter as the bell rang. Everyone began filing out, shaking their heads and grinning.

Say something, Sarah thought, slowly gathering her books. But what? *Excuse me, I know this sounds crazy, but were you in a tree house in the woods about seven months ago?*

The teacher was erasing the board. At the door Sarah paused, chewing her lip. The scent of roses was strong, almost dizzying.

"Oh, Miss Lucas . . ."

"Yes?" Sarah turned around.

"I have an assignment for you."

seven

Urgent Messages

"Don't be afraid." **The woman placed the eraser on the** ledge, removed her odd black spectacles, and turned to face Sarah.

There was no mistaking those eyes. Looking into their gray depths was like gazing at an ocean, boundless and serene and charged with power. The light around the woman's body grew brighter, and she held up one hand.

"Your brother is in grave danger. You must return the Stone to the Door."

"Danger? What do you mean?" Sarah clutched her books against her chest and stepped forward. "Is Sam hurt? Where is he?"

"The Stone will guide you."

"What stone?" The light flared, so brightly that Sarah had to shield her eyes. "Please, I don't understand—"

"The Umbra will oppose you, but you must resist with all your strength. Go now, and be on your guard."

"Umbra? What's that? Please, just tell me where Sam is so I can—"

"Go! Quickly!"

Sarah backed out the door into the empty corridor. What should she do? Where should she go? The old woman couldn't just— She pushed open the classroom door again. "Please," she began, "I . . ." But the room was empty.

She hurried toward the apartment, her head bowed against the October wind, going over in her mind for the hundredth time what the old woman had said to her. It didn't make sense. The only thing she understood was that Sam was in danger. She had to try to reach him.

Dead leaves scuttled down the sidewalk toward her like an army of crabs. The stout doorman, Mr. Beamish, stood under the canopy at the entrance to the building, his cheeks ruddy from the cold.

"You're home early," he said, opening the door for her.

Sarah nodded. "Is my aunt at home?"

"Went out about half an hour ago. Grocery shopping, she said. Didn't forget your key, did you?"

"No. Thanks."

"Oh, and the super's coming up in a minute," Mr. Beamish called as Sarah got on the elevator, "to fix the thermostat."

At least I don't have to face Aunt Helena right away, Sarah thought, unlocking the apartment door. She went straight to the kitchen and dialed Sam's number. With a sinking heart she heard the answering machine click on, and she hung up the phone before the recorded message ended, and dialed the Institute's main number.

"Cultural Institute," said a woman's voice. "May I help you?"

"May I speak to Dr. Samuel Lucas?"

"One moment, please."

Sarah leaned against the wall, twining the cord through her fingers, waiting.

"Experimental," a man's voice announced impatiently.

"Dr. Lucas, please."

There was a silence at the other end. "Who is this?"

"I'm his sister." Sarah pushed herself away from the wall and began to pace. "I've been trying to reach him for a long time. It's very important that I speak to him—"

"Just a minute," the man said.

Someone knocked loudly on the apartment door. "Superintendent!" a voice announced.

"Come in!" Sarah called, but the building superintendent was already unlocking the door with his own key. "Got my hands full," he said, brandishing a tool kit in one hand and a package in the other. "Brought this up with me—it just came for you. Careful, it's kinda heavy."

"Thank you." Sarah took the parcel from him. "I'm sorry, I'm on the phone—the thermostat's in the dining room."

"No problem. I'll only be a second."

Holding the phone against her ear, Sarah carried the package into the kitchen—it *was* heavy—and laid it on the counter. Wasn't anyone going to come back on the line? What could be happening on the other end?

Suddenly a voice broke in. It was the same man as before, only now he sounded less impatient than nervous. "Dr. Lucas can't come to the phone," he said. "He's carrying out some experiments, and the entire chamber is sealed."

"Unseal it, then! I need to talk to him."

THE DREAM OF THE STONE

"I'm sorry—that's not possible."

But Sarah scarcely heard the man. The package on the counter was addressed to her. It was Sam's handwriting, but it was messy, a mad scrawl. He must've been in a terrible hurry.

"Hello?" the man was saying. "Hello? Any message?"

"Just tell him to call me, please."

Sarah hung up. Why, why wouldn't they let her talk to Sam? Had something happened to him? She carried the package into the dining room, where the superintendent was replacing the cover of the thermostat.

"That ought to do it," he said, hoisting his toolbox. Sarah saw him to the door, locked it, and sat down at the dining-room table, feeling shaky and scared.

She yanked at the flap of the mailer, scratching her finger on a staple. Inside an object was packed in shredded computer printouts. There was a note from Sam.

Here's a prize paperweight to add to your collection. Don't you dare trade it. I expect to see it appropriately displayed when I come to visit you.

Love,
Sam the Man

Sarah pulled away the strands of paper. Underneath was a stone, a gleaming, polished dome. She picked it up. It fit perfectly in the palm of her hand.

She held it up to the light. At first it had looked black and opaque. Now she saw it was not black at all, but a pure dark blue, the ethereal blue of a winter twilight deepening into night. Hidden in its depths, among veils of clouds, glimmered a universe of tiny silver stars.

The Stone.

"What's that?"

Sarah jumped. She hadn't heard Aunt Helena come in.

"Oh, nothing." She swept all the torn paper together in a heap, along with the Stone. "The super brought up a package for me when he came to fix the thermostat."

"Something from Sam?" Aunt Helena bustled into the dining room holding her shopping bag. She seemed anxious, as though she was afraid she might have missed something. "What did he send you?"

"Oh, just a paperweight," Sarah said, trying to sound off-hand. "I collect them."

"Really? I've never seen your collection, have I?"

That's because I don't have one, Sarah thought, but said, "It's in storage."

"Let's see."

"See what?"

"The paperweight, of course."

Sarah swallowed. "It's in here somewhere. . . ." She searched for it with one hand, dropping shreds of paper, and held it out for inspection. Was it her imagination, or had the Stone gone dark?

Aunt Helena examined it, squinting. "Looks like black glass," she said, handing it back. "An odd gift."

Sarah kept her eyes on the Stone. "I like it," she said. "I think it's beautiful."

"Well, as long as it makes you happy."

Who said anything about happy? Sarah thought, going to

her room. She dumped the trash in the wastepaper basket, retrieved Sam's note, and went into the bathroom. Then she locked the door behind her and flushed the torn pieces down the toilet.

In the bathroom mirror her eyes looked huge and dark and frightened.

"The Stone will guide you," she said to her reflection. But she could tell from the look in her eyes that she didn't really believe it.

Sarah stared at the glowing green numbers on the digital clock beside her bed, Uncle Bernard's clock: 2:32. She had been in bed for hours, trying to sleep, holding the Stone in her hand. But she couldn't sleep; she was too worried about Sam.

I should have made the old woman tell me more, Sarah thought. *No, not more. Everything: like where Sam is and how I'm supposed to get there, for starters.*

Grave danger. Life-or-death danger.

If I were in danger, Sam wouldn't lie around in bed. He'd do something.

But what? What am I supposed to do?

You must return the Stone to the Door.

What door? There were thousands of doors in the city, maybe even millions. Which one was it? Maybe it wasn't even in New York. Maybe the door was in California, at the Institute. Maybe they were keeping Sam locked up there, and the Stone was a kind of key.

But that couldn't be right. A stone couldn't be a key— could it?

She pulled her quilt up around her shoulders and turned

onto her other side, held the cool surface of the Stone against her cheek. Then, from the blackness behind her closed eyes, an image of Sam swam to the surface, an image so real that her eyes flew open and she cried out.

The vision disappeared. She lay rigid and still, afraid to move, afraid Helena or Bernard might have heard her. But there was no sound from their bedroom.

What was it? What had happened?

She had seen him. And not simply seen him. She had been where he was, felt the wind of that place against her skin.

He'd been outside somewhere, kneeling before a tall, oval mirror supported by metal uprights. Not an ordinary mirror; it was at least seven feet high, and instead of glass it was made of a shiny reflective metal. Behind his head clouds floated in a green sky. A steel case was open at his side, revealing a maze of electronic circuitry. Sam had a tool in his hand, a small hammer or maybe a wrench, but from the way he was clutching it, she knew he'd used it to smash something, or intended to. He looked haggard—worse than that. His face was bruised and swollen.

She had taken in all this in the split second before she cried out. Now she tried to get the vision back. She stayed in the same position, even tried to think the same thoughts, but it was useless. Finally she slid the Stone under her pillow and stared up at the ceiling, where the artificial stars on the map of the universe glowed in the dark.

The next morning Uncle Bernard insisted on walking her to school. Angel was waiting for her beneath the dripping awning in front of her building. When he saw Bernard, he turned and slipped away before she could even catch his eye. Bernard hadn't seemed to notice him, but Sarah couldn't be sure. She couldn't be sure of anything anymore. She hurried to keep up with him. His legs were short, but he sped along the sidewalk, jostling people aside as he dodged puddles, his briefcase swinging dangerously.

They paused at an intersection, Uncle Bernard almost twitching with impatience. When the signal changed, Sarah felt someone brush her arm, stick something in her coat pocket where she had hidden the Stone. She drew a sharp breath, and Bernard shot her a curious look. Behind him, Angel disappeared down the street.

She checked her pocket. The Stone was still there—and something else, a small square of thin, stiff cardboard.

At the entrance of the school Bernard glowered and muttered something about being on her "best behavior." She hurried up the steps and went to the girls' restroom, shut herself in a stall.

On the inside of a matchbook cover, Angel had carefully written: "Meet you outside school after fourth period."

When at last the bell rang after algebra, she raced through the halls to the front door. Outside, Angel was leaning against the wall, the hood of his poncho pulled over his head.

"Did your aunt and uncle find out?" Angel threw back the hood. A few tendrils of wet hair clung to his forehead.

"I—I don't think so. But we can't go now anyway. Something else happened."

Sarah glanced over her shoulder into the lobby and lowered her voice. "Remember the old lady I told you about?"

She recounted the story of what had happened in Latin class. "I couldn't figure out what she was talking about, but when I got back to the apartment, there was a package from Sam. This was in it." Sarah reached into her raincoat pocket and held out the Stone. She had the curious sensation that by showing it to Angel, she was testing him in some way.

He took the Stone and turned it over in his long, slender fingers. Watching him gave her an odd, dizzy feeling.

Suddenly he drew a sharp breath. "Good God."

"What is it?"

"I had a dream about this stone last night."

"*What?*" Sarah said, so loudly that a passerby turned to look at them.

"Come on." Angel handed her the Stone and took her arm. "Let's go somewhere we can talk."

They walked through the drizzle to the coffee shop, settled in a booth at the back.

"Any chance we can still get breakfast?" Angel asked the waitress.

She glanced at a clock on the wall. "Make it snappy and I'll see what I can do. We stopped serving at eleven thirty."

"Thanks," Angel said. They placed their order and the waitress left. Sarah took out the Stone and placed it on the table.

"In the dream," Angel began, "I was in a strange place. You were there too. There was a weird pointed arch, made of gray rock. It had things carved into it—animals and birds and plants—and at the very top there was a flower."

"Growing in the rock?"

"No. It was carved from the rock like the other stuff. The

flower had big, flat petals, and in the center there was a round place"—he touched the Stone—"where this was supposed to go. Only, it wasn't there. It wasn't there because it's here."

"But I thought you said you dreamed about the Stone? If it wasn't there, how—"

He cut her off with a wave of his hand. "This is the Stone. Don't ask me how I know."

"Then, the arch . . ." A thrill of revelation ran through her. "The arch must be the door the old woman was talking about. It has to be!" She seized his arm. "But where is it, Angel? Have you ever seen it before? Could it be here in the city?"

He shook his head.

"Maybe you saw a picture of it, then? In a book? Try to remember!"

Sarah saw the waitress approaching and scooped up the Stone.

"Pancakes?" the waitress asked.

"Here," Angel said. "And coffee. Thanks, Wonder Woman."

She rolled her eyes and tried not to smile. "So you're the blueberry muffin," she said to Sarah, "and a small OJ. Anything else?"

When they shook their heads, she scribbled on her pad, tore off the check, left it in front of Angel, and walked away, touching the back of her hair.

Angel stirred sugar into his coffee and gazed out the window at the rain. "It wasn't a picture," he said. "And I'm sure I've never seen it before in real life anywhere. But it's strange. The Door did seem familiar to me somehow. Like I'd dreamed about it before, a long, long time ago."

He looked down at his full plate, as if wondering where it had come from, and picked up his fork. Before he had eaten half the pancakes, he wiped his mouth, threw a handful of bills on the table, and stood up.

"Let's go," he said, hoisting his pack over his shoulder. "I want to show that Stone to someone."

"I'm not sure anyone else should know," Sarah said as they went out the door and started down the sidewalk.

He didn't look at her. "She won't tell anyone."

They walked quickly through the drizzle, past the high school, with its barred windows, and down the street, where two lean, dark men in greasy overalls stood at the open garage door of a car repair shop. "Hey, *didakai!*" one of them said to Angel, and laughed.

Angel turned around to face them, walking backward, and said something in a language Sarah didn't recognize. Their amused expressions faded.

"What's a *didakai*?" Sarah asked when they had turned the corner.

"What I am: a half-breed."

"What did you say? They looked so . . ."

"Shamefaced? I think that's the word. I was speaking Romany, the language of the Gypsies. I said that I spoke better Romany than they did, and that in my heart I am more of a true Romanichal—a Gypsy man—than they will ever be."

He stopped in front of the library. "This is where I live."

"Here? In the library?"

"Upstairs, in an apartment on the third floor. My father's the custodian."

He held open the heavy wooden door and they went in,

past the desk where a librarian greeted Angel, then up the curving staircase to the second floor. Angel led the way through the stacks to a door at the back of the building. He unlocked it, and they walked up a narrow enclosed staircase to another door at the top.

"Come in," he said, opening the door. Sarah stepped into a hallway that smelled of cabbage.

"The sitting room's in there," Angel said, nodding toward a doorway on the left. He put his pack down in the hall. "I'll be back in a minute."

Sarah stood in the middle of the room and looked around. There was a big, lumpy sofa, a kidney-shaped coffee table, and an enormous TV. But mostly there were books: stacks and stacks of books lined up against the wall, books that had been used as bricks to make shelves for other books, supporting boards that sagged under the weight of still more books.

She walked over to one shelf and peered at the titles: *The Voyage of Magellan*, *How to Work with Tools and Wood*, *Deciduous Trees of North America*, *The Collected Poems of Henry Vaughan*.

"My father's," Angel said from the doorway. "Discards from the library. Come on." They walked single file down the hall. It, too, was lined with stacks of books towering nearly to the ceiling.

In a room at the end of the hall, a high-backed chair covered in threadbare red velvet faced the window. A moment passed before Sarah realized there was someone sitting in the chair.

"This is my mother," Angel said, taking Sarah's hand and

leading her forward. "Mara." A woman sat staring at the gray sky, her hands folded in the lap of her long patchwork skirt. She must have been very beautiful once, Sarah realized. Even now something of her beauty persisted, like a flame that refuses to go out. But her large, dark eyes were sunken and dull, and the delicate bones of her face showed through. She had the look of a wild creature—some bright bird, Sarah thought—resigned to long captivity.

A red silk scarf was wrapped around her head and tied behind. Her black hair, shot through with gray, had been recently brushed and carefully arranged around her shoulders. Angel rested his hand on her head. "Give me the Stone," he said to Sarah.

Sarah handed it to him, and he knelt beside his mother's chair. He gently opened her fingers and placed the Stone in them, then closed her hand around it and murmured something Sarah couldn't hear.

Angel's mother stared fixedly at him. "What is this you're asking? This is for the foolish *gaji*, not for us."

"Just this once, for me. Please try."

Angel's mother closed her eyes and rested her head against the chair. The tension in her face drained away, leaving her features in repose.

There was silence in the room. Sarah noticed for the first time that the walls were painted white, the ceiling a bright blue, like the sky. A mattress lay on the floor, covered with what looked like an eiderdown quilt. A large, hand-lettered sign stood propped against the wall: MADAME ESPERANZA, PALMIST: DESTINIES REVEALED, RENOWNED THROUGHOUT THE BRITISH ISLES, PATRONIZED BY ALL CLASSES.

Suddenly Angel's mother opened her eyes and looked at him.

"Where did you get this?" she asked.

Angel, still kneeling, glanced up at Sarah. "Her brother sent it to her. We don't know where he got it."

"It comes from the great heavens." She raised her eyes to Sarah's. "It is as old as the stars. A holy thing, from a holy place. It wants to go back."

"But how, Mama?"

"You take it!" She thrust it at him, pushing him away from her chair. Angel rocked back on his heels.

"All right, all right," he said, holding the Stone to his chest. "Don't get upset. Calm down. Think of something else. Good things. Remember the campfires in the evenings? And the rivers. The fish—you caught the fish with your bare hands! You were the best in the whole *kumpania*, Mama, better than any of the boys."

She began to hum, unevenly, a sad melody, picking at the threads of her skirt with her thin fingers. "The water was so cold. The fish were beautiful, like silver."

Angel looked briefly at Sarah, a look of such sorrow that she felt her own heart contract with pain.

"She'll be all right now," he said. "Let's go."

There was the sound of heavy footsteps on the stairs. A door opened and closed.

"It's my father," Angel said. The footsteps moved slowly down the hall. A man in a one-piece gray uniform appeared in the doorway. He was a big man, so big that his head came within inches of the top of the doorframe. He had wary blue eyes and a mane of faded red hair combed straight back.

"What's this, then?" he said when he saw them. "I thought you'd be halfway across the country by this hour, lad."

"Sarah, this is my father, Will Muldoon. This is Sarah Lucas."

"Hello." Sarah stepped forward, and they shook hands. His hand felt enormous.

"Sarah Lucas, Sarah Lucas." He repeated her name in his lilting Irish brogue, trying out the sound of it.

"I'm not going to California after all," Angel said.

"Oh, no? Had a change of plans, have you?" Mr. Muldoon crossed the room to stand beside his wife's chair. "How's my Mara this afternoon?"

"She's all right. Da, Sarah and I were just about to leave—"

"What's your rush? I'll put the kettle on. You know, lad," Mr. Muldoon said, turning from his wife and looking hard at Angel, "when we were discussing your travel plans, I don't recall any mention of a young lady."

Angel flushed. "If I had mentioned her, would you have let me go?"

"Glory be to God! Have you taken leave of your senses? Don't you know what happens to boys like you who lure young ladies like her from the homes where they've been so carefully brought up?"

"I didn't lure her from anywhere," Angel said.

"You'd better go home, Miss Lucas," said Mr. Muldoon. "Or to school. You go to school, don't you? To Saint Somebody-or-other's or Miss So-and-so's Academy?"

"Go on, Sarah." Angel glared at his father.

"Without you?"

"I'll catch up with you later."

"But where?" she asked, conscious of Mr. Muldoon, standing, arms folded across his big chest, regarding them.

"I'll find you, don't worry."

"Okay," Sarah said doubtfully, and left the room.

She was all the way downstairs and out on the wet side-walk before she realized Angel still had the Stone. She looked up at the third-floor windows of the library, rain stinging her face. She didn't want to leave him there, him or the Stone.

She wiped the rain from her eyes with the back of her hand. There was nothing she could do. If she went back, it might only make things worse for him. "I'll find you, don't worry," he had said. But he could do that only if she was where he'd expect her to be: at school, and then at the stable, and after that, back at the apartment.

She turned and started down the street, water seeping through the soles of her shoes.

Then she felt a hand grip her arm.

eight

Enter Zvalus

For a moment Sarah was too puzzled to be afraid. She looked up into the man's face, thinking he must have mistaken her for someone else.

It was a face that at first glance seemed handsome, like a face in an advertisement. But there was something wrong with it: his eyes. They were so pale they appeared almost colorless, and their gaze was flat.

She had seen him somewhere before.

He hurried her down the sidewalk, nearly lifting her off her feet. "There's no cause for alarm. I simply want to talk to you about your brother. I am Dr. Zvalus, the head of the Institute."

"Where is Sam? What's happened?"

"Get in the car." He pushed her toward a dark sedan with tinted windows and opened the rear door.

Suddenly she knew who he was. He wore a gray raincoat, not a white shirt, but he was the man she had glimpsed on the library stairs weeks ago.

"No." Sarah tried to pull away. "We can talk right here."

"In the rain?" *Be reasonable,* his smile said. In one swift movement he twisted her arm behind her and shoved. She slid all the way across the backseat and banged her head on the opposite door. Zvalus got in after her, shut the door, and nodded to the driver. The car pulled smoothly into traffic.

Sarah sat up, touching the sore spot on her head.

"Don't bother trying to get out that side." He adjusted his raincoat underneath him. "The lock is controlled by the driver. And I assure you, Oskar has no intention of opening the door."

All she could see of Oskar was the back of his head. He had a bulldog's neck, and hair like a stiff black brush. Their gaze met for a moment in the rearview mirror. His small, shiny black eyes looked her over with the mild interest of a cook inspecting a fish on a cutting board.

She turned to Zvalus. "What do you want?"

"Right to the point. Very good. You know that your brother has been working on an extremely important project for us. Several months ago he began experimenting with the equipment in secret. This was a very foolish and dangerous thing to do. It appears he has paid a price for it already."

"What are you talking about? Where is he?"

The car turned left on West End Avenue, heading south.

Zvalus took a tin of peppermints from his coat pocket, slid open the top, and offered her one.

"They have not been poisoned," he said when she refused. Without taking his eyes off her, he removed one of the mints—they looked like pills—and placed it carefully on his tongue. He sucked thoughtfully on the mint and spoke.

"From what we can gather, he made several journeys

between Earth and another planetary system, possibly in another galaxy."

There was silence except for the steady rhythm of the windshield wipers sweeping across the glass. "I see this does not come as a complete surprise," he said, clasping his hands together. The odor of dry-cleaning fluid rose from his raincoat. "I know, of course, that your brother has had at least one secret communication with you, using a . . . cleaning woman as an emissary."

Her surprise must have shown on her face.

He leaned over and rapped her forehead with a knuckle, hard. "You know it was me in the library that day. What do you think I was doing there, if not attempting to intercept the letter? We cannot permit such violations of security. It could be very dangerous."

"It was you, then, on the street that night? Looking up at my window?"

"Indeed it was. I've taken a special interest in you. Now, I assume your brother told you of his clandestine plans. What you may not know is that he made contact with an alien civilization. On one of these trips he brought back a certain artifact. This is the object you received from him yesterday."

How did he know? Who could have . . . For an instant the thought that Angel might have betrayed her turned the world inside out. And then she knew.

Helena! That's why she was so interested in the package, Sarah thought, *why she was so flustered that I intercepted the delivery. If it had come earlier, she would've opened the package herself. Maybe even hidden it. She's part of CIPHER. She*

*and Bernard, too. They've been spying on me all along. . . .
Helena must've called Zvalus last night as soon as I went into
my room. She must've told him where to look for me today.*

A drop of rain raced down the car window before a gust
of wind flattened it against the glass and blew it away into
nothingness. Sarah lifted her hand and touched the place
where the raindrop had been. *Somebody help me.*

"Now the aliens want it back," Zvalus was saying. "They
are holding him captive until it is returned."

He caught her gaze and held it, and she felt herself slowly
drawn into those strange transparent eyes like a swimmer at
the edge of a whirlpool.

Could he be telling the truth? Sarah thought. *Your brother
is in grave danger,* the old woman had said. *You must return
the Stone to the Door.* Had she been saying the same thing,
just using different words?

"We have very little time. I needn't remind you that your
brother is a most unusual person. My organization has
invested a great deal of time and money in him. As its head,
I must protect our investment. Where is the object he sent
you?"

Think, Sarah! "At home, I think. At my aunt and uncle's.
In my sock drawer."

He slowly shook his head. Was he smiling? "We searched
your room. Thoroughly."

"Then, I must've left it in my locker. At school."

The pale eyes never flickered. He reached into his coat
pocket and threw something on the seat between them. It slid
off and landed at her feet.

Her combination lock. The hasp had been neatly severed.

They were driving along the mist-covered Hudson, by the piers. A barge drifting by in the middle of the river sounded its foghorn. The car turned and headed down a narrow space between two warehouses. Oskar pulled in behind one of the warehouses, out of sight of the street. He switched the car's engine off but didn't move.

Zvalus turned to her. The rain running down the windows cast ribbons of shadow on his face. "Lying is a bad habit, Miss Lucas. Bad habits must be broken. It can be a painful process."

Sarah closed her eyes. Bitter saliva flooded her mouth. She swallowed it, feeling sick. *It's no use,* she thought. *There's absolutely nothing I can do.* She didn't know whether he had a knife, a gun, something worse than either—but she didn't want to find out.

"It's with a friend," she said finally, "at the library."

The door leading from the second floor of the library to the Muldoons' apartment was locked. Zvalus took a long, thin piece of metal from his pocket and inserted it in the lock, and a moment later the door opened.

"Go on," he said. She climbed slowly up the narrow, linoleum-covered steps, frantically trying to devise some sort of plan. Sam had trusted her with the Stone, the old woman had told her to take it back to the Door, and now she was about to turn it over to this . . . this gangster. She was a coward. She should have refused to tell him anything.

"Knock," Zvalus ordered.

She knocked. No one came. She felt a surge of hope. Maybe they were all out.

"Harder." Zvalus had turned away from her to watch the stairs.

She knocked again. This time there was the sound of movement inside the apartment. *Think of something! Quickly!*

The door opened suddenly. Mr. Muldoon looked at them, then at the door at the bottom of the stairs. He scowled and narrowed his eyes.

"It was unlocked," Zvalus said.

"Was it indeed? I'll have to speak to the doorman about that," Mr. Muldoon said, his tone heavy with sarcasm.

"May we come in?" Zvalus asked pleasantly.

Mr. Muldoon crossed his arms. "Looks as if you're already in."

"I'm Miss Lucas's guardian," Zvalus said.

"I've already told the lad to stay away from her." Mr. Muldoon started to close the door, but Zvalus held it open with his foot.

"He has something that belongs to Miss Lucas. We'd like to have it back."

"Is that so? Well, he isn't here."

"Where might we find him?"

"He's gone to work."

Sarah, who had stepped back to stand a little behind Zvalus, shook her head and mouthed, "No." Mr. Muldoon frowned at her.

"Who is that? Who is at the door?"

Angel's mother came toward them, the hem of her skirt trailing along the floor. She had taken off her scarf, and her long hair, black and silver, hung around her face in coils like Medusa's.

"Back to your room, Mara," Mr. Muldoon ordered, still looking at Sarah.

"I want to see," she said. She crowded in beside him at the door, looked at Sarah, and smiled. "Shall I tell your fortune? And you, sir?"

For a few seconds, as she looked at Zvalus, the practiced, charming smile held. Then, like a shadow of a cloud racing across the ground, a change came over her. Her smile faded. "You," she said. "You smell of evil."

"Mara, settle down—"

She leaped at Zvalus, clawing at his face. *"Beng! Beng!"*

Zvalus swore and grabbed her wrists. They struggled, crashing into Sarah. She lost her balance for a moment on the stairs and caught herself.

"Mara, for the love of God!" Mr. Muldoon stepped in, pushed Mara aside, and seized Zvalus by the lapels of his raincoat.

Sarah ran.

She flew down the stairs and out the front door of the library, pushing past a woman dragging a baby stroller backward up the steps. A car door slammed. Oskar came after her at a full run.

She darted across the street in the middle of traffic and ran inside a hotel, dodging people and suitcases, heading for a revolving door at the far end of the lobby. She struggled through it and was out on the street once again, zigzagging through the crowd.

There was a subway entrance at the corner. Hurtling down into the dank, windy darkness, she searched her pockets for her Metrocard, afraid to look back. A crowd waited on the platform. She slipped in front of a knot of people, glancing quickly over her shoulder at the entrance. No Oskar.

From far down the tracks came the first distant rumble of a train. She hid behind a concrete pillar and stole a quick look. Oskar cleared the low swinging gate of the wheelchair entrance, strode along the platform, searching the crowd.

The train roared into the station. The doors opened and people surged forward. Sarah stood with her back pressed against the pillar. Once more she edged around the corner and looked. Where was he?

For an instant her heart seemed to stop beating. He could be anywhere. If she couldn't see him, she couldn't tell if he was getting closer.

Then she spotted him, standing back from the crowd, scanning the length of the train.

There was no way out. If she got on the train, he would follow her, pushing his way through the cars until he found her. If she stayed on the platform, he would stay too, and once the train pulled out, the two of them would be left.

She had to make him get on the train.

She waited until he was heading toward her but still some distance away. Then she stepped out from behind the pillar, joining the crowd, careful to keep looking straight ahead. She boarded the train and struggled to keep her position next to the door as people pushed past her. A blond woman in high heels, carrying a shopping bag, ran wildly toward the closing doors. Sarah caught and held the door open as the woman edged her way through. At the last possible moment Sarah squeezed past the woman and jumped back onto the platform as the doors closed behind her. The metal wheels screeched. The train pulled away.

Oskar was nowhere in sight.

She sprinted up the stairs two at a time, pausing an instant to look down into the black hole of the entrance, unable to believe her luck.

Then she took off, running as fast as she could through the rush-hour crowd, expecting with every backward glance to see Zvalus's face. She was halfway to the stable when she remembered Bernard—Bernard, who sometimes left work early on Friday and who might be making his way home along this same street. To avoid any chance of an encounter, she would have to take a longer route.

She crossed Central Park West and ran beside the low wall bordering the park, under the dripping trees, blood pounding in her temples, a stitch in her side, too frightened to stop or even slow down. The early autumn dusk that slipped so quickly into night had already begun to envelop the city. The tops of the buildings were invisible, shrouded in mist.

Past the playground, left across the avenue again.

Jody was locking the stable office, closing up for the day. "Is Angel here?" Sarah asked breathlessly, holding her aching side.

"Upstairs." Jody looked her over but didn't comment. "Wait till you see what he's got in the stall."

Sarah started up the ramp, still panting. Dim light fell from the small, high windows. The dampness intensified the stable's familiar odors: manure and hay and leather and the horses themselves. The stalls were dark and shadowy, the horses partly hidden from view by the doors, but Sarah could feel them there, big and solid and warm.

Angel stepped out of one of the box stalls, his face like a pale moon in the dimness. At the sight of him the tears she had held in check for hours broke through. She ran to him and pressed her face against his denim jacket, holding him tight.

"Sarah, what is it? What happened?"

"The man—the man in the white shirt—when I came out of the library, he grabbed me. . . ." She could barely speak. "The Stone! Have you got it?"

"It's right here." He touched his jacket pocket, then held her by both arms. "Did he hurt you?"

"No! But he would have if—" Somewhere a board creaked. Sarah jumped. "What was that?"

"One of the horses. Don't worry—the doors are all locked downstairs. Jody locks everything when she leaves."

"But he can get in! He will! He picked the lock of the downstairs door to your apartment—your mother—"

"What about my mother?"

Sarah covered her face with her hands. "She's all right. Your father was there. Your father hit him, I think. That's how I got away." She told him, her words tumbling over one another, about the ride in the car, about the things Zvalus had said. "I was so scared! I was afraid he would hurt me. I was afraid that what he said was true—that if I didn't give him the Stone, something terrible would happen to Sam. But I knew I shouldn't tell him where it was—I knew I shouldn't—because then he'd come after you! I was afraid he would hurt you, too."

"Sarah, listen," Angel said, taking both her hands and

looking into her eyes. "I know what it's like to be scared. But you can't give in to it, understand? It will make you do things you don't really want to do. It's a weapon. Fear belongs to *beng*, to the devil."

"*Beng? That's* what your mother said! That's what she called Zvalus!"

Sarah described the scene at the top of the stairs and her escape from Oskar. "I don't think he could've followed me. But what if your father told Zvalus where to find you?"

"You're joking! Da probably threw him out on his ear."

"Zvalus could still track us down here! My aunt and uncle have been spying on me. They're part of CIPHER— they may know I've been coming here!"

"If they come, we'll get away."

"But how?"

Angel opened the door and they stepped into the stall. The horse inside circled around and regarded them with dark, shining eyes, his small ears pointed forward.

"He's a stallion," Angel said. "His name's Altair. The owner told me it means 'flier' in Arabic."

"He looks like he could fly! Angel, he's . . . magnificent." Sarah stroked the velvet muzzle and gently scratched the crest of his mane with her fingernails. His coat was a shimmering, ghostly white, like frost on the ground. "Where did he come from?"

"We're only boarding him overnight. The owner is a friend of Pam's. Some rich lady." Angel ran his hand along the smooth curve of Altair's back. "She just thinks she owns him, though. Nobody really owns horses—especially not one like this." Altair tossed his head in agreement. "Oh, stop showing off," Angel said. The stallion flicked his long tail and returned to his grain.

Angel took the Stone from his pocket, cradling it in his hand. "So this really is from beyond the heavens."

"And it wants to go back. The old lady in Latin class said I had to take it back. But what about Sam?"

"Sam?" Angel asked blankly, lifting his gaze from the Stone.

"Yes, Sam," Sarah insisted. But Angel was looking at the Stone again, lost in it. She couldn't expect him to be as worried about Sam as she was. He could think only about the magical part, the way everything seemed to be fitting together. She'd never seen him quite like this. It was as if the Stone had brought him alive in some new way.

"All we have to do now," Angel was saying, "is figure out how to get to a door in a dream." Altair ambled over and nibbled at the scuffed toe of his boot. Angel rubbed the wide forehead. "Not on horseback, that's for sure, hey, Altair?"

"Maybe not," Sarah said. "But I think I know how."

nine

Escape

"**Last night,**" Sarah began, "**when I was lying in bed** thinking about Sam and holding the Stone, something happened. I had this . . . I don't know—a vision of Sam. It was more than a picture. I could hear things. I could even smell the air. And then it was all gone."

Angel pulled a piece of straw from Altair's mane and rolled it between his fingers. "Go on."

"So I thought . . . maybe if I concentrated hard on Sam while I was holding the Stone, I might find him. And if you and I tried it together . . . Does that sound crazy?"

He turned and stood looking out through the bars of the stall door at the passageway.

"What is it? What are you thinking?"

"Before I left the house today, my mother said, '*Bahtalo drom—ja develesa*'—'Lucky road—go with God.' I told her I wasn't going anywhere, but she kept saying it and crying. I figured she thought I was still going to California. And then she told me my name—my real name."

"Your secret name? But why? Why today?"

"I don't know." He glanced at her and looked away again. "It's funny—ever since I was a little kid, I've had this feeling that one day something was going to happen to change my whole life. There's always been this voice inside me saying, 'Wait. Don't give up. Hold on.' Did you ever feel that?"

"I don't think so," Sarah answered.

"I think it's starting to happen." Angel turned to her with a grave expression. Then, putting one hand on the small of her back, he kissed her. Sarah felt herself growing weightless, floating up into a blue wash of light, anchored only by his hand. When they drew apart, she said, "Again."

He smiled, his eyes as black and full of secrets as the water at the bottom of a well. Then he gathered her to him, kissing her forehead, her eyelids, her mouth.

Suddenly Altair's head flew up, his ears flicking back and forth.

Angel pulled her down. "Someone's here."

"It's Zvalus, I know it! Jody was the last one here, and she was on her way out when I saw her! What are we going to do?"

Without making a sound, Angel stood up and lifted Altair's bridle from a hook. "Put this on him," he whispered. "When I go out, I'll close the door behind me, but I'll leave it unlatched. When I give you the signal, ride down the ramp as fast as you can. I'll have the big bay door open. Head for the park. Here . . ." He took her hand, put the Stone into her palm, and covered it with his own hand.

"*Bahtalo drom. Ja develesa.*"

He buttoned his jacket and opened the stall door.

"Angel!" she said. He couldn't just go. . . . "Be brave."

As silently as smoke he slipped out the door and swung it shut.

Sarah flattened herself against the stall, listening. She belted her raincoat, trying to keep the metal buckle from jingling, and slipped the Stone into her pocket. Somewhere a board creaked. Altair nibbled at the toe of her sneaker. The bridle. She had to get it on him.

Now he was nudging the door. She stepped closer, holding the bridle, praying he wouldn't give her a fight. "Come on, boy," she pleaded in a whisper. To her surprise, he lowered his head and accepted the bit. She slipped the leather strap over his ears and drew his long forelock through.

A moment later she heard footsteps.

She crouched down behind the horse, hiding as much of herself as she could in case someone opened the door. "Sarah?"

Aunt Helena!

"Sarah, you can come out now. No one's going to hurt you, dear. We just want to talk to you."

We? Did she mean Bernard? Or Zvalus? Sarah squinted through a crack in the boards, peering down the long passageway between the stalls. Aunt Helena stood at the end, holding her purse to her chest like a shield.

Go away, Sarah ordered her silently. Sarah braced herself against the stall and stared up at a spider's web in the rafters.

The cobweb trembled. A draft was coming from somewhere.

"Listen here, young lady. . . ." It was Uncle Bernard, using his courtroom voice. "We've had just about enough—" There was the sound of someone falling, and Aunt Helena cried out.

"Are you all right?" Sarah heard Bernard ask.

"My ankle . . ."

"I told you not to wear those ridiculous shoes. Can you walk?"

"She will walk," a third voice said quietly.

Zvalus!

"Get up, Helena," he ordered. "Now."

Sarah peered through the crack again, her forehead pressed against the rough boards. A paralyzing chill spread over her. All those months Helena and Bernard had been watching her every move, prying into her thoughts, reporting back. . . .

"We know you are here, Sarah." Zvalus's voice was smooth, confident. He moved unhurriedly down the passage. "There is no point in hiding. Tell your friend to come out too."

Where was Angel?

Altair tossed his head, nearly yanking the reins from her hand. He had submitted to the bridle because he wanted to get out, to run, and he didn't like being made to wait.

"Easy," she whispered, rising slowly from her crouch, her legs trembling. "Easy, boy." She was going to need something to stand on. With one hand she reached for an empty bucket in the corner of the stall and turned it over.

A stall door opened and closed, then another. Zvalus was four, maybe five, stalls away at most.

She thrust her fingers into her pocket and wrapped them around the cool Stone. *Please,* she prayed silently, her forehead resting on Altair's withers. *Please . . .*

From downstairs she heard a faint, familiar rumble as the bay door, where the horses went in and out to the street, was quietly raised. Sarah grabbed a handful of Altair's mane and stood on the bucket. The bottom buckled, making a loud click.

"What was that?" Bernard asked.

Zvalus opened the door of the stall next to Altair's.

Sarah jumped, knocking over the bucket, and wriggled onto Altair's back.

"Sarah, come out at once!" Zvalus commanded.

"Now!" Angel's whisper came out of nowhere, like a ventriloquist's. She kicked sideways at the door. Altair wheeled around and shot out of the stall.

Helena screamed.

Zvalus leaped toward Altair, grabbing for the reins. Sarah looked down into the cold transparency of his eyes for a split second before the stallion reared, shook him off, and raced down the packed-dirt ramp into the ring, with Sarah clinging to his neck.

A cloud of mist rolled through the open door.

From the shadows in the rear of the ring sprang a horse and rider: Angel, mounted on Foxfire, a spirited red mare who liked nothing better than to run.

Zvalus came running down the ramp, shouting directions at Oskar, who stood with arms outspread, blocking the bay door.

"Go!" Angel yelled, heading for the door. Oskar lunged. Angel aimed a kick at his face and missed, hitting him on the shoulder and knocking him off balance. Foxfire pinned her ears back and spun around, kicking savagely.

Almost at once they were outside, careering up the rain-slick street. Oskar stumbled after them, jumping into the driver's seat of the sedan.

A wino sprawled on a stoop cried, "Hi-yo, Silver!" as they clattered past.

The fog had thickened, shrouding the streetlamps, making it impossible to see more than a few yards. Up ahead Sarah could hear the traffic on Columbus, the first of two avenues they would have to cross before they reached the park.

Behind them the haloed headlights of the sedan drew closer. Oskar leaned on the horn.

They flew through the intersection. A taxi slammed on its brakes and honked.

"Slow him down!" Angel cried from behind her. "Pull his head in!"

Sarah pulled back with all her strength on one rein and then the other, but Altair had taken the bit in his teeth. His hooves pounded the shimmering pavement. There was nothing she could do but hold on.

A truck veered to avoid them and smashed into a lamppost. They thundered across Central Park West beneath a hailstorm of broken glass and headed into the park, up a hill, into the trees. The sedan gunned up the hill after them, crashing through the bushes.

Somewhere a siren began to wail.

"Look out!" Angel shouted.

Sarah ducked as a low-hanging branch rushed at her out of the fog.

They galloped down a path lined with tall, arching trees. The reins burned her palms, and her legs ached with the strain of gripping Altair's sides. Fog rose like a wall in front of them, the black trunks of phantom trees moving in and out of the mist.

She gathered Altair's reins in one hand and slipped the other inside her pocket, found the Stone. *Please,* she begged, holding it tight. *Please, take me to Sam!*

Nothing seemed to change. Then, so gradually that at first she scarcely knew what was happening, every sound—the traffic, the siren, shouting voices, even the horses' hard breathing—was absorbed into a low, steady roar, like a distant ocean. As if the fog had taken on substance, the horses slowed, plunging soundlessly into the mist. Sarah could no longer feel the ground beneath them.

"Angel!" She made a fist around the Stone and flung her arm toward him. Somehow he reached across the space between them and covered her hand with his own. The roaring grew louder, pressing in on them from all sides.

"Look!" Angel called. "Up there!"

Ahead of them the mist swirled and thinned and parted, but beyond it the familiar landscape of the park, the trees and lampposts and benches, had vanished. In its place lay an immense, glittering darkness. Sarah cried out. There was nothing below them. The horses leaped from an invisible ledge and flew down a corridor of stars.

At the end of the corridor stood a great stone arch.

"The Door!" Angel's voice was joyful. "The Door in my dream!"

They moved toward it in slow motion. At the peak of the arch Sarah saw a flower, hewn from the pale gray stone, its broad, flat petals radiating from a round center. The flower's outer leaves twined down both sides of the arch, where the carved figures of creatures Sarah couldn't name grew in and out of one another: Some had wings, others bore elaborate,

coiled horns, and still others seemed to be sea animals, trailing fins. Their eyes were everywhere, all fixed on her. For an
instant she had the powerful sense that they had been waiting
for her, expecting her, for longer than she could imagine.

The flower began to bloom. New petals budded, unfurled,
and gave way to newer ones, all in a slow, continuous rhythm,
like waves falling on a shore.

Only the flower's center was still, waiting, Sarah knew, for
the Stone. But if she gave it up now, how would she ever find
Sam?

The Door drew them closer.

"We're almost there!" Angel tightened his grip on her
hand.

"No!" Sarah cried. Beneath her, Altair pitched headlong
into a rushing void that sucked the breath from her lungs.
She could see nothing, feel nothing except her hand locked
around the Stone.

From the edge of the world Angel's voice rang out:
"Hold on!"

But she couldn't hold on. With the force of a gigantic
wave an invisible power bore down on them and tore her
hand from Angel's grasp. In the moment before darkness
swept her away, she felt the Stone slip from her fingers.

ten

Under a Green Sky

Sarah dreamed she was a little girl and someone was carrying her up an endless flight of stairs in the dark. The staircase was outside, and when she looked down, the ground was so far away she felt frightened. But she knew she wouldn't fall because whoever was carrying her was very strong. After a long time they stopped climbing, and she was lowered down, down, down, until her head lay on a pillow and she slept.

The light woke her. She squinted and shaded her eyes. She lay on her back, looking up into a tree, its branches drooping low all around her, a pavilion of rustling gold. For one joyful moment she was at home again, on the tree house roof. But these leaves were long and slender, golden petals, not like oak leaves at all.

She sat up, groggy, as if she'd been asleep for days. Memories came rushing at her: the horses pounding along the path, the leap into space—but where was Angel? He'd been holding her hand when . . . when what?

"Angel?"

No one answered.

"Angel!" She stood up faster than she should have, and the blood rushed from her head. She placed one hand against the tree trunk, then jerked it away. The bark was warm and smooth, uncomfortably like skin, and something like a mild electric current had issued from it. She eyed the trunk, rubbing her tingling hand on her jeans. Then the wind blew, shaking light from the tree and parting the leaves, revealing a patch of green sky.

Sarah pushed aside a branch. The sky was a vast expanse of pure, burning green, like the green at the heart of a flame. The same sky she had seen in her vision of Sam. The Stone had taken her to where he was. The Stone's magic was real!

Her hands flew to her raincoat pockets. Flat, empty. She jammed her fingers into the depths, into every pocket in her jeans, fell to her knees and frantically cast aside twigs and leaves in the sandy ground where she had slept. Finally she sank back, empty-handed. She would not find the Stone because it wasn't there to be found. It had slipped from her hand into that roaring darkness.

She had lost the Stone. Sam had given it to her to keep safe, and she had lost it. And now she was alone on another planet with no way to find him, and no way of getting back to Earth if she failed. A chill ran through her.

"Sam?" she called. "Angel?" *Oh, please be here, please.* She stumbled out from under the tree. Between banks of scarlet blooms a sandy path curved out of sight. She followed it as it wound among the flowers and then alongside a high wall of rosy quartz.

She came to a wide break in the wall, where below her

sloped a steeply terraced hillside, the terraces marked off by stone walls and linked by a network of paths like the veins in a leaf, endlessly dividing, disappearing at the foot of the hill into a sea of white vapor. Here and there other hills rose like islands from the mist.

She cupped her hands around her mouth and called for Sam, then Angel, again and again until her throat was sore. There was no answer. A flock of white birds sailed over the ocean of mist. Sarah followed their flight until she could see them no longer and finally turned and went back into the garden.

The hair on her arms rose like tiny antennae. Someone— or something—had built this place, had leveled those hillside terraces and laid stone on stone for the walls and walked along those forking paths. Whatever it was might be lying in wait for her.

She returned to the place where she had slept. There was a depression in the sand where her body had been. The tree's roots spread out around its trunk like long, bumpy toes, sprouting coarse hairs like a coconut's. She nudged one of them with the tip of her shoe. It was spongy. Even through the rubber sole of her sneaker she could feel the peculiar current.

Suddenly she remembered her dream and the pillow under her head. The pillow must have been a root. But what about the rest, the endless flight of stairs? The terraces! Had someone carried her up that terraced hillside and laid her here?

Calm down, she told herself. *It was only a dream. There's nobody here.*

A deep stillness seemed cast over everything, as if layer after layer of silence had accumulated through the centuries, like snow. She stood motionless beside a pool of water near the tree, watching the breeze etch the surface, listening to the small waves lapping against the bank.

She was suddenly thirsty, unbearably thirsty. Was the water in the pool safe to drink? Surely if she took only a tiny sip . . .

Sarah knelt and scooped up a little of the water in her hands, sniffing it before she drank. It was cold and sweet.

She backed away from the water's edge, wiping her mouth on her sleeve. The surface of the pool reflected clouds floating overhead. She leaned over and saw her face among the clouds. The girl in the water stared back at her, grave, unsmiling.

There had been another time, long ago, when she had seen her face among the clouds. She'd been helping Sam wash the windows of their house, and he had lifted her on his shoulders so she could wipe the top row of panes. Then he stepped back to survey their work, Sarah still perched on his shoulders.

The glass panes reflected the sky behind their heads, where fat clouds floated past. At the same time she could see into the house. There was the piano, the china cabinet, and the gold-framed mirror over the fireplace, like a mirror in a fairy tale.

At the far end of the dining room the door to the kitchen stood open. Her father sat at the table, reading aloud from a newspaper to her mother, who stood at the sink peeling potatoes.

Finally she saw herself, and Sam. They were all there, all caught up in the sky and the clouds, as if the house had been loosed from its moorings and were sailing through the heavens like a great, weightless ship.

"Look, Sam!" Sarah had cried. And he had squeezed her ankles in reply.

A wind wrinkled the surface of the pool. Sarah gazed into its depths and saw her mother's soft, flyaway hair catch the light. Her mother looked up at Sarah through the dark water and smiled. . . .

Then she was gone.

"Mother!" Sarah cried. She felt a pain in her chest, as if her heart might really be breaking, and sat down on a rock at the edge of the pool.

A fitful wind rose out of nowhere, tearing leaves from the tree and sending them whirling into the sky. It had been warm before, so warm she had thought of taking off her raincoat, but now there was a distinct chill in the air. Sarah pulled her coat closer around her. Why couldn't you turn back the pages of your life like a book? If only she could! She would walk up the flagstone path as the barn swallows swooped around her, feel the old brass doorknob beneath her hand as she opened the door. The house would smell of lemony furniture polish and flowers and her mother's scones in the oven. And there would be the peculiar, interesting smell that always seemed to cling to her parents, the smell of newspaper ink and photographic chemicals, the smell of their work. She would hear the murmur of their voices as they puzzled over some detail of a story, but they wouldn't mind being interrupted when she came in. . . .

Tears slid from her eyes. *I'd give anything to be home again*, she thought. *I'd give anything to go home and find it all the same as before. Anything . . .*

A cloud passed over the garden. The sky was getting dark. Was it going to storm?

On the other side of the pool, among the flowering bushes, Sarah saw something move.

Just a shadow, she thought.

But the shadow seemed to grow denser, snaking across the pool in slow, looping motions, like a hand carefully tracing letters. And for a moment after the shadow withdrew, Sarah thought she saw written across the water in wavery script that might have been nothing more than a trick of the light: *Anything?*

She covered her face with her hands and wept. She had lost them all, first her parents, then Sam, and now Angel—and the Stone. When at last she finished crying—it was odd, Sarah thought, but no matter how unbearable something was, you couldn't keep crying forever—she found a wadded tissue in her coat pocket and wiped her streaming nose. Crying was supposed to make you feel better, but she felt only a sodden hopelessness weighing her down like wet clothes.

"Chin up, old thing," she said aloud, in exactly the same tone her mother would have used. She scooped some water from the pool, splashed her face, and drank.

Stone-Bearer, a voice within her said clearly, *what have you seen in the Vision Pool?*

She sprang to her feet and slid partway down the bank, soaking one sneaker. From a nearby bush a cloud of what she had earlier taken for white blossoms rose and scattered, fluttering into the dark reaches of the garden.

"Who said that?" she managed to ask. Her heart thudded furiously against her breastbone. "Who's there?"

Although the mysterious words had come to her as silent impulses, like her own thoughts, she knew they were not her own.

Nothing moved.

She walked around the garden until her heart stopped its wild pounding. She was still frightened when she went back to the tree beside the pool, but she made herself take off her shoes and wring out the wet sock. Then she lay down on her side with her knees drawn up and her cheek resting on her hands. Her muscles ached with exhaustion, but she was too jittery to sleep.

Slowly the last of the green left the sky, and darkness fell. From behind the wall of the garden there rose the rim of a great, peach-colored moon, many times larger than Earth's, its surface pitted by enormous craters. Moments later a second, smaller moon joined the first. Mother and child, Sarah thought.

The sky grew thick with stars, more stars than she had ever seen. She searched for the constellations she knew, the familiar Big and Little Dippers, Pegasus, Orion. Sam had taught her to find them. It had frustrated Sarah at first—many of the constellations looked nothing like the things they were named for—but Sam kept making her look until, finally, she saw.

She couldn't find them now. "They're too far away," she could almost hear Sam saying. If they were up there, her stars, they were so distant they now formed part of other, new constellations, ones whose names she could not know. She could be millions of light-years from home now. She might never see the stars from Earth again.

If only she could have held on to the Stone! She went over, again, the moments before the terrible force had torn her hand from Angel's. They had been so close to the Door— Angel had called out. And she . . .

The wind blew and the leaves of the tree made a pleasant sound, a sort of taffeta rustle. She rolled onto her back, looked up. The bark of the tree was smooth in places, and in others, baggy and wrinkled, like the skin of an elephant. Here and there the skin—no, bark, Sarah corrected herself—came together and formed a bump, like a knothole, only roughly triangular instead of round or oval.

One of these knotholes was directly overhead; in the bright moonlight she could see it quite distinctly. It looked remarkably like an eye, staring down at her from beneath a crinkled lid.

Then it blinked.

Sarah cried out and covered her mouth with her hand.

Another eye opened, and another, in the crook of a branch. The eyes were everywhere, numerous as the knobs and whorls of an ordinary tree but utterly, dreadfully unlike them, and each one—liquid and black and ancient—was focused on her.

As if waking from a deep sleep, the tree stretched its limbs. The knobbed tip of a branch moved slowly toward her. Papery leaves brushed her face. The tree's fingertip, soft as the bud of a pussy willow but pulsing with life, touched her forehead between her eyes.

Then words unfurled in her mind:

In the Name of the One Whose Name Cannot Be Spoken, peace.

In the Name of the Amarantha, Sower of Dreams, peace.

In the Name of the Stone in the Door of the Worlds, peace.

The tree withdrew its branch. The spot on her forehead burned, but tranquillity flowed into Sarah like a river, coursing through her, carrying away her fears like so much debris.

The tree turned majestically and began gliding toward the opening in the garden wall.

Come, it said in Sarah's mind.

And she followed.

eleven

Miladras

Catching the tree's messages in her mind was like riding a bicycle, Sarah thought; it was what you didn't do that mattered. The bicycle would balance itself as long as you didn't make jerky movements and tip it over. In this case what you didn't do was think.

The tree's name was Miladras. Sarah had followed him out of the garden (the tree must be a him, she had decided, with that deep, rivery voice), walking behind him as he made his way down the endless, forking paths between the terraces, using his long roots to move himself forward in gliding steps. It had taken hours for them to learn to talk to each other, and dawn was breaking when at last they returned to the garden and the pool. Sarah could not quite believe any of it, even after the hours they had spent under the stars, asking each other questions ("Why have you no roots?" the tree wanted to know) and puzzling over the answers. He had "read" her messages much more quickly than she deciphered his, but she had kept at it, trying again and again to empty her mind to allow his messages to come through. It was trickier than it seemed; as soon as she tried not to think, stray thoughts swarmed out of nowhere. If she shooed them away, they only multiplied. Finally she discovered that if she ignored them and let them remain in the background, they would settle down one by one, like birds coming to rest. And then the one thought Miladras was trying to send her would emerge from the silence and she would understand. Each time it felt like a small revelation, like the sudden coming of light.

"Explain the part about the dreams once more," Sarah said now, massaging her temples.

"I belong to the kindred of the Thealkir," the tree said patiently inside her head. "We are the Dreaming Trees. For us there are two seasons: the Season of Walking and the Season of Dreaming. When we walk, as now, we wander along the forking paths, and each one tends his own garden. When we dream, we are rooted. We dream together, each one the same dream, season upon season. Are you understanding?"

Sarah nodded. "And someone called the Amarantha sends the dreams? Is she a sort of queen?"

There was a pause while the tree seemed to absorb this, and then the image of a queen in her mind was replaced by a flower that seemed made of light, burning with white-hot brilliance.

"She's a flower?" Sarah asked.

"She is like a flower," the tree answered.

"A flower." She still couldn't grasp what he meant, not really, but if they kept going on like this, she'd be in the garden forever, and she had to look for Sam and Angel. She lay back on a rock beside the pool and stared at the sky, her arms cushioning her head.

"We dream of the beginning in the Dream of the Sowing," the tree went on, "and of the end in the Dream of the Harvest of Light. We dream of the Wayfaring King. But of all the Great Dreams the greatest is the Dream of the Stone. It tells of the Stone-Bearer."

Sarah's heart fluttered against her ribs. She had almost forgotten his first words to her. "You called me that."

"Yes," the tree said. "You are the one we have awaited."

"Me?" She sat up. "But how could . . . I never even saw the Stone until yesterday—or was it the day before?—it came in a parcel! It doesn't make sense that I could be the one you mean. I'm only fifteen, and you've been dreaming those dreams for . . . for ages, haven't you?"

Sarah waited as Miladras seemed to ponder this. Time must be something very different for a tree than it was for a human being, she thought. Did the Dreaming Trees have growth rings, one for each year, like trees on Earth? If they did, they might not know it. After all, the only way you could see a tree's rings was to saw through—

A current of wild alarm ran from Miladras to her. "Oh, I'm sorry!" she said, realizing he must have picked up her thought. "Where I come from, the trees aren't human—I mean, they can't walk or talk or anything—people use them to make houses and paper. They give off oxygen. We couldn't live without them. And of course they're very beautiful," Sarah added lamely. From Miladras's point of view, it must have seemed that the trees on Earth got pretty shabby treatment from the human beings. She wondered if she should mention her tree house or books or Christmas trees, but he spoke first.

"They do not dream, the trees?"

"I don't think so."

"And your own kindred, the rootless ones?"

"Oh, we dream—but not in unison, like you do. Everyone dreams alone." It sounded sad somehow, put that way: *Everyone dreams alone.*

"I think your dreams must be very different," Sarah went on. "Ours are mostly just a jumble of things—except sometimes. But if you knew that . . . that someone was coming with the Stone, that means you must see into the future."

"Which future?"

"Is there more than one?"

"*S'ath emay na-kir!*" This exclamation, Sarah had learned, was untranslatable, something like "In this one the sap runs in the wrong direction!" It was sort of a cross between "Holy smoke!" and "How dumb can you get?" though she knew Miladras was far too polite to say it.

"Look at the forking paths," he said. Sarah found a place in the wall where she could get her footing, then climbed to the top, straddling it. The sun had risen over the horizon, but the air was still cool and damp and full of sweet perfumes from the flowers. The sandy paths spread out among the terraces, dividing and dividing again.

"Do all the paths lead to the same place?" asked the tree.

"No. They go in different directions."

"Just so. The future is like that: not a single path, but many possibilities."

"Is that what the dreams show you? All the possible futures?"

"The dreams reveal but one."

"The real one?"

"It is no more real than the others, until we make it so."

"How do you do that?"

"*S'ath!*" Miladras waved his branches. "At every moment the path divides. We go this way, we go that, and each time turn aside a thousand futures."

"Because we can only choose one?"

"Only one."

"But sometimes things just happen, things you'd never choose, things you can't control. . . ."

"It is so," the tree agreed. "But at every turn you must seek the Light, asking, 'Where is the path that leads to the Light?' The dreams bring us the Light. We follow the Light. Are you understanding, Sarah-kir?"

"I guess so." Sarah drew up her legs and rested her eyes against her knees. There was so much to understand. Earlier Miladras had explained that *kir* meant any creature who could speak or think, and *ela* meant anything living. The grass and flowers were *ela*, birds and fish were *anda-ela*, the Dreaming Trees *kir-ela*. A kindred of *kir-ela*, called the Loriakir, lived in the sea and could sing. A third kindred, the Wrakir, had wings.

He spoke again: "The Stone-Bearer must choose to bear the Stone. She will carry it through a great darkness. This we have known from the first Season of Dreaming."

Sarah raised her head. "What darkness? What do you mean?"

"The darkness of the Umbra."

"The Umbra?" Where had she heard . . . the old lady in Latin class! *The Umbra will oppose you, but you must resist with all your strength,* she had said.

"This is crazy," Sarah said, shaking her head.

"Crazy?" In her mind the tree nudged at her, questioning.

"Mixed up. Bizweird." Sam's word.

"You mean you are not understanding it."

"You're right." She managed a tired laugh. "I am not understanding." She shivered and tucked her hands into the sleeves of her raincoat. There was a small tear in one arm; she had a vague memory of having caught it on a board in Altair's stall when she was hiding from Zvalus.

She could almost smell Zvalus, smell the leather interior of the car where she had been trapped, the scent of dry-cleaning chemicals that had risen from his clothes, the sharp, nauseating odor of peppermint. Was he the Umbra, or part of it? He had wanted the Stone; wanted it so desperately, he'd been prepared to torture her. But why? For what? Why had Sam sent the Stone to her, anyway? And how had he gotten it?

Below her the sea of mist swirled in slow motion around the foot of the hill, sending up feathery sprays of white. Farther out the surface was unruffled, shimmering with iridescent tints of lilac and rose. Out there, somewhere, was Sam.

Your brother is in grave danger, the old woman had said.

"Listen." It was Miladras's voice, flowing among her thoughts like a current in a stream. She found the current and let herself be carried along by it.

"The Umbra," he explained, "is the Shadow That Walks by Itself. It roams the universe. It darkens some worlds. It swallows others. The Dream of the Stone tells us that many will come to our planet, Oneiros, from a world that lies beneath the Shadow. You are the second. The first from that world came not through the Door but by another way.

It is he who has taken the Stone from the Door."

"You must mean Sam, my brother! But he wouldn't steal anything—"

"He has taken the Stone from its place."

He must have, Sarah thought. *He sent it to me.* But why? Sam didn't want *things,* the way some people did. He wouldn't have taken the Stone unless he had a good reason. Maybe he'd been trying to make sure Zvalus wouldn't get his hands on it. What did Sam know about CIPHER? He'd broken into the files after he had that dream about Daddy, whatever it was . . . had he discovered something else? But none of that mattered right now. "Miladras," she said, "Sam and Angel—they're here somewhere, aren't they? Did the dream show you where? Are they all right?"

"You are not understanding. Without the Stone in the Door the way is open to the Umbra, and even the vision of the seers is darkened. I know only that your brother walks here still. I can see no more because already the Shadow has begun to fall. Did you not see it in the Vision Pool?"

Sarah drew a sharp breath. "I did see . . . something. It wrote on the water."

"It will use your heart's desire to work its will. To prevent you from returning the Stone to the Door. For you alone can save Oneiros from doom."

"Doom?" *Doom?* What was he talking about? Once, riding the subway, a wild-eyed man holding a poster board had walked through the aisles muttering to himself. Sarah had tried to read what was written on the board but caught only one word, scrawled in big black letters: DOOM. A crazy person's word. It sent booming echoes through her head.

She shook off a sudden chill. "Now you are not under-standing," she said. "I only came here to find Sam. Angel came with me. I did have the Stone, but on the way something knocked it right out of my hand, and Angel and I got separated, and the Stone fell into some kind of huge, windy hole. I'm sorry," she added, "but it was an accident. If I had it, I would take it to the Door. But I don't. So I'll just have to find Sam and Angel without it."

"How did you come to lose the Stone, Sarah-kir?" His voice, gentle but grave, seemed no longer in her head but somewhere deep inside her, as though her own heart were speaking.

I didn't lose *it*, she wanted to protest. *It wasn't my fault!*

The tree waited for her answer, an answer she was certain he already knew.

"We were almost to the Door," she said finally. "And I got scared. I couldn't think about anything but finding Sam. So I . . . I said no. And then everything went all wrong. Don't you see? I thought if I gave it back, I'd never find my brother! And I have to find him!"

"Your brother and all of Oneiros will be lost if the way remains open to the Umbra."

"There must be some mistake." She held her head with both hands. "I can't save a whole planet. I can't save any-body. I'm just an ordinary girl—"

"Ordinary?" the tree interrupted. "What is 'ordinary'?"

Sarah waved off his question. "Please try to understand! All I want to do is find my brother and Angel and go home!"

The tree said nothing. Sarah felt the steady gaze of his eyes. "Miladras . . ."

"You do not know who you are?"

"Yes—I mean no—oh, never mind."

He turned slowly and began to walk away. She watched him for a moment, then slid down off the wall and hurried after him. She didn't want to be left alone. "Wait! Where are you going?"

"To the high place."

"May I come?"

"As you wish."

She followed him. His muscular roots gripped the path, propelling him forward, leaving tracks in the firm, damp sand before the next stride swept them away. The tracks formed the same branching pattern as the forking paths among the terraces.

This way or that way, she thought, eyes on the ground. *I'd look for the Stone if I had the faintest idea where it was. At least I know Sam's here on the planet somewhere.*

Miladras led her to a place she had not been before, a knoll covered with silvery gray-green grass that came up to her knees. When the wind blew, the grass shimmered.

"You must eat now," he said.

She looked around. What was she going to eat? Except for a flowering vine that climbed the rosy wall, there were no plants growing here.

Miladras's eyes closed, and he held out a three-fingered branch. A swelling appeared between two of the fingers, at their base. It slowly grew larger, stretching the skin taut.

Sarah backed away, unable to take her eyes off the thing growing between his fingers. When it had swollen to the size of an orange, the skin, so thin now it was transparent, split open and the thing inside emerged, glistening. Miladras caught it before it fell. It was an irregular sphere, covered with a silver skin. He offered it to her.

She shook her head.

"You must eat my fruit."

"Oh no, please—I can't."

"The Shadow has already darkened your mind with fear and confusion. If you do not eat, you will be powerless against the Umbra."

"Isn't there something else?"

"There is only this."

Sarah stared at the fruit. The moisture on its surface had evaporated in the breeze, leaving only a faint sheen. She took it from him. It was heavy in her hand.

"Eat now, Sarah-kir, and be blessed."

She closed her eyes and raised the fruit to her lips. The skin broke easily. She took the smallest possible bite and held it in her mouth without chewing. The warm flesh melted on her tongue, tasting of bread and honey.

She ate the fruit, and as she did, a memory came to her. She remembered the Door as she had first seen it from space, the creatures carved into the arch, the sense she'd had that they were waiting for her, had been waiting for a very long time.

Tears slid into the corners of her mouth, salt mingling with sweetness. Miladras wiped them away with the tip of a branch.

"It is well that you have eaten, Sarah-kir. Now we are one. Now I will speak to you of the Stone."

"Yes," she answered, "speak to me of the Stone."

All that long afternoon she lay in the tree's golden shade beside the pool, her head pillowed on a root, and listened.

"Before the beginning," Miladras told her, "there was nothing, an abyss: neither star nor sky, ground nor seed. Nor was there time: Before and after, there was none; Season of Dreaming and Season of Walking, there was none. The One Whose Name Cannot Be Spoken dreamed a dream and said: 'For my joy, I shall be a Sower.' And from his heart the Sower drew a Seed and sowed it in the abyss. All that is made, time before and time after, Season of Walking and Season of Dreaming, star and sky, root and leaf, all spring from the Seed and dwell within it.

"I dwell in the Seed, and the Seed dwells in me. In me the Seed calls itself Miladras; in you the Seed calls itself Sarah. Through us it knows itself and brings forth flower and fruit, dream and deed."

Miladras struck the surface of the pool with a branch, sending ripples racing across it. Sarah sat up and watched as the water grew still. From its depths an image of the Door rose toward her.

"Look there, at its peak," the tree said.

Sarah peered into the water and studied the flower with its broad petals. At its center was the empty circle, where the Stone belonged.

"The Sower formed me and called me out of the darkness of the ground into the Light before I knew my name. This same One formed you from the dust of stars and gave you breath. It is his power that calls you to bear the Stone to the Door, where it belongs, and it is his power that will give you strength to bear it."

"What troubles you?" the tree asked after a moment.

"Why me? Why am I . . ." It was the first time she had said it. "Why am *I* the Stone-Bearer?"

"It is not given to me to know the mind of the Sower. But perhaps in saving Oneiros, Sarah-kir, you will deliver yourself."

"From what?"

"When you have carried the Stone to the Door, you will know."

"But how can I take it back if I don't even know where it is?"

"When you are ready, the Stone will guide you."

"But—"

"Are you not weary of so much speech?" The tree touched her forehead.

Sarah sank back, cradled between the roots of the great tree, her cheek against his smooth, warm bark, soft as old leather. She released a long, pent-up breath, and with it her questions. There was nothing she could do right now.

A sound came from deep within Miladras, low and rushing, like the wind, but it rose and fell like the notes of a flute. It came up from his roots, through his trunk, and out, somehow, through his long branches, so that it seemed to be coming from every direction at once, filling her ears with its music. This was his voice too, Sarah realized with surprise— a second voice, the voice of earth and rain and sunlight and wheeling centuries of time.

The tree was singing. She was caught up into the song, lifted and carried along, drifting with it down among the branching paths of the ancient garden, this way, that way, through the mist. . . .

"Come," Miladras sang. "I will show you chasms of ice and palaces of cloud."

Which way is home? Sarah thought. *I want to go home.* But she couldn't hear his answer. The sound of his voice grew fainter, as though she had turned down a different path and was wandering out of reach.

twelve

Stray Cat

Sarah was walking up Strawbridge Lane. The wild rosebushes in the empty fields had overgrown the fence, reaching across to snag her coat with their long, thorny fingers. Brown puddles stood in the ruts of the road. She was so happy she started to run toward the house. Her mother would be waiting inside.

She ran to the front door, turned the knob, and pushed.

On the other side of the door lay nothing but a huge, gaping hole. The ground gave way and she slid down into it. Someone she couldn't see was shoveling dirt over her. She tried to breathe and couldn't.

Then, suddenly, air, sweet air. Something soft brushed her face. Mrs. Woodley's feather duster, she thought, and woke.

Inches from her nose, a small, whiskered face. Unblinking golden eyes stared into hers.

"Ozymandias?"

He answered with a silent meow.

She sat up. "It's really you—it is!" The cat rose on his toes, purring, nudging her hand with his head. She picked him up, cradling him against her chest, rocking to and fro. "Oh, Ozzie, Ozzie . . . I missed you so much!"

"It's my cat," she told Miladras, who stood over her. "My kitty!"

"Does kitty-ela dream?"

Sarah laughed, and Ozzie tried to escape. "I don't know! Do you, Ozymandias?" She touched her nose to his. "I still can't believe it! Miladras, how did he get here? Did you find him?"

"He has come along one of the forking paths."

"Which one? I have to know! Don't you see, Ozzie was with Sam! It's the only way he could've gotten here from Earth. If I can get back to the place Ozzie came from, maybe I'll find Sam, too!"

She followed Miladras to the entrance of the garden, where they stood looking out over the terraces and the paths running between them.

"In the gardens of the Thealkir," he began, "the Old Magic still lingers. In the Vision Pool, along the paths. The paths are the way in and the way out. From here one may journey anywhere in Oneiros in the blink of an eye."

"Like shortcuts? But there are so many! Where do I start?"

Miladras lifted a branch and pointed to the fine white sand at her feet, delicately etched with a pattern of cat paw prints.

"Follow the tracks? That's it?" Sarah settled Ozymandias in her arms. "All right, let's go."

Miladras did not move.

"Aren't you coming with me?" Sarah laid her hand on his

smooth trunk. "Miladras?" Beneath his hide she could feel the tension.

"The Umbra is near. We Thealkir must remain in our gardens."

"But how will I get back here? How will I find the Stone without you? Or get to the Door?"

"The Stone will guide you to itself. But be on guard. Your dream was a warning."

"How did you—Ozzie, be still!"

"There is danger in your heart's desire. The Umbra will surely turn that desire to its own purpose; that is part of its cunning. When it saw that your will was divided as you drew close to the Door, it struck and cast the Stone into the Place That Is Neither Here nor There. But only you can carry it from that place. The Umbra cannot take possession of the Stone unless you relinquish it. Are you understanding?"

"But how do I get to this . . . this place?"

"It may be that the Umbra will devise a way; I do not know for certain. Once you have found the Stone, do not tarry, but make haste to the Door. Your will must be one with the will of the Stone."

"I understand."

"There is one last thing. If you are to carry the Stone to the Door, your hands must be empty; you cannot cling to anything else. Again I say: Be on guard against the craft of the Umbra! Now, come."

"Miladras, wait! When I get to the Door, will you be there?"

"This is as we have dreamed."

"We'll take the Stone to the Door together!"

One dark eye gazed solemnly on her. "May it be so, Sarah-kir."

"Oh, Miladras!" Sarah put Ozymandias on the ground and embraced the tree, feeling the warm life pulsing within him. "I don't want to say good-bye."

"You have eaten of my fruit. I am always with you." Slowly he drew away. "There . . ." He pointed. "The path begins."

Sarah followed the small marks of Ozzie's paws in the glittering sand. The cat trotted beside her, his tail waving. Here and there the trail broke off, in places where Ozymandias had leaped up onto a terrace wall and down again on the other side, but after a few minutes of searching she would spot the tiny prints once more. She and Ozymandias descended the path together, mist swirling around Sarah's ankles, growing thicker as they neared the foot of the hill.

Finally they came to an opening in a wall where the tracks disappeared altogether. "Is this it, Ozzie? Is this where you came through?" She peered through the entrance. Nothing out of the ordinary: Like the other terraces, this was a miniature version of the big garden at the top of the hill, surrounded by a low stone wall with plants growing in its crevices.

"Well, kitty, here we go." She took a deep breath, scooped up Ozymandias, and walked to the middle of the terrace. Ozzie began to squirm. She rearranged him and scratched his head, trying to keep him happy. It was awfully hard to make a cat do anything he didn't want to, she thought, staring at a brilliant scarlet flower growing in a cleft of the wall. Was it her imagination, or were the stones in the wall around it moving, breathing slowly in and out? Ozymandias tensed, his claws in her arm.

Now, Sarah thought. She felt a lifting sensation in her stomach, as though she were riding in an elevator, and shifted her feet to keep her balance. The red of the flower grew more intense, flaming like a sun, and then she saw it *was* the sun, sinking through fiery clouds. She was standing at the edge of a lake. All around it rose towers of rock in fantastic shapes, as if a giant's child had been making drip castles with wet sand. The setting sun hammered out a path of beaten gold across the water, ending at her feet.

Something floating among the reeds caught her eye. Holding Ozzie firmly in one arm, she stepped on a rock, reached over, and caught it. It was a bandanna like Angel's.

Angel! She felt a surge of hope, then fear. Where was he? She stared at the water. The lake was miles across. It would be deep and cold. If he had fallen from space, at night . . .

Ozymandias wriggled free and trotted away from her along the shore.

thirteen

Starlight and Shadow

"Wait, Ozzie! Wait!" The cat was heading toward the nearest of the bizarre towers. Sarah followed the bright flag of his tail up a spill of broad, flat rocks ringing the shore. If she wasn't quick, she would lose sight of him.

She slipped and hit her knee. When she glanced up a moment later, he had disappeared over the top of the low bluff. Moving more cautiously, she made her way from one rock to another until she was overlooking a sheltered cove with a crescent of sandy beach.

A white horse stood up to his fetlocks in the lake, his long neck arched to drink. Altair! A few yards away the mare, Foxfire, pulled at a patch of tall grass.

A man crouched on the sand, building a fire. The skin of his bare chest glowed in the fading light. His hair grew in a wild tangle, sticking up in an odd way all around his head. No, not his hair—a garland of leaves. He took a piece of kindling from the pile and held it toward his other hand, as though to light it. A flame leaped up, illuminating his face.

"Angel!"

He rose in an instant, and she saw that he was naked except for his crown of leaves. A dark line of hair led down his flat belly to a darker mass and the complicated bundle beneath it.

"Sarah? Is it you?"

"Angel!"

He darted across the sand and struggled into his jeans, and then he was scaling the rocks, his face lifted toward her, lit with joy. He threw his arms around her, embracing her so fiercely she thought her ribs would crack. A mysterious, wild smell rose from his skin, horses and moss and sunlight and lake—a green, summery sort of smell.

"Sarah," he said into her hair, over and over. "I thought I'd never see you again! I looked everywhere!"

"I wasn't here. I was . . . somewhere else, in a garden."

"How did you find me?"

"Ozzie showed me. Ozymandias. My cat." She pointed to him, sitting nearby on a rock with his tail arranged neatly over his front paws. "I told you about him—he had to go live with Sam out in California . . . where *is* Sam?"

Angel looked blank. "I haven't seen a sign of another human being. The cat just appeared. Yesterday, I think. I was fishing. He dragged off the biggest one before I could stop him, the little thief."

"Then, where . . ." Sarah twisted the kerchief in her fingers, trying to think.

"Hey, you found my bandanna! I hung it on some reeds yesterday when I was swimming—"

"I thought you had drowned!"

"Do I look like a ghost?" He grinned, tucked the kerchief

in his pocket, and took her hands. "But what about you? The last thing I remember, we were headed for the Door—when I woke up here, you were nowhere to be found."

Sarah looked down at their clasped hands. The gold ring on his finger, the ring his mother had given him, glinted in the last light. So he didn't remember how she had drawn back at the last moment before they reached the Door, didn't know that she had lost the Stone.

She thought it might be easier to say the second time. It wasn't. She stumbled through the story and waited for him to speak.

"You mean the Stone is gone?"

She nodded, afraid to meet his eyes.

When she dared to look up, he seemed strangely composed. "So we won't be going back," he said.

"Yes we will! I'll find the Stone. And Sam, too. I have to!"

He tightened his grip on her hands. "It's okay, don't you see? Now that you're here, everything is perfect. Look at this place!"

Across the lake the sky glowed green, as if underwater, and silhouetted against it were the rock towers. It was beautiful. If she had her paints . . .

Angel was gazing at the landscape, still wearing the crown of leaves.

"I like your hat," she said, teasing.

"Oh." He took it off, and she saw she'd embarrassed him.

"Just something to do, I guess." Before she could protest, he flung it in a wide arc over the water, and it landed, scattering a flock of long-legged birds. "They lay good eggs."

Sarah studied him as he watched the birds fly low across

the glassy water. "You look different. Older. No, not older, but—I don't know." She suddenly felt shy. "Look at that rock way over there," she said, changing the subject. "It looks like a dragon, doesn't it?"

"That's what I call it: Dragon Rock. And that one"—he put his arm around her shoulder and pointed—"that's the Maiden. See her long hair?"

Sarah nodded and turned in the circle of his arm. "I can't believe I found you."

"Believe it." He lifted a strand of hair from her face, tucked it behind her ear, and kissed her forehead.

Angel caught three fish for their supper and cooked them over the fire. The flames spit and crackled, sending tiny sparks drifting up into the blackness overhead.

"How did you get the fire started?" Sarah asked.

"Oh, Gypsies are born knowing how to make fires." He winked and pulled a lighter from his pocket. "My father taught me a gentleman should always carry two things: a pocketknife and a lighter."

By the time the moons rose, they had finished eating and fed the scraps to Ozymandias. They lay together on a flat rock overhanging the lake, their sides touching, looking up at the sky, brilliant with stars.

Just as he had on those long afternoons in the stable, Angel listened now as Sarah told him about Miladras and the garden and the branching paths. He wanted to know everything about Oneiros, but he was most interested in the dreams of the Thealkir, especially the one about the king.

"I don't know much about it," Sarah told him, "except

that it's one of the Great Dreams. And the king is called . . ."
She thought hard. "The Wandering King or the Wayfaring
King—something like that."

Angel grew quiet again. *He's changed*, Sarah thought,
looking at him. He'd always seemed strong, with something
brave and utterly determined at his heart. But sometimes she
felt he was acting a little, playing a part for her sake, so that
she would feel safe. Like the way he had said, "I won't let
anyone hurt you," the first time they really talked. And when
she had been so scared in the stable and he had assured her
they would get away. But now, as though this place had
worked some magic in him, he seemed to have become the
person he'd once pretended to be.

"Tomorrow," he said, "we'll take the horses out and start
looking for Sam. There's bound to be some sign of him."

They fell into silence. They were alone together for the
first time, truly alone. All the sensation in her body seemed
concentrated in her side where his arm lay against her. There
was more she needed to tell him, but she wanted to wait, to
prolong this moment.

Ozymandias sprang up beside them, purring, poking his
nose in Sarah's ear, tangling her hair with his claws. "Ow."
Sarah pushed him away. At last he settled down, wedging
himself between the two of them like a chaperone on a sofa.

"I've dreamed of this," Angel said, gazing at the sky.

Of being together? she wanted to ask, but she knew it
wasn't what he meant.

"Of being free," he went on. "My mother used to tell me
wonderful stories about the campfires and sleeping under the
stars and catching fish with her hands. I spent a couple of

summers traveling around with cousins of hers—fifth or sixth cousins, ten times removed or something. But it wasn't the way I thought it would be. For one thing, I didn't belong really. Because I'm a *didakai*. But here it doesn't matter." He turned on his side and propped his head on his hand, stroking Ozzie's back. "Here I'm a Gypsy."

And what am I? she thought. Out of the silence the answer came: *You are the Stone-Bearer.*

She thought of Miladras, alone in his garden, and of the Stone. Somewhere it waited for her.

Angel ran a fingertip along her cheekbone. "You look different too."

"I do? How?"

"I'm not sure. Something . . ." He lifted a strand of hair from her lips, where the wind had blown it, and bent over her, looking into her eyes for a long moment before he kissed her. Her lips yielded to the gentle pressure of his mouth, and desire spread through her. Ozzie, squeezed between them, growled deep in his throat. They fell apart, laughing, and the cat leaped nimbly over Angel's chest, perched on a rock just above them, and with a vexed air began to lick himself.

She lay back, looking up at the stars. She wanted Angel to kiss her again but was frightened of what might happen if he did. Maybe he was afraid too. He had drawn away from her a little, just far enough so that their sides no longer touched, and lay with his arms crossed under his head.

"I wonder what happened to the Stone," he said.

"Miladras says it's in the Place That Is Neither Here nor There," Sarah said.

"What? What does that mean?"

"He says it will guide me to itself. And give me the power I need to carry it back to the Door."

"Then it will. It got us here, didn't it?"

"But what if I can't do it? What if . . ." She paused. She hadn't told Angel about this part. It was almost too frightening to think about.

He turned on his side to face her. "Tell me."

"There's a . . . an evil force. The Umbra. It's like a shadow. The old woman in Latin class knew about it, too. When I pulled back from the Door, I must've given it . . . I don't know, an opening. Because that was when something came out of nowhere and tore our hands apart, and I lost hold of the Stone."

"Has the Umbra got it, then?"

"No. I . . . I'm the only one who can take it from that place. The only way the Umbra can possess the Stone is if I turn it over."

He searched her face, as if looking for the answer to an unspoken question. "Then the Stone is safe."

"But without it the Door is open to the Umbra. It's already making its way in. Miladras said that unless the Stone returns to the Door, doom will come to Oneiros."

"What do you mean?" He sat up suddenly. "Are you saying this place may be destroyed?" He stared hard at her and twisted away. "A shadow! How are we supposed to fight a shadow?"

When she touched his back, his muscles were rigid.

"We'll get back to Earth somehow," she said. She would find Sam; he would figure out a way. He had the Looking Glass.

"Think so?" Angel nodded to himself. "And then what? I'll go on riding somebody else's horses around the park for the rest of my life?"

Was that how he saw his future? There was so much she did not know about him, so much he kept hidden.

"You know that big meadow in the park, the Sheep Meadow?" he asked without turning around. "I call it the Grass Museum. A few more years and there won't be anything left but grass museums and forest museums and beach museums. The earth used to be like this once." He opened his arms to the lake and the stars. "Before the *gaji* slaughtered the animals and poisoned the rivers and filled the air with so much filth you can't breathe and you can't see the stars."

"It's not all like that—you could get away, out of the city. You could travel, like you said, in your *vardo*."

"You mean my Winnebago. That's what Gypsies travel in now. That picture I showed you came out of a library book. I used to tell people the man in it was my grandfather."

She paused. "Did you know him?" she asked gently. "Your grandfather?"

Angel drew a deep breath, looking out over the lake. "My mother was a little girl during the Second World War. She and her whole *kumpania* were traveling through Croatia, hiding in the woods. She was drawing water when soldiers came and rounded everybody up. Nobody knows what happened— whether they all got sick or the guards killed them—but Mara never saw any of them again. My father says that's why she's crazy: because she lived and everyone else died."

Sarah imagined Mara as a little girl, left alone in the

woods. *Like me,* Sarah thought suddenly. *After the state trooper told me about Mother and Daddy . . .*

Why did such terrible things have to happen? Why was the world like that?

Her heart ached for Mara, for Angel, for herself. There was nothing she could say, no promise that everything would be all right. She touched his back. He turned to her and she took him in her arms.

"Please, Sarah," he whispered, his head against her breast. "Find the Stone. Take it back."

fourteen

Wrakir

At first light Sarah and Angel set out on the horses, leaving Ozzie asleep in the cave where they had spent the night. Sarah rode Altair, who wanted to run but could be persuaded to canter at an easy pace, and Angel rode Foxfire. They loped beside the edge of the lake, plumes of vapor rising from the water like phantoms.

They slowed to a walk. The horses' ears flicked back and forth, listening while Sarah and Angel talked.

"The Great Dreams of the Thealkir," Angel said. "Like the one about the king—it hasn't come true yet. But will it? Can the trees see the future?"

"It's not that simple. I think the dreams are more like important stories. Maybe by dreaming them over and over, the trees help them come true. But Miladras says there are thousands of futures, and every time we make a choice, we turn all but one of them aside. So nobody can predict what will happen. It depends on the choices we make." She went on, thinking aloud. "Maybe they see things that way because they have branches. Sam told me

once that our number system is based on ten because
humans have ten fingers. The trees' branches divide, and
divide again, like the forking paths. Like the pattern in
their leaves. So that's how they see life: You're always
coming to a place where the path divides and you have
to choose."

"Except that when their branches divide"—Angel held
out two fingers—"they go both directions at once."

"Too bad we can't! Then we could decide which future we
liked better."

"*Yekka buliasa nashti beshes pe done grastende,*" Angel
said, smiling at her. "It's a Gypsy saying: 'With one behind
you cannot sit on two horses.'"

They laughed.

"Anyway, if the Thealkir are right," Sarah said, "the future
isn't already decided, something you can jump out of the
present and look at."

"Like reading the last page of a book before you get to the
end? But it *is* a little like a book, isn't it? We're the characters,
and what we do really changes the story, but we don't know
what's going to happen in the next chapter. Or even the next
paragraph."

"Because we're not writing the book?" Sarah asked.

"Of course not. It's God's book."

"But maybe even God doesn't know what happens.
Miladras says the Sower chooses not to know everything."

Angel appeared to be thinking this over. "That makes
sense," he said after a moment. "Why go to the trouble of
creating these complicated beings who can make choices if
you already know what they're going to do?"

Again they laughed, and Angel nudged Foxfire into a canter. The sand along the water's edge was firm, perfect for riding.

"Let's race!" Sarah caught Angel's look of surprise as Altair shot past Foxfire, kicking up clumps of sand. Sarah leaned over him, the wind whipping his silvery mane into her face as they pounded along the shore, the powerful body beneath her like an extension of her own. "Fly, Altair," she said in his ear. "Fly!" And for a moment, as she closed her eyes, she felt as though they were soaring into the sun.

They dismounted in the shadow of Dragon Rock to eat and let the horses graze. Angel had wrapped a piece of cooked fish in wet leaves and gave her a handful of berries he'd picked from the same sort of bush whose leaves made his garland. The berries were fat and juicy, with a thin skin, like grapes, but they tasted like licorice.

He went around the other side of the rock to relieve himself and came back looking puzzled. "Come here," he said. "See what you make of this."

He pointed to a patch of earth where the grass was flattened. "Something big must've been lying here. Over there's a print. . . ."

She squatted to get a closer look. It was partially erased, but she could see a V-shaped print with a fainter line down the middle and deep holes at the base of the V and the ends. It was twice the length of her sneaker.

"What could it be?" Sarah asked. "It's much too big to be a bird's, but it looks like a claw print."

"There're some droppings over here."

Sarah inspected the mound of shiny greenish black pellets.

She nudged one with her sneaker, and it crumbled to dust. "They're all dried up," she said. "I wonder if that means they're old."

"Maybe." He frowned. "Didn't the tree say something about creatures with wings?"

"The Wrakir. They're one of the three kindred of *kir-ela*. He said they live on a volcanic island. But they like to be around still water. They like to look at themselves. Miladras thought that was funny because they're so ugly. . . ."

But Angel was crawling up the side of the rock toward a cave at the top. Sarah stood still as he disappeared into the black hole, her heart thumping against her rib cage. From the corner of her eye she saw the horses suddenly raise their heads, ears at attention. They wheeled and bolted.

What was it? What had they heard that she couldn't?

A sound came from behind her, a whirring like a rope being twirled through the air, only louder. A dark, winged shape appeared in the sky.

"Angel!" Sarah screamed. The thing kept coming. Angel slid toward her in an avalanche of small rocks. "Get down!"

She covered her head with her arms. Above her there was the wild beating of wings. She felt a blast of hot breath and smelled something rank and oily.

"Go!" Angel shouted at it, throwing up his arm. "Get out of here!"

The thing, bigger than any man, fell back, ribbed wings flapping furiously. It had the stubby snout and round nostrils of a dragon. It hissed and drew back its lips, showing sharp little teeth.

"Go!" Angel commanded once more. The yellow blood-shot eyes stared, blinked. Then, miraculously, the creature turned and flew away, growing smaller and smaller until it was no more than a black speck against the green sky, disappearing at last into a bank of clouds on the horizon.

Angel, panting, dropped beside Sarah. Gradually the wild drumming of her blood slackened. The horses made their way back. Altair stamped his front feet and blew through his nostrils, his hide twitching as if he, too, were trying to shake off the memory of the thing they had seen.

"How," Sarah said finally, "how did you make it go away like that?"

"I don't know."

"It was as if it knew you! But how could it?"

"I don't know."

She studied him for a moment. He was still staring at the clouds where the thing had disappeared. *But you do know,* she thought, *or at least you have an idea. It's something to do with you and this place.*

Angel had risen to his feet. "Must have been a Wrakir," he said, as much to himself as to her. "A Wrakir," he repeated, sounding somehow pleased. "Didn't you think it looked a bit like a dragon? A real one, I mean. Not the cartoon sort."

"It was horrible! Horrible!"

"Oh, I don't know." Angel smiled over his shoulder. "I've seen guys in the subway uglier than that. Come on, let's go back to camp."

There had been no sign of Sam anywhere. They would look again tomorrow, Angel said, following the direction the crea-

ture had taken when it flew off, and if they still found nothing, they would go farther the next day, set up camp somewhere else.

Angel caught two fish, and they cooked them over the
fire, as they had the night before. When they had finished
and fed the scraps to Ozzie, Angel took out his pocketknife
and began to whittle, humming to himself, a sad-sounding
melody that Sarah thought must be a Gypsy song. The flames
cast mysterious lights and shadows on his face, while around
him everything else melted into darkness.

Sarah lay on her side in the sand, staring into the fire,
thinking of all the times she had lain like this in front of the
fireplace in her bedroom at home. She saw the scene as if she
were a stranger looking through the window: the room glowing with yellow light, the bed with its blue and white quilt
turned down invitingly, and herself—the girl she used to be—
dreaming before the fire.

Home. If only she could go back, if she could be that girl
again, and everything could be the same. . . . Longing swept
over her, so sharp it was a physical pain. *I should be happy,*
she thought. *I'm with Angel, in this beautiful place.* . . . She
drew in her breath and blinked back tears.

"You okay?" Angel stopped whittling.

Ozymandias appeared and sniffed delicately at her face,
inquiring. She drew him to her.

"I'll recite something for you." Angel rested his knife on
his knee and looked off toward the water.

> As I came over Windy Gap
> They threw a halfpenny into my cap,

For I am running to Paradise;
And all that I need do is to wish
And somebody puts his hand in the dish
To throw me a bit of salted fish:
And there the king is *but as the beggar.*

. . . .

The wind is old and still at play
While I must hurry upon my way,
For I am running to Paradise;
Yet never have I lit on a friend
To take my fancy like the wind
That nobody can buy or bind:
And there the king is *but as the beggar.*

"Like it? It's by Yeats. Willie Yeats, Muldoon used to call him."

"Muldoon? Oh, you mean your father."

"Yes." Angel went back to his whittling. "Da taught me the poem. He used to be an actor in Dublin. But when we moved to America, to New York, he couldn't get parts. So when I was a kid, we'd stand on the sidewalk with this sign that said 'The Poetry Man Recites Your Favorite Poem from Memory,' with a list of all the ones we knew and the prices. Muldoon knew hundreds. The long ones cost the most. I did mostly the short ones and ones that rhymed, like 'Annabel Lee.' There are two more verses in the middle of that one I just said, but I can't remember all the lines now." He blew the shavings from the object he was carving.

"Your parents must be worried about you," Sarah said.

"Mara knows I'm all right."

"How?"

"The same way she knew I was going on a journey. She'll tell Muldoon."

"How did the two of them end up together?" Sarah asked.

Angel smiled. "Muldoon likes to say he saved her life. The acting troupe came across her in Gibraltar after the war. Mara was maybe nine—Da was eighteen. She'd been wandering around for a couple of years, begging, living off scraps, stowing away in boats. Once or twice the authorities picked her up and put her in an orphanage, but she ran away. Anyway, Muldoon took her back to Ireland, and Mara lived with Muldoon's granny—my great-grandmother—and worked as a kitchen maid in the big house in the village. One day Muldoon came back from Dublin and saw she'd grown up, and they got married. They used to go around to fairs and she'd tell fortunes—when she wasn't in one of her crazy spells—and he'd do scenes from plays."

"Madame Esperanza," Sarah said, remembering the sign in Mara's bedroom. She traced the name in the sand with a stick.

"Right. The thing is, she really does have the Sight. Most gypsy fortune-tellers, it's just a scam, but she would see things."

She knew about the Stone, Sarah thought. *A holy thing, from a holy place. It wants to go back.*

"She has this set of tarot cards," Angel was saying, "old, old cards handed down from her great-grandmother and blessed by Sara la Kali, the saint of the Gypsies. There's this legend that two relatives of the Virgin Mary drifted all the way to France in a boat, and Sara was with them. She was an Egyptian servant

girl—dark-skinned—that's why she's called Sara la Kali: Sara
the Black. Every year in France the Gypsies make a pilgrimage
to the place where the boat washed up. The statues of the saints
are dunked in the water three times, and if you dunk your tarot
cards in the sea at the same time, they're supposed to be
blessed." He stretched and looked at the lake. "Speaking of
being dunked . . ."

"You want to go swimming now? At night?"

"There's plenty of light."

There was. Both moons were full, bathing the cove in silver.

She looked away as Angel walked down to the water's
edge and undressed. A moment later she heard a splash.

He glided through the black water, sending the moonlight rippling toward her across the surface, beckoning. She
scratched an itchy spot on her scalp and another on her
back. It would be wonderful to be clean. She imagined the
feel of the water on her bare skin.

Quickly—because she knew unless she did it quickly, she
would not do it at all (even undressing in gym, in front of
other girls, made her face get hot)—she stood up, turned her
back, and slipped off her blouse. When she got to her under-
clothes, she hesitated. Should she leave them on? She would
feel less naked, but it seemed silly, and somehow more
embarrassing than taking everything off, as she was sure he
must have done.

She unsnapped her bra, yanked at her underpants, and
threw them on top of the pile with her other things.

He wasn't looking. He wasn't even there. She stepped
into the water, arms folded across her breasts, and gasped. It
was cold. She would have to get in anyway, and fast, too,

before he came back up. At least the bottom of the lake was hard and sandy, not spongy or slimy. She gritted her teeth and waded in up to her neck. Where was he?

"Angel?"

Hands slid up her legs as far as her knees. She screamed. They thrashed around in the water, breathless and laughing. He grabbed her by the ankle and pulled her down, and when she came up, she found his shoulders and dunked him, hard.

"Race you to the rock!" Angel said. They swam furiously to the rock and held on, catching their breath. "I won!"

"You had a head start," Sarah protested, wiping the water from her eyes. "Look at the horses!" she cried. They were racing back and forth along the shoreline, snorting and whinnying and kicking up their hind legs.

Angel whistled. "Hey, Altair! Want to swim? Come on! Come on, boy!" But the horses would wade in only as far as their knees, where they stood with ears pricked forward. Altair tossed water at them with his nose, jerking his head up and down.

Sarah laughed and turned to find Angel looking not at the horses, but at her.

Carefully holding his body away from hers, he leaned forward and kissed her, once and then again, a deep kiss that left them both breathless. He broke away. "God!" he said, resting his head against the rock, his eyes closed. "I'm going to burst into a million pieces!"

"If you do," Sarah said, "I'll spend the rest of my life searching for every last piece. Then I'll put them in a box on the mantelpiece—a box made of silver and ivory—and when I'm an old, old lady, I'll take down the box—"

"And say to your fat, deaf husband," Angel broke in, "'This is Angel Muldoon, dear. He went so mad with lust for me that he popped, like a big red balloon.'"

"And he'll say"—Sarah tried not to laugh—"'What's that you say, Mother? You found a dead loon?'"

"Then you'll smile enigmatically," Angel said, "and put the box back in its place." He grew quiet, scooping up the moonlit water and letting it run like quicksilver through his fingers. It seemed a long time before he spoke. "You know what I wish? I wish we could stay here forever."

Here, forever? Sarah looked up at the two moons floating among ragged clouds. If she lived to be a hundred, this could never feel like home.

"Sarah?" Angel turned to her, his face serious. "You've never . . ."

She shook her head. "But you have?"

"Yes. It never meant very much. But if I—if we . . . it would mean forever. We'd be married, and we can't be, not . . ."

Not yet, she waited for him to say, but he didn't.

"You're shaking." He took her hand and kissed the palm. "Come on, we'd better get out."

He waited in the water while she got out and dressed. When she had finished, she went to the cave where they had slept and lay down on the moss that was their bed. Ozzie appeared from out of the shadows and began kneading a patch of moss next to her, purring and purring. Sarah lay still, listening to the moan of the wind blowing through the rock. It was an eerie sound—"like a mermaid's song," Angel had said when he first showed her the cave. She slipped her hand under her blouse and felt her heart beating fast.

Angel stood in the entrance of the cave in his jeans. "I made something for you," he said, holding it out toward her.

"A present?" She sat up. "A comb! Oh, Angel—I've been dying to comb the tangles out of my hair. I've been using my fingers. How did you do it?"

He shrugged. She could tell he was pleased and trying not to show it. "I just kept whittling. Let's see if it works."

She sat with her back toward him while he removed the elastic band from the end of her braid and carefully combed her hair, the right way, starting with the ends. When there was a bad snarl, he held the section above the knot so he wouldn't be tugging at her scalp.

"Tell me if I'm hurting you."

"You're not." Sarah felt dreamy and light-headed, the way she always had when her mother brushed her hair with her special black oval brush that had MASON PEARSON, LONDON, ENGLAND written on the handle. "Somebody must have taught you how to comb long hair."

Angel's hands fell still. "I used to do my mother's."

Sarah had a sudden picture of the little boy Angel must have been, patiently combing his mother's hair, taking care of her instead of being taken care of, the way Sarah had been.

"Your hair's thick, like hers. There." He spread her hair out on her shoulders and handed her the comb and the elastic band. "Leave it down for a while so it can dry."

She twisted around to face him. "Thank you."

"You're welcome." He stroked her cheek with the side of his hand. Then he got to his feet.

"Where are you going?"

"I'll sleep on the beach."

"But why?"

"You know why."

"Couldn't we just lie together, like last night?"

He laughed. "No."

At the entrance to the cave he paused. He stepped back inside, took her face in both hands, and kissed her once more. Then he was gone.

She stretched and lay blinking at the sun, already well up over the horizon. She'd been dreaming about food: In the dream she was at the aunts' house in Oxford, and they were having high tea, a real Yorkshire high tea like the ones the aunts had had when they were little girls growing up in the country. The first time she'd heard someone mention high tea, she'd thought it must be a very grand sort of occasion, with everyone sitting primly in the dining room in their Sunday best. But it wasn't that at all. It was really an early supper, a feast of wonderful things eaten at the kitchen table: crumpets with melted butter swimming in the little holes, gingerbread, almond custard cakes called Richmond maids of honor, gooseberry tarts, a leek-and-bacon roly-poly pudding, ham and cheese, pickles, "fat rascal" cookies studded with currants, and toad in the hole, which sounded terrible but turned out to be delicious—plump sausages baked in batter. Sometimes Great-aunt Sophie could be persuaded to make the griddle cakes they called singin' hinnies. The aunts called Sarah "hinny," which was the Yorkshire way of saying "honey," and although the cakes didn't have any honey in them, they did squeak and "sing" when they were sizzling on the hot griddle. The aunts would wrap a coin in greased brown paper and hide it inside one of the hinnies; if you found it, it was supposed to bring you good luck.

In the dream Sarah ate some of everything, just as she had whenever she visited the aunts, but in the dream she didn't make herself sick; she could just keep on eating and eating.

Her stomach grumbled and she got up, hoping Angel had found something for breakfast. But he was nowhere in sight, nor were the horses. She fought down a flutter of panic.

A stick stood upright in the sand with Angel's kerchief tied to it. There, written clearly in the firm white sand, was a message: LOOKING FOR EGGS BACK SOON LOVE GUESS WHO P.S. STAY IN CAVE.

Relieved, she let herself smile, untied the kerchief, and stuck it in her pocket. The sun was burning off the mist on the lake, and overhead, in the spaces between golden clouds, the sky shone green. She took a deep breath and waded an inch into the clear water, wiggling her toes. Her toenails needed cutting. Angel's pocketknife had a tiny pair of scissors—maybe they would work.

She bent down and splashed some water on her face to wake herself up, then turned to walk back to the cave.

At the edge of her vision she glimpsed something move among the rocks that jutted out into the water. Nothing there. She took another step toward the cave and froze. The rocks themselves seemed to be moving. The creature they had seen yesterday, its wings folded, crept among the boulders.

Don't move. Don't breathe.

It worked its way to the very tip of the promontory and

crouched there like a gargoyle, staring down at the water and making squeaking sounds.

It's looking at itself, Sarah thought, *it doesn't see me.* . . .

She inched toward the cave, never taking her eyes from the creature. She was halfway there when Ozymandias darted out from a stand of reeds near the water and leaped up onto the rocks.

Sarah cried out.

The creature spread its wings and hissed.

Sarah raced toward the cave. The thing swooped in front of her. She turned and ran back toward the lake, feet sinking into the sand. She lunged toward the water, threw herself under. Something tore at her scalp and shoulder and pierced the skin between two ribs. She felt herself being seized, clumsily dragged out of the water. She screamed. Before she could understand what had happened, she was in the air.

fifteen

To the Island

The Wrakir struggled to rise, grasping Sarah around the middle, and the ground tilted and slid sideways. Suddenly there was no up or down: Clouds, rocks, sky, lake, all tumbled over one another. She beat her fist against the Wrakir's belly, screamed, tore at the talon embedded between her ribs, but the Wrakir rose still higher, and the ground fell farther and farther away.

In a swirl of vertigo she looked down. Scattered silver pieces of a puzzle. The lakes. She closed her eyes, but the dizziness only grew worse. She could not faint. If she fainted . . . She clung with both hands to the creature's scaly leg as its wings beat in a steady rhythm.

On and on they flew, the wind stinging her eyes. The clouds thinned, and the meandering channels that fed the lakes grew broader, and the lakes spilled into one another, forming inland seas. Sarah could see through the clear water right to the gray bottom, ridged and whorled like the hide of some gigantic slumbering beast.

The air gradually grew colder. They entered a limbo of

dense gray cloud. The Wrakir fought to make headway, buffeted by gusts that blew stinging mist into Sarah's face and roared in her ears. The pain in her side grew worse, but she was afraid to yank out the single talon piercing her skin. The creature might dig deeper—or lose its grip altogether. A faraway droning sound reached her ears and grew more distinct: waves, waves crashing against rocks. An alien smell engulfed her, not salty like the seas on Earth, but sharp and metallic, like an iron pan left on the stove. Suddenly they emerged from the clouds, and the wrinkled carpet of ocean lay spread out below them.

The island towered above the churning water, a natural fortress ringed by peaks that rose as sharply as stalagmites. The highest pinnacles pierced the clouds and soared above them. There were caverns in the peaks, black holes like eyes and mouths.

They flew low over the water toward the sheer cliffs at the island's edge, and the Wrakir made its way between two peaks. Beneath them lay the center of the island, a crater filled with pools of ooze that steamed and bubbled and burst into flame, filling the air with oily fumes. Dozens of the creatures were bathing in the ooze, flapping their bat wings, oblivious to the fires igniting around them. One flew up, settled on a rock, and began to lick itself clean with a long, forked tongue.

Straight ahead, in the side of a peak, yawned a huge black hole. Sarah's captor flew toward it, hurtled into the blackness, dropped her, and crashed into a wall.

She somersaulted wildly and lay still, one leg bent awkwardly underneath her. The Wrakir scuttled away. A dank wind blew over her, as if the cave were breathing. She hurt all over. Cautiously she unfolded her leg, flexed it, then the other. Left leg and right leg. Arms. Right, left. Nothing broken, but everything bruised and scraped and bumped. Pain sang along every nerve. She gingerly touched the place where the Wrakir's talon had pierced her. Her blouse was stuck to her skin with what she guessed was clotted blood.

From deep within the cavern came sharp, birdlike cries and a faint answering murmur. It sounded like a voice. A human voice. She lay perfectly still, her whole body straining to hear. Out of the silence came footfalls. Something was moving toward her.

She struggled to her feet, holding her hands in front of her, cried out as her fingertips grazed something and her wrist was seized and held.

"Don't move."

The fingers holding her wrist loosened. There was the sound of a match being struck and a painfully bright flare of light. The flame wavered, then steadied. A man's face sprang from the darkness, squinting fiercely at her. He held the match higher and inched closer. "*Sarah?*"

"Sam!" She threw her arms around her brother and burst into tears. "I can't believe it! It's really you!"

"Shhh, it's okay," he was saying, rocking her from side to side. The match spluttered and went out, and once more they were surrounded by darkness.

"Sam, what is this place?"

"Let's go outside, Sarah, I've got a lot to—"

"Those things are out there!"

"They won't hurt you."

"It did! It grabbed me to pick me up. Its claw went in my side."

"I've got something we can put on it. Wait here."

"No!" She reached for his arm in the dark. "I want to go with you."

"No! We don't have much time—"

"What do you mean?"

"If a Wrakir comes along, just be still." He hugged her again. "I'll be back in a minute." She listened to his retreating footsteps, her heart beating uncomfortably fast. *Take a deep breath,* she told herself.

It caught in her side with a sharp pain that made her wince. What did Sam mean about their not having much time?

"Got it," Sam called out to her in the darkness. "Where are you?"

"Right here."

"Come on." He pulled her to her feet. "The air's not a lot better outside, but at least we can see."

She held on to his belt as they shuffled forward. "Watch your head," Sam said. "Bend down." They rounded a corner. Blank gray sky filled the mouth of the cavern.

Sam climbed down the sloped face of the peak to a patch of flat ground below. Sarah followed, cautiously placing her feet, her knees watery.

A group of Wrakir crowded around an object leaning against the side of the peak, shrouded in a tarpaulin. They jostled for position, making excited squeaks.

"Kray, *shala.*" Sam beckoned to one of the bigger Wrakir. "*Shala.* Come." The creature crept through the crowd on all fours and then sat up on its hindquarters in front of Sam and lifted its snout, snuffling. Sam stroked the Wrakir's stomach and back, rubbing the place between its wings.

How could Sam bear to touch it? But he had never minded snakes, either, and the skin of the Wrakir was something like a snake's: scaled, marked by faint patterns, and with a dark sheen that caught the light when the powerful muscles shifted underneath.

The Wrakir's barbed tail switched back and forth with seeming impatience. Sarah quickly moved out of its path.

"This is Kray," Sam said, thumping the Wrakir as if the creature were a big dog. "He's the one who found you."

"You sent him after me? How did you know I was here?"

"I didn't. I was banking on the Stone to bring you here. Hoping. Praying. Only I had no idea where you might end up, so I sent a whole posse of Wrakir to search for you. Since Kray brought you back, he gets a reward." Sam drew the tarpaulin away.

Underneath was a tall metallic oval, the mirror she'd seen in her vision of Sam, the first thing the Stone had shown her.

The Wrakir drew close to the mirror and extended his neck until his snout nearly touched the surface. He turned his head from side to side, making faces and murmuring with pleasure at his wavery reflection. When a second Wrakir approached, Kray made a warning growl deep in his throat and swiped at the other creature.

"Kray!" Sam grabbed the Wrakir's foreleg just above the five-clawed foot. It looked both remarkably like a hand and horribly different, with its long, scaly toes and curving, yellowed nails.

Sam said something in a low voice and let go of the Wrakir, who looked down for a moment before his eyes slid back to the mirror.

Sarah studied Sam's haggard face. He looked awful. His cheeks were shadowed with stubble. A clump of dirty adhesive tape held his glasses together on one side. And how had he gotten that black eye?

Kray began to talk softly to the Wrakir in the mirror.

"Sam," Sarah asked, "is this the Looking Glass?"

"That's what's left of the auxiliary unit. The rest of it's over there." Sam pointed to a heap of broken machinery, then quickly looked away. "I smashed it. I wanted to make absolutely sure no one from CIPHER could get back to Earth from here, just in case. . . ."

She stared at a piece of metal glinting in the weak sunlight. He had destroyed the Looking Glass. Their only way off the planet.

"We need to get out of the open." He scanned the ridges surrounding the lake. "Come on." He turned and started climbing toward a more sheltered spot among the rocks. Sarah followed him, glancing over her shoulder at the jumble of electronic circuit boards sprouting colored wires.

"You okay?" He reached for her hand and helped her over a boulder. She had to step carefully; she wished she hadn't been barefoot when the Wrakir snatched her into the air.

"Sam, if CIPHER can't use the auxiliary unit, that means we can't use it either."

"We won't have to. We can use the Stone."

She stopped where she was, wobbling.

"It got you here from Earth, didn't it?"

"Yes, but . . ."

"But what?"

She paused, braced herself. "It got lost. On the way here."

"It got lost? You lost the Stone?" He grabbed her elbow.

"I was trying to use it to get to you!"

"Sarah, do you know what this means?" His hands flew to his head. "We'll never get back! We'll be here forever!"

"You don't understand!" she cried. "First Zvalus tried to get it—he practically kidnapped me, but I got away, and then he found me again and chased us through Central Park, and that's when—"

"Zvalus! But how did he know you had it?"

"Helena called him, Sam! I'm sure of it. She and Bernard are part of CIPHER!"

He looked stunned. "Then, the will . . ."

"Bernard probably forged it."

He sank down on the edge of a flat rock and held his head. "I should've seen that! I should've seen a lot of things."

Sarah sat down next to him. More Wrakir had climbed out of the ooze to gather around the mirror. Most had no chance of getting so much as a glimpse of themselves, but they crowded in nevertheless. A gusting wind carried the oily scent of the fiery lake, and a host of gray clouds fled toward the horizon. Sarah took Sam's hand. "Tell me," she said.

"Yeah, okay," he said, rousing himself. "You need to know this. But we'd better do something about your side."

While he opened his first-aid kit, Sarah tried to peel her blouse away from the wound. She worked most of the cloth out of the sticky blood, but one ragged bit seemed glued to the spot. If she pulled it away, she knew the bleeding would start again, but there was no way Sam could apply the sterile dressing unless she did.

"Want me to do it?" Sam asked.

"No." She would show him she could be brave. Then he would believe she had been brave when Zvalus caught her.

"You don't have to prove anything to me, Sarah," Sam said.

She raised her eyes to his. Sam always knew. She closed her eyes, clenched her teeth, and yanked at the cloth.

"Holy smoke, Sarah."

She squeezed back the hot, stinging tears. He lifted her blouse. "Hold this out of the way." He dabbed the area with something that felt mercifully cool and soft. "What I wanted to tell you . . ." He broke off, listening.

"It's the wind. Go on."

He ignored her, his eyes searching the landscape. For what?

"Sam?"

He turned back to her with a distracted air and resumed his dabbing. "I probably should've disabled the Looking Glass a long time ago," he said. "The main unit, I mean, the big one, back at the Institute. But I didn't. Maybe it's a lucky thing. In the end I had to use it to escape."

"You've been here before?"

"Four times. This is my fifth. The others were round-trips. Looks like this one may be one-way." He glanced up. "Sorry. That wasn't meant as a jibe. Honest. I knew the whole thing was a tremendous gamble, counting on the Stone to bring you here, betting that I'd find you. . . ."

And that I would have the Stone, Sarah added silently.

But she knew Sam wasn't blaming her. That wasn't his way. "Think of it, Sarah!" he was saying. "I traveled from Earth to here and back four times, and every time the Looking Glass worked perfectly! The equations, the ones in the tree house—they were all I needed."

Sarah smiled. This was her old Sam, the Sam who kept her up late at night, pacing the floor of her bedroom in his red plaid bathrobe, tripping on the trailing sash, explaining how the universe had been created out of nothing, how the atoms in her body had once been part of the stars. Her dear, funny, brilliant brother. Here, now, sitting beside her. It seemed too wonderful to be true. How had it happened? For a moment she had the powerful sense of an invisible force working through all the events of the past, guiding them toward each other through the vast reaches of space.

Sam folded the square of gauze he had been using, exposing a clean surface, and gently wiped away a smear of blood. "I was scared of the Wrakir at first—just like you—so I stayed hidden and observed them. Then I realized they had a language, and little by little I started to communicate with them. They told me about the Stone in the Door. They thought I'd come by way of the Stone, you see—they didn't understand about the Looking Glass. It's just the *mee-wah* to them."

He blew softly on her wound.

"Mother used to do that," Sarah said, smoothing Sam's cowlick into place.

Sam held up one hand. "Wait—did you hear something?"

Sarah shook her head.

"Get down, behind that boulder. I'm going to go see what it is."

Before Sarah could obey, two Wrakir came clambering over the rocks and joined the crowd around the mirror. Sam exhaled loudly. "False alarm," he said, sitting beside her again and opening a foil packet.

"Sam, what is it? What are you afraid of?"

"I'm trying to tell you. I managed to get here and back the first three trips without anyone knowing I'd been gone." He took a cotton swab and began to probe the puncture itself. Sarah clenched her teeth and forced herself to concentrate on what he was saying. "But by then I knew enough about CIPHER to realize I couldn't let them have the Looking Glass," Sam went on. "I'd been accessing their files, and although I couldn't figure out precisely what they were up to, I knew it wasn't good. With the Looking Glass CIPHER could spread through the whole universe. So I stalled. I said there were a few minor hitches. I knew I was going to have to destroy it. But I couldn't make myself do it. Here was this perfect thing, this thing that made it possible to do something that human beings had dreamed of since the first one of us looked up at the stars. How could I destroy it? I thought maybe I could convince somebody in the government to help me expose CIPHER, but I didn't know who to trust." He sat back, looking at the wound with a thoughtful expression. Then he squeezed a bit of ointment from a tube onto his fingertip and smoothed it on her skin.

"And then I started thinking about the Stone." He sighed deeply and replaced the cap on the tube. "I thought, 'Suppose what the Wrakir say is true?' Suppose that, compared with the Stone, the Looking Glass was nothing, the Looking Glass was like . . . like Icarus, with his wax and feathers, compared to a spacecraft with hyperdrive? That's when I realized I had to go back and get the Stone and test it. If I didn't test it, I had no choice but to destroy the Looking Glass right away. Because if the Stone could do what the Wrakir said, I couldn't take any chances—CIPHER might use the Looking Glass to come here, and they might discover the Stone and steal it. You follow?"

She nodded. "So you came back one more time?"

"Yes. Here, hold this in place." She took the gauze pad he offered and cautiously held it against her skin, watching him tear a strip of adhesive tape from the roll with his teeth.

"My fourth trip," he said, pressing the tape into place, "the Wrakir were so happy to see me—it was easy to convince them to take me to the Stone. But this time Zvalus was on to me. He used the Looking Glass himself and followed me. When he got here to the island, he forced one of the Wrakir to tell him where I'd gone, and then he came after me."

Sam tore a second strip of tape from the roll. "He must have been watching me when I took the Stone from the Door. I don't know where he was hiding—he just seemed to . . . materialize. I didn't know what to do, how to get away from him. He started coming toward me, closer and closer, talking to me in that phony hypnotist voice he uses sometimes, and I took a step backward through the Door and *boom!* I was back at the Institute. In the men's room!" He laughed.

"Just like that?"

"Just like that. So I walked right into my office, found a mailing envelope, scribbled a note to you, and intercepted a UPS guy on his way out of the compound. Then I didn't know what to do. Now that I knew the Stone really worked, I had to do something about the Looking Glass, but I was certain Zvalus must've alerted the place before he left. The only reason I hadn't been caught right away had to be that the Guardians were waiting for me to show up in the staging area, where the Looking Glass main unit was. But I knew there wasn't much chance of getting out of the compound and then getting back in. So I figured I'd hide. I wanted to do three things before Zvalus got back: call you, disable the Looking Glass, and get away from the Institute before anybody realized I was there. But I couldn't get through to you, and I couldn't get to the Looking Glass—there were too many Guardians around. And then Zvalus did come back."

"He caught you?"

Sam nodded grimly.

"Did he hurt you?"

He didn't answer.

"Oh, Sam."

Sam closed his eyes. "It was . . . bad. I almost told him. And then, just when I thought I couldn't hold out any longer, Zvalus stopped coming to the cell. I knew then he must've found out you had the Stone, but I couldn't figure out how."

"What happened then?"

"The old woman—the one who smuggled out a letter to you—she helped me escape."

"Sam, she must be the same old woman who was in the tree house! She came to New York the same day the Stone came in the mail. She told me you were in danger and that I had to return the Stone to the Door. Miladras said that too—"

"Who's that?"

"Oh, Sam, he's the most wonderful . . . I landed in his garden—he's sort of a cross between a tree and a person. They're called the Thealkir, the Dreaming Trees. They use mental radio to communicate."

"Telepathic trees?" Sam's eyebrows shot up.

"And they can see the future—well, possible futures. They knew the Stone would be taken from the Door by someone from another world, and they knew someone from that world would return the Stone. It's me, Sam. I have to find it and take it back. It's dangerous for the Stone to be out of the Door."

"Why?"

He stared intently at the ground as she explained. "Listen, Sarah," he said when she had finished. "The Umbra, CIPHER—they must be part of the same thing. The Umbra's working through CIPHER, using it. Like a branch office of evil on Earth, with Zvalus in charge." He paused, his expression somber. "I should never have taken the Stone from the Door. I was too focused on finding out if what the Wrakir had said about it was true. I should have thought about the possible consequences. But," he went on, talking to himself as much as to her, "somebody must've wanted me to come here. The equations in the tree house led me directly here. . . ."

Sarah's mind was racing. If Zvalus was somehow part of the Umbra, what would happen if he somehow managed to capture the Stone?

Doom. Images of devastation rose in her mind: Miladras's garden laid waste, the lakes on fire, the stars extinguished. Darkness, forever and ever. "Sam," she said, seizing his arm, "does the main unit of the Looking Glass still work? Could Zvalus use it to come here again?"

He looked at her as though he had forgotten she was there, and blinked. "That's what I've been trying to explain. When I escaped from the cell at the Institute, I made it back to my quarters and tried to call you to warn you about Zvalus, but I couldn't get through. Then the alarm sounded. I knew the only chance of escape I had left was the Looking Glass—if I stayed on Earth, I was a goner. I had to gamble that the Stone would transport you here and just hope we'd find each other. So I grabbed Ozzie—he was dozing on the windowsill—and we hightailed it to the staging area. By the time I activated the Looking Glass, the Guardians were on my heels, but it was too late for them to do anything—the fail-safe element had already locked in. I told them not to follow me—I told them I was going to destroy the auxiliary unit and make it impossible for anyone to return to Earth. But I don't know if they believed me." Sam replaced the adhesive tape in the first-aid kit and snapped the case shut.

"But Sam, even if they did believe you, and even if they convince Zvalus that you meant it, Zvalus thinks I have the Stone! He'll figure that the Stone will get him back to Earth, the same way you did."

Sam was pacing, thinking aloud. "If I could just determine the ratio of time between here and Earth . . . it's variable, but if I had enough data, I might uncover a pattern. . . ."

"Sam, what are you talking about?"

"I'm wondering how much time has passed back on Earth—whether Zvalus could've returned to the Institute by now. You see, weeks ago I set up a delayed-action virus in

the Looking Glass as a precaution. I had it programmed so
that I could activate it with a single command when and if
the time came that I needed to destroy everything. I gave the
command just before I left Earth. It's a fatal virus—once it's
introduced, the whole system starts to break down. But it's
slow-acting." He wiped his glasses on his dirty shirttail and
held them up to the light, frowning. "I wanted it that way so
I could use the Looking Glass one last time if I was in a tight
corner. I also wanted to make sure nobody would notice
anything was wrong until it was too late. But the system
could remain intact for a while." He replaced his glasses and
stood staring at her.

"So Zvalus may have had time to use it? He could show
up here any minute?" Sarah jumped up, clutching her side.
"Why didn't you tell me before?"

"Because I knew you'd react the way you're reacting
now."

"We've got to get out of here, Sam!"

"Without the Stone and without the Looking Glass there's
only one way off this island, and that's the way you came.
Besides, I don't want to leave the Wrakir." He pointed to one
of them in the crowd around the mirror. "See that one there,
with gray around his scales?"

"Which one?" Sarah asked impatiently, glancing over the
group. She couldn't believe he was worried about the Wrakir
now, when the two of them were in danger. "They all look the
same."

"You're not looking closely enough."

At first they really did look the same, but as she studied
the group, she saw they were all slightly different, and here

and there a smaller one clung to what Sarah guessed must be its mother. Then she saw, standing a little apart from the others, one whose scales were peppered with gray, like the muzzle of an old dog. There was something odd about the way he held one front leg against his chest, protectively. Suddenly she saw that he *had* only one front leg; the other was a stump. She drew a sharp breath.

"Zvalus did that," Sam said. "I guess he got frustrated, you know? Trying to get them to tell him where I'd gone when they took me to the Door. If I'm not here when he comes back, he'll torture the whole lot of them."

"But the Wrakir can fly! They can get away."

"It's not that simple. This is their habitat—I think the ooze contains certain soluble minerals they need to survive. And they're not used to defending themselves. They look scary, but they're not aggressive really."

"But Sam, we have to do something!"

"I've rigged some traps, and I've warned the Wrakir to keep watch. But I can't go on running away from Zvalus. Sooner or later he'll find us."

"If only I knew where the Stone was," Sarah cried, "or how to get there! Miladras said it would guide me, but he didn't say how."

"How did you lose it?"

"We were running away from Zvalus, in Central Park, on the horses. But I didn't lose it in the park, it was afterward, when we were between Earth and here—"

"Who's 'we'?"

"Angel and me," Sarah said. "He's . . . a friend."

"A boyfriend?"

"What's so astonishing about that?"

"Nothing, I guess. You just seem awfully young. How old is he?"

"Seventeen. Almost eighteen."

"An older guy?" Sam's expression grew serious. "You've been alone here with him?"

"He's back where the Wrakir grabbed me," Sarah said. "With the horses. And Ozzie."

"Our Ozzie? But he was here with me. How did he—"

"The shortcuts! The ones that run from the gardens of the Thealkir to other parts of the planet. They're sort of like those wormholes you told me about. That's how I found Angel, and it must be how Ozzie got from here to the lakes and from there to Miladras's garden. Haven't the Wrakir said anything to you about them?"

"They told me about some 'disappearing' places on the island. But they wouldn't show me where they were. They're afraid of them."

"But you could persuade them to show us. Then we might be able to get back to Miladras's garden. He could help us, Sam—"

"I'm very much afraid," said a voice, "that no one can help you now."

Sarah sprang to her feet and whirled around. On a ledge above them stood Zvalus.

sixteen

Underground

Sam grabbed Sarah's hand. "This way!" He hauled her through a crevice between two slabs of rock at the edge of the clearing. A steep slope littered with rocky debris fell sharply toward the lake of ooze. They half ran, half slid down it and raced along a narrow ledge skirting the lake.

Heat from the ooze rose and beat against Sarah's face. Her heart felt as if it might jump out of her chest. The Wrakir were screaming, scattering and disappearing among the huge boulders.

"Hurry!"

But she couldn't go any faster; it was like running in a dream.

"It's pointless to run away!" Zvalus sounded close by, but when she threw a terrified glance over her shoulder, she couldn't see him.

Ahead of her Sam yelled something she couldn't catch and rounded a corner. She willed herself forward and made the turn just in time to see his legs disappearing into the wall next to the ledge. She wriggled into the hole after him, using her forearms to drag the rest of her.

It was dark. There was not enough air. She couldn't lift her head. Her hunched shoulders grazed the roof of the tunnel each time she pulled herself forward.

"Are you all the way in?" Sam whispered. "Make sure!"

"Sam, I can't breathe!" The unyielding rock walls seemed to squeeze her as she inched her way through.

"Keep going!"

Something crawled across her scalp. She jerked her head up and banged it against the roof of the tunnel. "Ow!" Hot tears sprang to her eyes.

"What happened?"

"I hit my head. Sam, I can't—"

"You have to! Come on!"

She started again. The backs of her forearms were scraped and sore. She could feel her bandage tearing off.

"A few more feet," Sam urged. "You can do it."

At last she felt his hand.

"Watch your head."

He found her elbow and helped her sit up. The wound in her side throbbed. She reached under her blouse and tried to press the bandage into place. She looked back the way they had come. The entrance to the tunnel was a small, dim key-hole of light. Had Zvalus seen them come in here? "Sam, what are we—"

"Shhh!"

She felt rather than heard the footsteps above their heads. Then a muffled shout and a faint answer. Zvalus *and* Oskar?

"Sam, what if they block the entrance—"

"Listen: There's an underground cavern where the Wrakir

lay their eggs. If we can make it down there, we should be safe for a while."

"Does Zvalus know about it?"

The shouts were more distinct now. Two voices.

"I'm not sure," Sam said, "but we can't stay here."

The next hours passed in a slow procession of minutes: minutes when she crept or crawled or slid or hung, dangling from a ledge, before she finally let go and dropped through darkness. Sam went first, using a stick he had left in the tunnel to gauge the distance to the ledge below, and only when the stick met empty space did he fire up one of the precious matches. The caverns grew larger as they descended. In the brief flare of a match she saw moisture glistening on rock walls and a narrow stream that threaded its way downward. Always they moved down, down, and farther down, deeper and deeper into profound darkness, listening for any sound that might mean Zvalus had found a way in. But they heard only their own breathing and the sound of trickling water.

After a long, exhausting descent—she tried not to think about what would happen if one of them fell and broke a leg— they reached a place where the cavern floor sloped gently downward and the stream ran along a narrow ravine. Then, so gradually that at first she thought she was imagining it, the blackness around them grew lighter by infinitesimal degrees until it was like being in a darkened theater.

"Where is the light coming from, Sam?"

"Wait till you see. . . ." He took her hand and led her beneath a low arch.

Sarah caught her breath. They were standing in a cavern the size of a cathedral. High above their heads the great vault was pierced by oddly shaped openings, through which fell long shafts of gray light. An animal smell hung in the air.

"The Wrakir females come in and out through those holes to get to their nests," Sam said. "Up there." He pointed to ledges near the roof. "They lay their eggs, and then they seal off the nest with a kind of sticky stuff, like cobwebs, only denser. And then when it's time for the eggs to hatch, they come and eat the cobwebs"—he smiled at her expression of disgust—"and the young climb on their backs, and they fly out."

"How did you ever find this place?"

He craned his neck to look at the ceiling. "I nearly fell through one of those holes."

"Sam! You would have been killed!"

"That's what gave me the idea for the traps. I left some holes open so the Wrakir could get in, but I covered a lot of the others with brush. See?"

She looked in the direction of his pointing finger and saw the several patches where only dim light filtered through. No one could survive a fall from that height. She imagined Sam falling, falling. . . . It made her feel weak.

Stop it, she chided herself. It was bad enough being afraid of the future. She couldn't start worrying about things that had never even happened. Somehow they would get out of this place and go back . . . no, not back home—that was impossible, she thought, feeling the old ache return. But surely there would be some place for them, somewhere to call home.

She felt Sam's hand on her arm. "Sarah," he said quietly, never taking his eyes off the vault, "there's somebody up there."

seventeen

A Great Fall

"Hello down there!" Zvalus sounded almost cheerful.

Sam and Sarah edged back into the shadows.

"Can you see me?" Zvalus called. "I can see you!"

They looked at each other, then at the roof. Where was he?

"Let's not be tedious about this," Zvalus said. "It's unpleasant enough having to shout, without having to wait for answers to our questions. You've nothing to fear. We want to help you!"

"Right," Sam muttered.

"We thought you might be hungry after your long climb, so we've brought you something to eat! We'll just toss it down, shall we? Stand clear!"

A moment later a large, dark object plummeted through one of the openings and hit the floor with a sickening impact.

"Oh, God," Sam breathed. "Don't look." Sarah turned away, but she had already seen the broken body of the Wrakir and, beneath its skull, the spreading pool of dark blood. She covered her mouth with her hand. She thought she might be sick.

"It's Freeg, the one he tortured before," Sam said.

"Hardly escargot, but we do the best we can," Zvalus called down. "I have good news, Professor Lucas! We're not stranded here after all, despite little Sarah's unforgivable carelessness."

Sarah's heart jumped. "He knows!" she whispered. "He must've overheard me tell you I lost the Stone—"

"Shhh!" Sam's gaze was fixed on the opening through which Freeg's body had fallen.

"We've brought spare parts for the auxiliary unit," Zvalus continued. "As soon as you've reconstructed it, we can all go back to Earth."

"Why should I do that?"

"You don't want to stay here, surely? And we must get back ourselves. We have so many things to do!"

Sam scanned the cavern ceiling, then cupped his hands around his mouth and called up to Zvalus, "Maybe we can work something out."

Sarah glanced at Sam. What was he thinking?

"There's a Wrakir up there," he said in a low voice. "It must be Freeg's mate."

"Excellent, Professor! It's always a pleasure to deal with a man of intelligence like yourself."

A dark form filled one of the holes, stared down at the body on the floor, and let out a wail of grief.

"She sees Freeg," Sam said. "*Wrakir-ma!*" he called. "*Maranam! Druyati!*"

Freeg's mate drew back from the hole. A moment later Sam and Sarah heard a cry of surprise from Zvalus. "Get away from me!"

The Wrakir cried out, an angry, high-pitched shriek.

"Go on, back! Back! Get away, I tell you, or I'll—"

Sarah heard the crack of branches breaking and the scream before she saw Zvalus, falling with arms outspread like useless wings, turning in the air, turning and falling and screaming.

Sam grabbed her, pushed her head down against his chest. She felt his heart pounding furiously.

"It's all right," he said, again and again. "It's all right. It's over."

She opened her eyes. Shreds of dry grass floated down in the shaft of light, and dust hung in the air. She would not look at the thing that lay on the cavern floor next to the body of the Wrakir. She felt no sense of relief; she was still too shocked and afraid.

"Are you sure he's dead?" she whispered. Sam drew away from her.

"Be careful!" She looked up. Where was Oskar? Had he heard the scream?

Sam was walking slowly toward Zvalus's body. He stood over him for a moment, then walked away.

Sarah stared. She took one step, then another. Zvalus lay on his back, his eyes open. In the growing darkness his skin looked pale, almost as white as the shirt he wore.

She drew closer. A trickle of blood ran from the corner of his mouth, bright red against the whiteness of his skin, but there was no blood anywhere else. He was staring at the roof. He looked surprised. She hadn't known dead people could look surprised.

"What do we do now?" Sarah asked. The thought of

spending the night in the cavern with Zvalus's corpse sent a chill through her.

Sam didn't answer. He was crouched beside the dead Wrakir, his hand over his eyes. Was he crying?

She shivered. The air had grown cold, very cold. A draft? No—the air was still. Nothing moved.

A foul smell flooded the air, the smell of sulfur.

She looked down at Zvalus. His eyelids fluttered.

"Sam," Sarah opened her mouth to say, but no sound came out.

Zvalus's head rolled to face her. "Hello, Sarah."

His hand shot out and seized her ankle.

Tea with Dr. Zvalus

In a split second Zvalus sprang to his feet, twisted Sarah's arm behind her back, and threw his free arm around her neck, holding her in front of him. The slightest pressure from his arm against her throat would choke her.

"Let her go!" Sam cried. "Let her go, and I'll repair the unit! I'll do whatever you want!"

"'Humpty Dumpty had a great fall,'" Zvalus said in a singsong voice. "'All the king's horses and all the king's men couldn't put Humpty together again.' But look at me! Good as new! What do you make of it, Professor?"

"Let her go, Zvalus."

"You're hardly in a position to negotiate. You will repair the unit." He tightened his hold on her neck. "Though when we have the Stone, we will have no more need of such clumsy mechanical devices, will we, Sarah?"

Sarah couldn't speak.

"Don't worry," he breathed in her ear, "we will help you find it."

A light moved toward them along the passageway. Oskar

stepped into the cavern. He held a flashlight and carried a coil of rope slung on his shoulder. The beam of the flashlight blinded her.

"Doctor, are you injured?" Oskar touched his own mouth. "You have blood here."

"Do I?" With the same arm that was hooked around her neck, Zvalus reached toward his mouth, pressing her to him. She felt him wipe his lip and, from the corner of her eye, saw him look at the smear of blood and smile.

They started the long climb back to the surface the way they had come, with Sam in the lead. Oskar went second, and Sarah followed him, with Zvalus bringing up the rear.

She was conscious of him behind her, humming tunelessly, the strange sulfurous odor rising from his skin. What was he going to do with them? They couldn't possibly overpower him in a fight; his strength seemed superhuman.

She'd been certain he was dead. He had to have been. But he hadn't stayed dead.

Above her, Sam scaled a ledge while Oskar watched. If Sam repaired the unit, would Zvalus take them back to Earth as his prisoners? Or would he kill them? Either way she would never find the Stone, never take it to the Door, as she had promised Miladras, as Angel had begged her to do.

She dragged herself through the tunnel once more and stood beneath the night sky. Sam gave her a look: *Are you okay?* She nodded. Oskar shoved him away.

They set up camp in the cavern where Kray had dropped her, carrying in the supplies Oskar and Zvalus had brought from Earth and hauling up the metallic oval mirror. The Wrakir stayed out of sight, though Sarah glimpsed a tail slithering away among the boulders. Zvalus supervised the operation from a camp stool while eating the dinner Oskar had prepared for him. When the last of the supplies had been hoisted up to the cavern, Oskar tied Sam's hands, hobbled his feet, and led him toward a passageway at the rear of the cavern.

"Where are you taking him?" Sarah cried. "What are you going to do?"

"Leave her alone," Sam said to Zvalus just before Oskar yanked him into the passage. "I'll do what you want." His voice rose. "Do you hear me, Zvalus? Sarah, don't believe anything he says—"

And then he was out of sight, silenced. A moment later Oskar returned.

"Tell me what you did to Sam!" She tried to run past Oskar, but he snatched her wrists, tied them and her ankles with cords, and pushed her down among the supplies.

He took a tube of something from one of the bags. "Open your mouth," he ordered, and when she refused, he grabbed her jaw with one meaty hand and forced it open.

"It's food," he said, squeezing the paste onto her tongue, where it dissolved, leaving an aftertaste of liver.

Zvalus pulled his chair up close to Sarah, set a kerosene lamp at his feet, and gazed at her with his colorless eyes, one finger pressed against his lips. The light from the lamp at his feet cast spectral shadows on his face.

"You ought to be grateful, you know," Zvalus said. "Had I not overheard your confession, you might have found it difficult to convince me that you truly had lost the Stone. That could have led to all sorts of unpleasantness. But," he went on, "I have a theory. It came to me after my fall. I think you know where the Stone is."

"But I don't!"

"It's an intuition I have—a little glimmery fish, a notion fish. They swim through my mind"—he smiled—"and I grab them by the tail. Oskar . . ." He twisted on the stool to look over his shoulder. "Is that water hot yet? Bring us some tea." He turned back to her. "How about a nice cuppa?"

Oskar set a tray beside Zvalus. On it were two metal mugs, a spoon, a jar containing white powder, a box of sugar cubes, and something wrapped in a striped dish towel.

"We'll let it steep," Zvalus said. "I can't abide weak tea. Do you take milk?" He lifted the jar. "Powdered, of course, but better than nothing. No?" He waggled a finger at her. "You think I'm trying to drug you? That's why you refused my peppermints the day we met." He spooned the powder into his own mug. "See? Now, shall I put some milk in yours?"

The idea of taking anything from him, of drinking from a mug he had touched, made her recoil. But saying no would only irritate him, and that could be dangerous, for her and for Sam. And she was very thirsty.

"Yes," she said.

"Very good. You are your mother's daughter, I see. I met her, you know. Your father, too. When they came out to the Institute. I, too, prefer milk in my tea. One must take one's lead from the British in all matters having to do with tea, I think. Sugar?"

She nodded.

"Excuse my fingers. Oskar neglected to pack sugar tongs."

Zvalus pinched a corner of the dish towel between two fingers and snatched the cloth away, revealing a dented tin pot. "I'll be mother, shall I?" he said, pouring a cup of tea for each of them. "I can help you remember where the Stone is, you know."

"It's not a matter of remembering," Sarah protested. "I dropped it in space! I don't *know* where it is!"

"Not here, perhaps"—Zvalus tapped her forehead with the handle of the spoon—"but deep inside you know. We must reach down and bring it to the surface. I'm a psychiatrist." He raised his pale eyebrows. "I've spent years peering into human souls. Most of them," he said, making a face, "are rather like those mounds of dirty snow you see in the city near the end of February. You know the ones I mean—all covered with soot and litter and all manner of nastiness. What will I find in your soul, I wonder?" He dabbed at the corners of his mouth with the towel.

Sarah stared into her tea.

"You're not drinking? Oh, how thoughtless of me. Your hands."

Sarah held her hands over the tray as he untied the cord. She rubbed her wrists.

"Such a lovely woman, your mother. The classic English rose, I thought to myself: that porcelain complexion"— Zvalus raised a hand to his own cheek—"that cloud of hair. And so clever with a camera. Terrible thing, the plane crash. You think about it a great deal, don't you? Imagine the minutes before they died?"

Sarah said nothing. She had thought about it, countless times. The scene replayed itself over and over in her mind.

"I expect they had time to think about it before they went down. Would they have panicked, do you suppose? Or prayed? Evidently God didn't hear them. He appears to be deaf at times."

"Stop it," Sarah said.

He tilted his head and regarded her. "Death interests me." Then he leaned across the table, sniffed, and wrinkled his nose in distaste.

"How curious," he said. "My fall seems to have sharpened my olfactory sense. I can smell him on you—the Gypsy's son. Where do you suppose he is now?"

"I don't know." She looked down to hide the fear she knew must show in her face.

When she raised her eyes again, Zvalus was staring at her, his face empty of expression.

He's waiting for me to say something, to give something away. It was an interviewing strategy; her father had told her about it. "You need to know when to keep quiet," he'd said. "Silence makes people a little uncomfortable. If you don't speak, the other person will feel they must, and sometimes they'll say something they might otherwise have kept to themselves."

Sarah took a sip of the lukewarm tea and looked down at her hands in her lap. *Good girl,* she could almost hear her father say. *You've shown him two can play that game. Now catch him off guard: Ask him a question of your own.*

"How do you get people like my aunt and uncle to join CIPHER?"

Not a flicker of surprise showed in his face. "The same way I recruited your brother," he said, draining his mug and pouring a second cup. "We offer them the thing they most desire." He smiled. "What do you want, Sarah?"

To go home, she thought instantly.

"It's not a secret, I hope? If you tell me, perhaps I can make it come true."

"I don't think so. But what did Bernard and Helena want?"

He shrugged. "I concern myself with recruitment only in special cases, like your brother's. But if I had to guess, I'd say the bait in Bernard's case was a senior partnership in his law firm, perhaps. As for Helena . . ." He laughed without making a sound. "Many look for power, of course. The idealists seek a cause to live for. The insecure hunger for security. They make up the majority of our followers. But a remarkable number simply want to walk out of their lives, leave everything behind, start over as someone else. Whatever they most want—or think they want—we can give it to them.

"And then," he continued, examining his reflection in the metal spoon, "they must keep their end of the bargain. If they are to be of real use, of course, they must have their minds and wills . . . reshaped."

"You mean you brainwash them."

Zvalus made a sour face. "Such a crude term! A crude concept. Our methods are refined, subtle. We clear the mind, rid it of petty preoccupations with self. We make each individual consciousness reflect a single mind, the mind of CIPHER. For most people it comes as a great relief. Human beings don't truly want to be free, you see. We lift that burden, and they are so grateful"—he spread his hands apart—"they give us everything."

A chill ran through Sarah.

"We chose not to process your brother's mind, of course," Zvalus went on. "Even with our advanced methods there may be occasional undesirable side effects. It wasn't worth the risk, and I believed his devotion to his work would keep him from straying off course. I was wrong, I admit. But no matter. Once we return to Earth and make a few adjustments, I'm sure the good professor will give us many more years of useful service. And perhaps you will as well?" He winked and snapped his fingers. "Oskar! It's well past Miss Lucas's bedtime."

Sarah's heart pounded as Oskar appeared from the shadows and tied her hands.

"Your brother can be dreadfully obstinate," Zvalus said, leaning across the table. "I hope it's not a trait you share."

She smelled alcohol. Something cold and wet brushed her arm. Oskar had rolled up her sleeve. She saw the needle and pulled away, but Zvalus seized her wrists.

He smiled. "Nighty-night."

She dreamed she was in the garden with Miladras, by the Vision Pool. He was tracing letters in the sand by the pool, but she couldn't read the words. Mara was there too, only she was a little girl, and she was trying to catch fish in the pool. "It's not that kind of pool," Sarah told her, but Mara wouldn't listen. "He's in there," Mara said. "You catch him." Sarah plunged her hand into the water. It closed around something slippery. *It's a notion fish,* Sarah thought. She pulled it wriggling from the pool, and it leaped from her hands to the bank, flipping frantically. Then she saw it wasn't a fish. It was a fetal pig, like the ones they had dissected in biology, only this one had a human face. Zvalus's face . . .

nineteen

Revelation

Sarah woke to the sound of waves crashing on rocks. For a moment she didn't know where she was, or why she was wedged so uncomfortably among duffel bags and metal chests. Then she lifted her hand to rub her eyes and felt the tug of the cord around her wrists.

A Wrakir was creeping about the cavern, sniffing at things: the kerosene lamp, an empty tube of liver paste. A canvas tarpaulin hung on a clothesline, curtaining off a small area beneath the cavern roof. The air was steamy and reeked of disinfectant. Beneath the hem of the tarp a pair of long, pale feet showed. Water sloshed in a pot. Zvalus was taking a bath, humming in that monotonous way he had.

Sarah squinted into the darkness at the rear of the cavern where she had seen Sam disappear. Where was he? Her ankles were still bound with cord, but if she could crawl or scoot . . .

The Wrakir had picked up something: Zvalus's white shirt. He sat on his haunches and began to turn it over in his claws. He found a pocket and opened it, peering inside. With a squeak of pleasure he withdrew an object.

"*Mee-wah!*" He held the small mirror close to his face, like a nearsighted man, turning from side to side to view his reflection from different angles, grimacing and wrinkling his snout. Despite everything Sarah almost laughed.

"Hey!" Oskar clambered into the cavern. "Get away!"

The Wrakir shrieked and jumped up, backing into the tarpaulin. There was a clang that sounded like a metal pot hitting the floor, and the curtain fell.

Zvalus snatched at the tarp. The fish-belly white of his chest was scored with angry red lines, as if he'd been scrubbing himself with a wire brush.

With a roar Zvalus hurled the pot at the Wrakir and struck him in the head. The creature cried out and backed away, falling over Sarah as he scrambled to escape.

Oskar hurried to hang the tarp again and brought Zvalus a clean shirt. "I beg your pardon, sir! I was only gone a moment—"

"Where's my brother?" Sarah demanded. Oskar, scooping up the articles the Wrakir had scattered, didn't answer. "Where is he? I want to see him."

"He's working." Zvalus emerged from behind the curtain, pink faced and glistening, buttoning his shirt. He took the little mirror from Oskar and tucked it into his pocket. "He mustn't be interrupted."

"I won't interrupt," she promised. "I only want to see him. Please. I just want to know he's all right."

Zvalus approached and crouched in front of her. He lifted her hands, and she flinched. With his index finger he stroked the back of her hand, softly, again and again, in one direction. She thought suddenly of how she used to catch lizards and stroke their bellies to put them to sleep.

"Tell us what you dreamed last night," he said.

Why? she wanted to ask. It had something to do with his wanting the Stone, she knew. As if her dreams held some clue only he could read . . .

"Tell us," he repeated, "and we'll let you see your brother."

She told him. Not everything, not that the pool was the Vision Pool in Miladras's garden, and not about Mara crying, "You catch him," but about the thing she caught, how it had a face, and the face was his.

He laughed. Then he told her Sam was outside, and he pulled her to her feet and watched as she hopped and shuffled toward the mouth of the cave and looked out.

The peaks stood watch over the crater of ooze like specters gathered around a cauldron. Ghosts of blue flames, barely visible in the sunlight, leaped from the bubbling surface. In the open space below, looking small and pale and out of place among the dark, scaly bodies of the Wrakir, was Sam. He was working on a circuit board. He wore no shirt, and Sarah could see his ribs. There were fetters around his ankles. A cloth lay spread on the ground next to him, with bits and pieces of machinery carefully arranged on it. He spoke to one of the Wrakir, and the creature grasped a tool in his claw and gave it to Sam.

"Sam!" Sarah cried.

He looked up.

"I trust you're making good progress, Professor," Zvalus called. "We must hurry back, before the nasty virus does its work. If you are tempted to dawdle, think about your little sister."

He hooked a finger through the belt loop on Sarah's jeans and yanked her back inside. She didn't care. Sam was alive. She was alive.

Just before nightfall Oskar led Sam through the cavern to the passageway at the back. He gave her an almost imperceptible nod and a furtive thumbs-up. Sarah lay back down, listening to the distant, monotonous roar of the ocean. How much longer did they have? The cord around her ankles was too tight, and the wound in her side was swollen, hot, and hard. She must have a fever.

She had to talk to Sam. If only Zvalus would go to sleep . . .

But Zvalus didn't sleep, she discovered.

He sat at the rickety camp table, scribbling in a notebook. He had been going at it for hours, talking to himself, hissing "yesyesyes" through his teeth and, once, something that sounded like "revolution," or maybe it was "revelation."

They had to escape. There had to be some way. If only she had the Stone . . .

She thought of Miladras, waiting for her in the garden—if he was still there. She closed her eyes and sent a silent message: *Tell me what to do. Help me!*

Minutes passed while she listened to the scratch of Zvalus's pen as it raced across the page of his notebook.

An image of the Stone rose in her mind. She saw it lying in her palm, glowing with its own inner light. *Where are you?* she asked. *Show me the way.*

Her palm grew warm, then hot. She kept her eyes shut, kept imagining the Stone as she had seen it the first time.

Outside the waves seemed to rise and fall in rhythm with her breathing. She felt light, weightless, as though she were floating on the waves under the stars, the same stars that glittered in the depths of the Stone. . . .

But it wasn't the waves, it was the wind in the pines. She was rising through space in a slow arc, and then she was upright, skimming over a surface that she saw was a road, a dirt and gravel road, and then her feet touched the ground and she knew where she was: on Strawbridge Lane, the road that led to home.

The sky was dark. She looked down and with her bare toe traced a line in the earth. It was smooth and soft as talcum. She took a deep breath. She was really here. The air smelled like rain. A drop fell and left a tiny crater in the dust. She was running, dodging the patches of gravel in the road, thinking of nothing but getting home, but she seemed to come no closer to the top of the hill, where the mailbox was, where the driveway turned off to the right and led down to the house. A flash of lightning lit up the sky, and for a moment everything looked like the negative of a photograph: The trees stood out, white and skeletal; milkweed blossoms on the fence were dark as blood.

A hand fell on her shoulder. She opened her eyes.

"Dreaming?" It was Zvalus. "Tell us."

She blinked back tears. "I was back home," she said, turning away from him to face the wall.

"You want to go home very much, don't you?" His voice was soft, meant to soothe. "You'd give anything to do that. *Anything . . .*"

The next morning, when she sat up, she felt something stuck in the calloused skin of her heel. She drew it out and held it to the light. It was a shard of gravel. But as she pressed it between her fingers, it crumbled into dust and blew away.

✾

"Teatime," Zvalus sang. "Come, Sarah. Quickly! Quickly!" Sarah shuffled to the table with the cord around her ankles and sank into the chair. Zvalus sat with his knees drawn up, arms wrapped around them. His eyes were closed.

Suddenly he uncoiled his body and pressed his palms together, looking at her over the tips of his fingers. "You look feverish." He sounded displeased. He reached to touch her forehead, and she shrank from his hand.

"I'm all right," she said.

"I shall tell Oskar to give you some medicine. We must keep you well." He unwrapped the towel from the tin pot and poured tea for both of them. "I myself am feeling well," he said, untying the cord around Sarah's wrists. "Quite well."

You don't look it, Sarah thought. The skin of his face was stretched taut over the bones, and his eyes were glassy and bright. He had just finished bathing. She watched him stir the tea. His hand was red and raw.

"You are wondering about my hands. They are clean. I must keep myself clean. Within and without. I must be ready."

"Is something going to happen?" she asked.

"Something beyond imagining."

"What is it?"

He laughed. "I might as well explain it to that creature!" He picked up a spoon and threw it at one of the Wrakir, asleep in a corner, striking him in the back. The spoon clattered to the floor. The creature twitched but didn't wake.

"Thick hides, thick skulls. I'm surrounded by stupidity."

Sarah stirred her tea. It would be a mistake to ask a lot of questions, to appear too curious. The tea was strong but failed to disguise the slightly salty taste of the water. She drank it anyway. If she pretended hard enough, she could imagine it was the real thing, the bracing, comforting, thirst-satisfying tea her mother used to make. Every day after school Sarah would get off the bus, walk up the lane to the old barn, and climb the stairs to the converted loft, where her parents had built a photographic studio. There, if the red light was not on over the darkroom door, she would join her mother at her work.

Watching an image emerge from the blank paper under the water had always been Sarah's favorite part of the process. First came an arm, the corner of a building, and then a piece of sky—and then, bit by bit, the rest appeared: It might be a pathetically young soldier holding a rifle, a child on the steps of a broken-down house. "Why do you take pictures of sad things?" Sarah had once asked her. And her mother had answered, "To make myself look."

While her mother finished up whatever she was doing, Sarah would plug in the electric kettle and get the tea things ready in the studio's galley kitchen. Sometimes there might be English digestive biscuits in a tin on the shelf. Sarah had always thought "digestive biscuit" was an awful name to give such a delicious, crumbly, not-too-sweet cookie. Sometimes they had only graham crackers, which tasted all right but disintegrated too quickly when dunked. Sarah would set the tea tray on an old sea chest they used for a table. She and her mother would sit in the two big overstuffed chairs and drink their tea and talk.

Her chest ached. She covered the place with her hand.

"A painful memory?"

She had almost forgotten Zvalus. That wasn't good.

"No," she said.

He shook his head. "Stop lying. You're not good at it. Now, tell us."

She thought of making something up, just to keep him out. But he might know, and it would make him angry. She told him, trying not to reveal anything he might somehow use against her.

"'O Death in Life,'" Zvalus declaimed when she had finished speaking, "'the days that are no more.'"

"Tennyson," Sarah said automatically.

"Excellent!" Zvalus studied her. "Perhaps you are not too stupid to understand."

"I want to understand."

"Do you?" He leaned across the table toward her, or rather, Sarah thought, his neck stretched forward while the rest of him stayed fixed. Like a reptile.

"Do you really want to understand?"

"Yes," Sarah answered, forcing herself not to lean back, away from his fetid breath. It seemed to smell worse all the time, as if something inside him were rotting.

He lifted his chin, eyes closed. "Shall I tell her? Shall I?"

Sarah glanced at the cavern roof. Whom was Zvalus talking to?

He moved and she quickly shifted her gaze back to him.

"I have been chosen," he said.

Sarah was silent.

"It's too much for you to grasp."

"Maybe if you explained a bit more?"

He sighed, a well-if-you-insist sort of sigh. But she could tell he was eager. "It's very simple, though it has taken me a lifetime to grasp it myself. I am the first of a new race of beings. I will usher in the new order."

He laughed, and for a second she saw the grinning skeleton beneath his skin.

"You are perplexed. Of course you are. You see before you a man. An intelligent man, perhaps even a brilliant man. A mere human being nonetheless. As a human being, I have reasoned and calculated and schemed to change the world, to shape it to my own ends. And I succeeded. I had great power—power that emperors and kings and tyrants would envy. But great as it was, it was merely human: small minded, petty. Cheap goods, d'you see? I was so foolish I could not see it. But now I do. I am being purified, in order that I might gain a power far, far greater." He gripped the edge of the table, his fingers arched. His fingernails, which she remembered as being short and well manicured, had lengthened and yellowed, curling over his fingertips. When had that happened? she wondered. But Zvalus was talking again.

"That is why I am here," he continued. "That is why I was brought to this dreadful place, why I fell and why I rose. This is my crucible. This is where the metamorphosis takes place."

Sarah looked into his eyes, unable to turn away. *It must be true*, she thought.

It is true, Zvalus's eyes answered.

"How?" Sarah asked.

"The very question I have asked myself, again and again. I do not know. I must wait and listen and obey. When he judges me ready, he will enter. He is very near now; he is waiting. He speaks to me of you, Sarah."

In the fading light of afternoon the flame of the kerosene

lantern wavered as a dank wind blew through the cavern. The Wrakir trembled in his sleep, dreaming. Sarah looked toward the entrance of the cave, where battalions of clouds were ranged across the sky.

The Umbra. The Shadow That Walks by Itself. The Umbra had revived Zvalus. It needed him. For centuries it had been searching for a way into Oneiros, and now at last, through Zvalus, it had found an entrance. And when it came, there would be no driving it away, no escape from its power . . . unless she could find the Stone and take it to the Door, block the way in before the Umbra possessed Zvalus completely, made him its own body.

All this Sarah understood in the time it took for the sun to emerge from behind a cloud and disappear once more.

The wind rose, scattering pieces of dried grass from the cavern floor. Sarah heard a soft hissing sound. The hair on her arms stood on end.

As if in a dream, she found herself turning toward the sound, in terror of what she might see but unable to look away. Zvalus was sitting very straight, arms held stiffly at his sides, head tilted back, lips parted. The sound was coming from his throat. But it was not his voice.

"Sssssssssss . . . ssssssssss . . ."

Zvalus began to shake. The voice that was not his fought to tear its way up through his throat, to claim the vocal cords, to master the tongue.

"Sssssssssssssssssssaaaaaaaaaaa . . ."

Then, all at once, the word drew itself out:

"Sssssaaaaaaaaccccccrrriiiiiiifiiiicccccccccccccccce."

Sacrifice.

twenty

Valley of the Shadow

In the ghostly midnight of the two moons Sarah bent over, picked up a rock, and staggered with it to the pile the Wrakir had made. Zvalus had ordered them—all of them, even Oskar—to build an altar. It had to be ready by dawn.

Sam passed her. Their eyes met for a fraction of a second. She searched his face for some sort of signal, some clue as to what he wanted her to do. But Zvalus was watching.

He paced along the edge of the clearing, brandishing a steel rod like a baton. A few feet from Sarah a Wrakir stumbled and fell. Everyone turned to look. The still form on the ground took a ragged breath. Zvalus pushed his way between two of the other creatures.

"Get up at once!"

The Wrakir lay motionless. *He's dead,* Sarah thought. She felt nothing; she was too exhausted to feel.

Zvalus brought the rod down, and the creature shrieked piteously.

"For God's sake, Zvalus!" It was Sam.

"Get up!" Zvalus bellowed again.

The Wrakir struggled to stand. One foreleg dangled uselessly at his side.

Sarah cried out. Zvalus came at her. She raised her arm to ward off the blow, but he did not strike. His hand stopped in midair. He leaned close to her.

Sam started toward them, and Oskar grabbed him by the shoulder.

The back of Zvalus's hand grazed her cheek. She recoiled and tried too late to hide it. An unreadable expression flickered in his eyes. "Are you ready, Sarah?" he whispered. "Ready to play your part?"

"Back to work!" Oskar shoved Sam away.

Her heart banged against her ribs. What did Zvalus mean? She had not really believed, until this moment, that he would kill her. They had talked. He'd given her tea. . . .

She'd been a fool. Zvalus was insane, capable of anything. Of course he would kill her. And when Sam tried to save her, Zvalus would kill him, too.

But the Stone . . . He wanted the Stone; he thought she could get it for him. He would keep her alive if only for that, wouldn't he? Unless something made him change his mind, convinced him she was useless. And sooner or later he would be convinced. Because no matter what he thought, no matter what he did to her, she couldn't tell him where the Stone was or how to find it. She *was* useless.

She crouched before a rock and struggled to loosen it from the ground, her leg muscles shaking uncontrollably. *I can't,* she thought. *I can't. . . .* She yanked the rock free, like a jagged tooth from its socket, and lugged it to one of the pillars. Her fingernails were torn and bleeding, and the wound in her side burned.

In the unreal brilliance of the moonlight she saw Sam adding a rock to a second squat column. Again they caught each other's gaze.

What are we going to do?

With a slight movement of his hand at his side Sam signaled her to wait.

It took a dozen of the Wrakir to shift the huge, flat slab of rock Zvalus wanted for the top of the altar table. Sam worked with them, giving directions in the Wrakir tongue as they grunted and strained.

When the slab was in place, Zvalus ran his hand across the surface. "I am pleased." He drew himself up and looked across the island to where a faint glow lit the sky beyond the peaks. "It will be at least an hour before there is enough light. I shall go and prepare myself. I suggest you do the same. Oskar, I shall need you."

Was he going to leave her alone with Sam? Sam shot her a look. Quickly they both turned away. Zvalus stopped, his back to them. He couldn't have seen them look at each other, but he had felt it, scented their hope, like a shark tracking blood. "Come along, Professor. We'll leave Sarah to her own thoughts, shall we?"

Sam disappeared into the cavern. Sarah watched him go and sank to the ground.

Before her stood the crude altar table, and beyond it lay the crater of bubbling ooze. A cloud of gas burst into blue flame, writhing like a spirit in torment. Looming over everything were the massive black peaks.

I'm going to die. She began to shake.

Inside her something twisted like a red-hot wire. A cramp seized her intestines, then another. Doubled over in pain, she lurched to her feet and struggled to drop her jeans in time to squat.

Humiliated and shaken, she looked around for something she could use to wipe herself. There was nothing. Her hands trembling violently, she ripped the lining of her pocket from her jeans and used that. She dug a small hole and buried the stinking rag, then kicked dirt over the rest and staggered away from it to the other side of the clearing.

A few of the Wrakir crouched nearby, gargoyles watching her through the yellow slits of their eyes.

Fly away, she wanted to cry. *Why don't you fly away?* But they would never fly away as long as the mirror from the Looking Glass waited in the cavern, shrouded in its tarpaulin, promising them the bliss they craved. Stupid, foolish things.

But was she any less foolish? If only she had done as the old woman had said and taken the Stone to the Door! She drew up her knees and rested her head on her arms. The darkness pressed in on her. In a matter of hours her life might be over, extinguished like one of the blue flames that sprang out of the ooze, burned for a moment, and vanished. Was that all she was? What had her life added up to? What had it meant?

Nothing, the darkness answered. *Nothing at all.*

Mother, Sarah thought. *Daddy.* But there was no answer, only the hiss and bubble of the lake and the drone of the sea.

"'The Lord is my shepherd; I shall not want.'" Her lips, dried and cracked, struggled to form the words. "'He maketh me to lie down in green pastures: he leadeth me beside the still waters.'"

What was the rest? She had to remember! "'The Lord is my shepherd. . . .'"

She had learned the psalm in confirmation class at Saint Julian's. It hadn't seemed important at the time. She'd gone to classes only because her best friend in sixth grade was going.

"'He leadeth me beside the still waters. He restoreth my soul. . . .'"

Everyone had had to memorize a Bible passage, and she had chosen the twenty-third psalm. Because it was easy.

She saw herself as she had been then, sitting in the creased red leather chair in Father Griffiths's study, waiting impatiently for him to finish so she and Caitlin could go for ice cream. And now she was filthy and helpless and terrified, linked to that Sarah of long ago by nothing more than these words.

The words came to her now. But they no longer seemed mere sounds, remembered marks on a page. For with them came the truth of why she had learned them. It was so that now, at this very moment, a moment she could never have known would arrive, the ancient words would be there, would come to her aid.

"'Yea, though I walk through the valley of the shadow of death, I will fear no evil: for thou art with me.'"

Are You? Sarah thought. And even as she formed the question, she felt the answering *yes* rise inside her, clear and calm.

Not far away a Wrakir perched on a crag, turning something over in his talons, sniffing it. When he saw her looking, he lowered his eyes, let it slip from his grasp, and silently crept away.

Sarah waited until his tail had slithered out of sight, and crawled toward the rocks where he had been sitting. She peered into a deep cleft, then reached in, stretching her arm as far as it would go. She scrabbled at the thing, finally managing to catch a corner between two fingers, and slowly raised it from its hiding place. It was a notebook, its leather cover worn soft from use. There was just enough light from the fading moons and the dim glow of the sky to decipher the small, cramped handwriting that went all the way to the edge of every page, line after line, page after page, obsessively precise.

Zvalus's notebook.

twenty-one

Desperate Measures

Sarah read, her eyes flying across the pages, faster and faster as the darkness gave way to a misty gray dawn. She wanted to scream, to cry, to storm the cavern and fly at Zvalus.

He had murdered her parents. It was recorded as a mere footnote, with no more emotion than he might have used to describe setting a mousetrap. He had contaminated the fuel in their plane with a substance difficult to detect. It had caused the engine to fail. He had done it because they were dangerous to him. They were probing and persistent, and they might eventually have persuaded Sam to abandon the Looking Glass.

And CIPHER wanted the Looking Glass. It had plans. Plans to seize power plants, television stations, military bases. In every country on Earth it had bribed and corrupted government officials. It blackmailed and tortured and assassinated. It had weapons, money. And with the Looking Glass it would have the perfect means to dispose of anyone who got in the way. Oneiros was to become a penal colony, a place where resisters who were not killed outright or deemed useful as slaves would be "rehabilitated" while CIPHER tightened its stranglehold on Earth. Eventually the Looking Glass would make it possible for CIPHER to reach other planets as well.

That would be impossible now if the virus Sam had set into action had done its work. But if CIPHER had the Stone . . .

The Stone was the ultimate prize. If it fell into CIPHER's hands, the whole universe would be in peril. Because CIPHER was merely the Umbra's human agency, and the Umbra would not stop until its shadow had blotted out the galaxies.

Fear of the Umbra, of its invisible and overwhelming power, swept over her, and she felt her heart shrink. What could she do, pitted against a force like that? It had torn the Stone from her grasp on the journey from Earth, and she'd been powerless to stop it. Even if she found the Stone again, would she be able to protect it?

There was nothing she could do about the Stone now. But, she realized suddenly, there was something else she could do. She had to act quickly. At the edge of the open space, beneath an overhanging ledge, lay the auxiliary unit. She removed the cover and stared down at it, the labyrinth of circuitry that looked like a city in miniature. Yesterday she'd overheard Oskar say that Sam was close to finishing the reconstruction.

Would it even work, now that the virus had infected the main unit back on Earth? Evidently Zvalus was counting on it to function well enough to get them back. She felt sure Sam would never have cooperated with Zvalus except to protect her. She couldn't let him complete the repair. She couldn't give Zvalus even a chance to get back to Earth, to make them his prisoners back at the Institute. She would have no hope of finding the Stone then. . . .

A Wrakir crept onto the ledge and stared down at her, a question in his eyes. The unit was Sam's thing; what was she doing with it?

She tried to lift it. It was not large—about twice the size of her father's computer—but it was heavy. She began to drag it across the open space. The Wrakir squeaked.

Wait. Think. Without the unit Zvalus will have no reason to keep Sam alive. . . .

Sam! A cry rose up inside her. *Tell me what to do!*

There was no way to be sure, no time left. She had to take the risk. What mattered more than anything now—more than her own life, more even than Sam's—was stopping CIPHER and the Umbra.

She pulled and pushed the unit the rest of the way across the flat ground and over some boulders. Two more Wrakir had gathered now, screeching and scolding her.

"Stop!" Oskar bellowed from behind her. "Stop!"

With a strength she did not know she had, she raised the unit over her head and hurled it into the lake of fire.

"Oh, my God! What have you done?" Oskar scrambled toward her over the boulders and stared, wild eyed, as the unit sank beneath the ooze. For a moment she thought he might jump in after it.

Behind him came Zvalus and a flock of Wrakir, hopping and shrieking with excitement.

Oskar grabbed her shoulders, shook her until her teeth

rattled. "Without that unit we are marooned in this filthy place!" He clutched his head and moaned.

"What is it?" Zvalus asked calmly from the edge of the open space. "What has happened?"

"Doctor! She has destroyed the auxiliary unit! I never dreamed—"

"Come here, Sarah." Zvalus beckoned. Then, when she stood before him: "Why would you do such a thing?"

"Because I know," Sarah said defiantly. "Everything."

Zvalus's hand went to his pocket. "My notebook . . ."

Sarah pulled the notebook from the waistband of her jeans. Let him have it. She would never forget what she had read there.

Zvalus was paging through the book, his eyes darting from one entry to the next, as if to make sure everything was in order. "The Wrakir," he said, looking up and smiling, "worse than monkeys, always getting into things." He tapped her chest with the notebook. His hands, which yesterday had been red and raw, were now covered with dark, scaly patches. "But you have no excuse. Didn't your parents tell you it is wrong to read someone else's private thoughts? Oh, but of course not! That's how they made such a name for themselves! Snooping around, spying on people. Taking photographs where no photographs were permitted?"

Filled with loathing she could not contain, Sarah spit at him. She was not good at spitting, and her mouth was parched, but a little spray hit him on the cheek. Oskar gasped.

Oh, God, Sarah thought, looking into Zvalus's eyes. *What have I done?*

Zvalus's lips compressed into a thin, tight line. He took a

handkerchief from his pocket and carefully wiped his face, never taking his eyes from hers.

"Doctor, what shall we do? Tell one of the creatures to recover the unit!" Oskar pleaded. "Perhaps there is some chance . . ."

Zvalus was still staring at Sarah. "Do stop fretting, Oskar," he said, replacing his handkerchief. "Fetch Professor Lucas. We will proceed with our plans for the morning.

"Poor Oskar," he went on, his eyes fixed on her. "He cannot see events for what they are: the working out of destiny. All will unfold as it must. Even the greatest obstacles will be swept away." He grabbed her hair and pulled her face close to his. "You will bring me the Stone, Sarah. You would not have destroyed the unit unless you knew where to find it."

There was nothing she could say; she was trapped. If she told him once again that she did not know and he finally believed her, he would kill her. If she told him and he didn't believe her, if he thought she was hiding something from him, it would be an invitation to torture.

He glanced at something behind her, over her shoulder.

"Do be careful, Oskar!" he shouted. "No mistakes!"

Oskar had climbed up into the cavern. He was fastening a rope around the shrouded Looking Glass.

The mirror? But why?

A few of the Wrakir noticed it and made small, excited noises.

Zvalus began to walk back toward the cavern, still holding her by the hair. "Oskar, untie the professor. I'll need him down here to help me as you lower the mirror."

Oskar went inside the cave and returned a moment later.

"Lucas!" screamed Zvalus. "Get down here at once!"

Seconds passed. Where was Sam? What was he doing?

"Lucas!"

Suddenly Sam appeared in the mouth of the cavern, blinking at the light and rubbing his wrists. When he saw Zvalus holding her, he quickly started down. She wanted to break away, run to Sam and tell him why she'd destroyed the unit, tell him . . .

Oskar lowered the mirror until it hung halfway between the mouth of the cavern and the open space below. It swung gently, bumping against a rock, reverberating like a tapped cymbal.

"I told you to be careful!" Zvalus shouted.

Dozens of Wrakir scurried toward the Looking Glass from all directions, some out of the fiery ooze, others flying from caverns in the surrounding peaks, converging like pigeons on a scrap of bread.

"Get back!" Zvalus shouted. The throng of Wrakir engulfed them, pressing forward toward the mirror. A tail twisted around Sarah's leg and she tripped. Zvalus pulled on her hair.

As she struggled to stand, one of the Wrakir called, "*Mee-wah!*" The others took up the chant: "*Mee-wah! Mee-wah!*"

"Hold it!" Zvalus called up to Oskar, shouting to be heard over their cries. He turned to the mob, brandishing his steel rod. "Silence! Do you understand? No *mee-wah* until you move back!"

For an instant she imagined the Wrakir surging forward in a great mass, knocking Zvalus over, trampling him underfoot. . . .

"Professor!"

Sarah couldn't see Sam through the press of bodies. "Talk to them!" Zvalus shouted. "Tell them they'll get the mirror if they stand back!"

"*Ree-darma, kayno!*" Sam's voice rang out. "*Mee-wah n'arit su kayno. Sreek!*"

Immediately the Wrakir fell still and moved back, forming a circle around the altar. Sam edged toward them.

"Now, Oskar, lower the mirror," Zvalus said. "Slowly. Lucas, come help me get it into position against the wall here."

Zvalus left Sarah standing among the Wrakir. "Be ready to run," Sam said to her in a low voice, and walked away through the crowd.

"Tell them," Zvalus said to Sam when the mirror stood leaning against the side of the peak, "that I am about to bestow a great honor upon one of their number. The one who comes forward to lie upon this altar shall gaze upon himself until the sun is overhead!" He pointed up with the rod, and all the Wrakir looked quizzically at the sky.

He's going to kill one of the Wrakir. We're safe! Relief poured through Sarah, relief and then a flash of shame that she cared so little about what happened to the creatures.

"Tell them, Professor!" Zvalus turned to her, his mouth twitching in what might have been a smile. How could she have thought, even for a second, that they were safe? The Wrakir would be just the beginning.

Sam looked out over the crowd and took a breath.

"*Wrakir-ma,*" he began, and went on speaking for some time, with gathering force.

At first the listening Wrakir seemed excited and eager, but as Sam continued, a change came over them. Their homely faces registered first confusion and then fear. Some of the mothers began to edge away, out of the crowd, clinging to their babies.

"What are you telling them?" Zvalus broke in hotly. "What are you saying?"

Sam took something from his pocket and struck at Zvalus. It was a needle, like the one Oskar had used on her. Zvalus deflected the blow, and the syringe went flying.

"Run, Sarah! Run!"

She wheeled and started to run. Behind her she heard the sound of the rod landing a blow. Sam cried out in pain.

"Sam!"

He crumpled and fell. Blood poured from a gash in his scalp. For a terrifying moment she thought he was dead. She ran to kneel beside him, found the torn flaps of skin, and pinched them together with her fingers as the blood soaked his hair and ran down his face. A bandage. She needed a bandage. . . .

"Get up!"

Sarah ignored Zvalus, reached into her pocket, and drew out Angel's bandanna. Oskar grabbed her arm and whipped her to her feet.

"What did you tell them?" Zvalus demanded. "I want the truth!"

Oskar yanked Sam upright.

"The truth," Sam said, blinking the blood from his eyes. "That's what I told them."

"Heroics," Zvalus sniffed. He prodded Sam with the rod. "Suppose we find out just how heroic you are."

"No!" Sarah cried. "Don't hurt him! Don't!"

"But perhaps it would spur that stubborn memory of yours. Besides, he wants to be hurt, don't you, Professor?" Zvalus asked in a smooth, hypnotic murmur. "Hmmmm? You want to do penance, don't you? Look at yourself!" Oskar shoved Sam toward the mirror. "The brilliant Samuel Lucas," Zvalus said, looking over Sam's shoulder at their reflections. "So young, so gifted. The man who made the greatest scientific discovery in history. But we know the truth, don't we, Professor? If it hadn't been for your obsession with that machine, your parents would still be alive. You killed them, Professor."

"That's not true!" Sarah threw herself at Zvalus and struck his chest with both fists. She heard him grunt in surprise and felt the sharpness of his sternum. He seized her and lifted her nearly off her feet, until her eyes were level with his. His pupils were tiny, two pinpoints of black in his colorless eyes.

"The truth is what I say it is."

"You killed them!" Sarah said. "You contaminated the fuel in their tank!"

Sam groaned.

Zvalus slapped her across the face, hard.

"Damn you, Zvalus," Sam breathed. "I'll kill you, I swear it."

"Sam," Sarah cried, "there's more—I read it in his notebook—CIPHER is planning to take over the world! That's why I had to destroy the unit. They've got weapons—they're all over the world—"

"That's enough!" Zvalus raised his hand to slap her again but appeared to change his mind. "If either of you moves or speaks . . ." He seemed to have difficulty forming the words. He worked his jaw, then went on, "The other will s-s-suffer for it."

Sarah stared. What was happening to him? It couldn't be the drug Sam had tried to inject him with—the needle hadn't even grazed his arm before he knocked it away.

Oskar tied Sam's hands behind his back.

A few of the Wrakir remained around the altar, sniffing curiously at the smell of blood in the air and edging closer to the mirror. "You like the mirror, don't you?" Zvalus said in a coaxing tone. "Yes, you do. I know you do."

Several of them took a few cautious steps toward it.

They've already forgotten what Sam said, Sarah thought in despair.

"That's right," Zvalus was saying. "Come along! Who's to be the l-l-lucky one?"

One of the larger Wrakir pushed another aside and stepped forward.

"Ah, here comes a handsome fellow." Zvalus gestured at the creature. "Very good. Come, come." Suddenly Sarah noticed that Zvalus's arms seemed to have become shorter, stubbier. And the fingernails had grown even longer and sharper.

Zvalus seemed unaware of this change in his body. He was intent on watching the Wrakir, who now stood entranced before the mirror, turning his head to admire himself, lifting his chin, wrinkling his forehead, baring his teeth.

The Wrakir did not see Zvalus come up behind him holding the knife.

With his hands still tied behind him, Sam lunged at

Zvalus, but Oskar tackled him. The two hit the ground just behind Zvalus, grunting and struggling in the dust. Zvalus paid no attention, moving toward the Wrakir's back, knife in hand, the blade held horizontal, the point glinting in the bright sunlight.

Sarah leaped at Zvalus as he plunged the blade into the Wrakir's spine. Without a sound the Wrakir straightened, turned on one hind leg, like a dancer spinning off balance, and fell. Sarah stared at the handle sticking out of the Wrakir's back, so confused that for a split second she thought she had stabbed him herself.

Zvalus crouched down and extracted the knife. He ran his finger along the blade, wiping off what little blood there was, and licked his finger. Then he tested the sharpness of the edge and, apparently satisfied, cleaned the knife with a handkerchief, replaced it in the sheath, and started to stand up.

Midway to his feet he cried out and hunched over, reaching for his back with one hand.

"Doctor!" Oskar cried. "What is it?"

"My back . . ." Zvalus dropped to his knees. He cried out again and fell forward.

Two circles of blood appeared on the back of his white shirt. Zvalus's shoulder blades strained against the fabric. The bones seemed to grow bigger and bigger, and the circles of blood spread. Zvalus tore at the collar choking him, ripped off his shirt. Oskar uttered a little cry. There, where Zvalus's shoulder blades had been, two fleshy masses had split the skin and emerged. But it wasn't human flesh. It was dark and oiled and folded into many layers, like a fan.

Zvalus pushed himself into a crouch and then to his feet,

awkward with the unfamiliar weight. Stepping over the fallen Wrakir, he stared at himself in the mirror, his shortened arms crossed over his bare chest.

Slowly the folded flesh began to open up into two enormous, batlike wings, streaked with blood. *A demon's wings*, Sarah thought suddenly, and in her mind's eye there flashed an old painting of hell she had happened upon in an art history book, its canvas crawling with grinning half-human monsters.

Zvalus looked in the mirror, turning from side to side, and smiled at himself.

Sarah met his gaze in the mirror.

She glimpsed, for an instant, what remained of the human being in Zvalus as it shrank away. Now, through his eyes, an infinitely more cunning and powerful intelligence stared out at her. Like an advancing shadow, it swallowed up Zvalus in darkness.

"I . . . know . . . who you are." The Umbra spoke slowly, still unused to the body in which it found itself. "Stone-Bearer."

The blood in her head roared. "Yes," she answered, "yes, I am."

He rolled his head as if to work out a kink in his neck, then jerked to a halt and fixed his eyes on her. "The Stone is mine. You will give it to me."

"No." It was Sam.

One of the Wrakir crept up and sniffed at the body of its fallen companion.

Behind them the sun, midway to its zenith, struck the mirror. Its light blazed out like white fire. Sarah raised her hand to shield her eyes. The light grew brighter, filling the mirror to its edges. She squinted into it, unable to see, unable to look away.

Gradually, like a mist dispersing, the light thinned, and in the mirror Sarah saw a narrow gravel lane wind its way between two fields, up a hill, where the tin roof of a barn glinted in the sunshine. The road home.

"Now," a voice said. "Go." But she could not tell whose voice urged her forward.

I'm afraid. The words hung in her mind. *I'm so afraid!* The fear lodged beneath her breastbone, growing, pressing the air from her lungs.

She took a step, her hands held in front of her. But where she expected her fingertips to meet the glass there was nothing. In a moment she was on the other side.

Lost in Illusion

Cool air touched Sarah's skin. She breathed in the sweet smell of rain and damp earth. At her feet lay a puddle. It trembled and grew still, reflecting the sky.

Somewhere a bird greeted the day with a perfect four-note song: *too-wit, too-wee.*

The blur of gold by the mailbox at the top of the hill was forsythia. She walked toward the flowers, slowly, as if one wrong step might make everything disappear.

Overhead the sky was the color of a sky-blue crayon. The puffy clouds had scalloped edges, like clouds in a child's drawing.

She hurried up the lane. Everything stayed in place, held together. But there was something . . . something not quite right—had the forsythia ever been quite that yellow, so yellow it almost hurt her eyes?

But it *was*. It was real, it had to be real, it was just the way she remembered it. . . .

She ran toward the mailbox. When she reached the top of the hill, she heard a car turn off the paved road and start up the lane behind her. As the gray station wagon drew closer, gravel crunching under its tires, she recognized Mr. Moss, the mailman. *He'll be surprised to see me. What should I tell him?*

He saw her and stopped, rolled down his window. "Morning, Sarah!" he said, just as he had hundreds of times. "How're you?"

"Fine, thank you," she said automatically. She watched as he sorted through the bag of mail next to him on the front seat.

He expected me to be here. He's not surprised at all. She reached for the bundle of mail he handed through the window.

"You saved up enough money for that horse yet?" Mr. Moss looked up at her, squinting against the sun and smiling. "I hear Gibson Mayfield's thinking of selling that little half A-rab filly of his. . . ."

"Star?" Star was the most beautiful horse she had ever seen, except for . . . except for . . . The image of another horse, a white one, raced through her mind and vanished before she could put a name to him. Along with him a whole host of other images seemed to gallop away and disappear. She put one hand against the mailbox to steady herself. What was happening?

"Star—that's right," Mr. Moss was saying. Sarah forced herself to focus on his broad, good-natured face.

"You ought to give Gibson a call—make him an offer."

When she didn't answer, he simply went on smiling.

"Well, I better get going." The car pulled away a few feet and stopped. "Oh, and Sarah . . ." He leaned out the window, looking back at her. "Don't forget to leave that package in the mailbox."

She stood staring after him as the car made its way up the road and disappeared from view.

Package? What package? Had she forgotten something else?

She shifted the mail from one hand to the other and wiped the sweat from her palms. *My name is Sarah Lucas. My birthday is May sixth, my favorite color is green. I live at Sycamore Farm on Strawbridge Lane. Right here. Look, there's the barn, there's the house, there's the crab apple tree. It's hot pink. Like the lipstick that girl in French class wears—what's her name?—Sue Ellen! Good. See? You can remember anything you need to. Everything's fine. There's Daddy's car, there's Mother's. Just where they're supposed to be.*

Daddy and Mother. At the thought of them her heart tightened into a knot of pain, and tears filled her eyes. *Run inside, hug them, never let go!* She could imagine how her father would look up from his desk, startled and pleased and trying not to show it. He was at his desk, wasn't he? Yes, of course he was. When she'd left the house to fetch the mail, he'd been working, typing something onto the computer screen . . . or was that yesterday? All the times she had done this very same thing seemed like cards in a deck, shuffled and reshuffled. Pick a card, any card.

Why was she feeling so *peculiar* this morning?

She swiped at her tears and walked toward the house, absently sorting through the mail. As usual, there were mostly bills addressed to her parents. A flier from the hardware store in town advertised picket fencing, tomato sets, garden hoses. *Why don't I ever get any mail?* Maybe it was because she never wrote any letters herself. She could write the aunts. They would be sure to answer, and they always used interesting English stamps. Or, even though he was a bad bet when it came to letters, she could write to Sam in California. . . .

Sam. She dropped the bundle of mail. Again the sensation of having just forgotten something, something important, something that lay a tantalizing fraction beyond the reach of her mind, but this time the sensation persisted, on and on, as though a switch had been thrown in her brain. When at last it stopped, abruptly, she could have cried with relief.

She stooped to gather up the scattered mail. She would go in and see if there was any tea left in the pot from breakfast, and then she would take a cup to her room and lie down. How had she gotten so tired between waking up and now? She could fall asleep this very moment and sleep for years and years, like Brier Rose in the fairy tale. Brier Rose had fallen under a spell. Maybe she was under a spell too.

The thought of bed lured her forward, and she almost missed the square of paper fluttering in the grassy circle in the middle of the driveway. She picked it up. Her name was printed in fine script on one side of the neatly folded square. She hadn't noticed the paper before, when she was sorting through the bundle. Had it been tucked inside something else?

She opened it.

"DANGER!" the note read. "COME TO THE TREE HOUSE AT ONCE."

A jolt like an electric current ran through her, shooting out through her fingers and toes.

She heard a window being opened, and looked up. There,

on the second floor, a shadowy figure peered through the ivy-covered screen.

"Well?" It was her father's voice. "Anything for me? A fat check maybe? A Pulitzer Prize?"

Danger!

"Sorry," Sarah managed to say. Did her voice sound as odd to him as it did to her? "Just bills. You already have a Pulitzer."

"I thought a matching pair would be nice." The figure stepped away from the window but left it open.

"Daddy?" Her voice was faint. Would he hear her?

"Yes?" He was back at his desk, but he had heard.

She paused. "Nothing. I just . . . I love you, that's all."

His chair scraped across the floor, and once again he was at the window. "I love you, too, sweetheart. You coming in?"

"In a minute." Sarah looked down at the paper in her hand. It was blank.

But there had been something! Something terribly important.

She put her hand over her eyes. "I'm going crazy," she said aloud. Crazy, crazy. How many times had she used the word, never understanding—this was craziness, this frantic scurrying of her mind back and forth, like an animal trapped in a box.

Only a few more steps and you'll be inside. You'll be home. Everything will be all right. You can rest, you can stop worrying.

Down the two stone steps between the hedges, along the flagstone walk. Her mother's windflowers were all in bloom along the edge of the yard, a sea of blue stars. . . . The door to the mudroom stood open, firewood stacked against the wall.

Go on . . .

She stepped inside. A breeze scattered a few dried leaves—the last of the winter—and they flew at the front door as if trying to enter. She put her hand on the tarnished brass doorknob.

Open the door, quickly!

If she'd been led blindfolded to this spot, she would have known she was home by the feel of the knob in her hand, loose in its fitting, as always, so that you had to fiddle with it before it caught, and you couldn't have locked it even if you'd wanted to. . . .

Hurry up!

She leaned her forehead against the door. Her fingers gripped the knob, aching, her knuckles white. *It's all right,* the voice insisted. *You're home!* Home. Home. But . . .

It is! It's just as you remember it, isn't it?

Yes, Sarah thought, *exactly the way I remember it.* She lifted her head and looked around the mudroom in a daze. *But why should I have the feeling I'm remembering?* Her next thought, when it came, came slowly, as if struggling up from some great depth:

Nothing is ever exactly the way you remember it. Nothing, ever.

She turned and ran.

twenty-three

Return to the Tree House

Sarah ran blindly from the mudroom, through the gate, and across the newly plowed field, her feet sinking deep in the soft furrows. Twice she nearly fell, but she kept on running, not thinking where, just away, away from the house. Then she was in the woods, running along the path strewn with pine needles, dead branches snapping under her feet, frightening the birds into silence.

She hadn't meant to go to the tree house; her legs had simply carried her there. She climbed the ladder, crawled inside, and pulled the door closed behind her. It was very dark. She sat against the wall, hugging her knees to her chest to make herself as small as possible.

My name is Sarah Lucas. My name is Sarah Lucas and I've been away somewhere, for a long time, and now I've come back and everything's just as I remember it and that's all wrong. Wrong because nothing is exactly the way you remember it when you go back to a place. Even though people sometimes say so, it never is. Things look smaller, like the time I went back to Cedar Grove Elementary, and the desks and chairs were so

*little I couldn't believe I'd ever sat in them. Or shabbier, or
there's something you recognize but it's different somehow, like
the Chinese box on Great-aunt Sophie's dresser, where she kept
her sewing things, the one with the gold dragon, only when I
saw it again, the dragon wasn't gold, it was red. . . .*

*Why does thinking about the dragon make me feel afraid? I
am afraid, I can feel all the hairs on my arms standing up. . . .*

A square of dim light emerged on the opposite wall. The
window. Below it stood a shelf, though she could see only the
barest outline. Two planks supported by bricks. She knew
what lay on the shelves: smooth stones from the brook, the
baby owl's skeleton.

Sarah sniffed the air. There was an attic sort of smell, of a
damp, closed-up space, and the faint odor of burned wood.
Mingled with them was the unmistakable perfume of roses.

What was that pile of stuff in the corner? Had Sam just
thrown his sleeping bag down without bothering to roll it up?

Something in the pile moved.

Sarah's heart leaped like a startled deer.

"Don't be afraid," said a clear, light voice. "Shall I show
myself to you?"

The dark shape began to glow with a green gold light like
a firefly's. Sarah shrank against the wall, too frightened to
speak.

It was an old lady, sitting on an orange crate. A very old
lady, judging by the wrinkled face and strands of white hair
escaping from her knit cap. She wore a duffel coat, fastened
at the neck with a diaper pin.

"I know you," Sarah said slowly. "Don't I?"

"Of course you do!" The old woman nodded sharply, and

the pom-pom on her cap bounced. Her sea gray eyes shone. "'Thursday's child has far to go'! Traveling shoes! *Tempus omnia revelat!*"

She spread her arms wide, trailing streamers of light. "Translation?"

Sarah blinked. The shabby clothes were gone, replaced by an old-fashioned suit and sturdy lace-up shoes.

"'Time reveals all things,'" the old woman said, removing a pair of round black spectacles and looking gravely at Sarah. "You must complete your assignment, my dear. We have very little time."

"I don't understand."

"Is that important?"

"I . . . I mean I can't remember things properly. I know I know you, but I don't know where I've seen you before. Or anything about an assignment."

"It's the place," she said. She reached for the skeleton of the baby owl and held it for a moment before replacing it on the shelf, where it sprouted feathers and feet and a beak and stared at Sarah with its enormous eyes before it flew up to a corner of the ceiling and perched there in the shadows. "The longer you're here," the lady was saying, "the more you'll forget. That's why you can't stay."

"What do you mean? It's my home—I don't want to go!"

"But you know there's something wrong here, don't you, Sarah?"

Sarah looked down. "Yes."

"That's because it's an illusion."

"You mean it's not real?"

"It's a real illusion."

"Then, are you . . . are you real?"

She laughed, and for a second Sarah thought, *Why, she's not old at all, she's young.*

"Oh, yes," the lady answered. "Quite real. As real, in fact, as it is possible for anyone to be. Except for the One Whose Name Cannot Be Spoken." The light radiating from her body intensified.

Sarah shielded her eyes from the brightness. "But none of this seems like an illusion at all. It's just the way I remember it." She paused and looked up. The light had faded a little, enough for Sarah to see without squinting. "That's what makes it feel wrong somehow."

"It *has* to be exactly as you remember it. It can't be otherwise. It's woven from your memories."

"But where did it come from? Did I make it?"

"The memories are yours. The craft is another's."

"Whose?"

"The master of illusions. The Umbra. It is his purpose to make you a prisoner, living among these shadows, Neither Here nor There, until you are no more than a shadow yourself."

"But why?"

"Because you are his adversary. You are the Stone-Bearer."

At her words something in Sarah's memory stirred painfully. She pressed her fists against her forehead. "I can't remember! I try and try, but I can't. Why does it make me think of a tree, a tree walking?"

"It must be such a nuisance to be a human being," the lady said. "Forgetting things you ought to remember, and remembering the ones you'd be better off forgetting. Just a moment." She shifted. Light poured from her, firing every hair to white-hot brilliance.

She's made of light, Sarah thought. *She belongs in it, the way fish belong in water and birds in air. She made herself solid only so I could see her.*

Sarah stared. Before her on the orange crate sat a beautiful woman in a filmy white gown strewn with blossoming flowers, a garland on her head. *Like the painting,* Sarah thought suddenly, *the painting of the goddess of spring . . .*

"*La Primavera?*" the lady prompted, her eyes full of merriment. "Oh, yes, I'm a great admirer of Botticelli."

"But who *are* you?"

"I am the Amarantha, the Everlasting Flower Who Never Fades. Miladras told you about me. You've forgotten, though, haven't you? Here." She took something from the folds of her gown and held it out to Sarah. It was a silver-skinned fruit.

"An apple of the Thealkir," the lady said. "You've had one before, only you've . . . well, never mind. Moon apples, they call them. I always like to have one with me. It will help you remember."

Sarah scooted forward and took it. The fruit was heavy in her hand, and she was suddenly aware of how terribly, painfully hungry she was. But when she raised the fruit to her lips, she hesitated.

"Will I . . . will I remember everything now?"

"Everything? Only those of my kindred—the Irissa, the Shining Ones—remember everything. But it will help."

"I don't know if I want to. Some of the things I forgot were bad things—I can feel them inside me. . . ."

"There is pain, yes."

"I don't want to feel it!"

"Be brave, Sarah! For human beings there can be no love without pain, no coming to life!"

"That's easy for you to say!" Sarah cried. "You're not a human being." Immediately she was sorry, afraid she had offended the shining creature. But when after a moment Sarah dared to glance up, the Amarantha met her with a look of infinite tenderness.

When Sarah had eaten the fruit, she and the Amarantha sat for a long time without saying anything. From outside the tree house Sarah heard the melancholy cry of a mourning dove. One by one all the things she had forgotten came back to her. She remembered the afternoon when she learned her parents were dead, remembered the state trooper holding his hat, Ozzie on the mantel. And Sam! Poor Sam, who had tried and failed to stop Zvalus, who waited for her now on the island. Sometimes she cried, looking at the calm, grave face of the Amarantha through a blur of tears, and though the Amarantha was silent, Sarah felt her light surround her like an embrace.

"They're not really in the house, then," Sarah said at last. "My parents?"

"What you have made of them in your heart is there," the Amarantha answered.

"But how can that be *bad*? How can the Umbra use it to trap me?"

"In itself it is good. But if you cannot let it go in order to take hold of a greater treasure, then even what is good becomes a means of evil. Do you understand?"

"I think so." Sarah released a long, shuddering breath. "Is it time for me to go?"

"Yes. Find the Stone. Take it to the Door. Let nothing keep you from it."

"But where is the Stone?"

The Amarantha rose, crouching beneath the low roof of the tree house, and opened the door. A breeze blew in. The cobwebs trembled. There was a rustling sound, and the baby owl flew out the open door. Sarah got up and stood bent over in the doorway, beside the Amarantha. Through the budding trees she could just see the roof of the house, the brick chimney, and, beyond it, the gleaming surface of the pond.

"There," the Amarantha said.

"In the house? But why?"

"Where else could it be certain to be found by you? And you alone can carry it from this place."

"Miladras warned me. When I dreamed of coming home. He said there was danger in my heart's desire." She turned and looked at the Amarantha. "But I have to go back now, don't I?"

"You must go back. One last time."

twenty-four

The Hiding Place

Sarah collected the scattered pieces of mail from the stone floor of the mudroom and opened the front door. The house was quiet. She put the mail in the brass bowl on the hall table, on top of her parents' car keys and a jumble of coins, and rested her hand on the banister. In the stairwell, jewels of colored light from the stained-glass window quivered on the landing.

The Amarantha had known only that the Stone was somewhere in the house. "The Stone will guide you," she said, just as she had said before, in Latin class. Just as Miladras had said. Sarah called on the Stone now, conscious of her weakness, already feeling the power of the place exert its pull, like gravity, with every step she took up the stairs. The fruit she had eaten—Miladras's fruit—would keep her from losing her memory again, but there would be other dangers. The Umbra would not give up easily.

Upstairs she paused in the hall to look out the front window, remembering the snow, the black-and-white state trooper's car parked in the driveway. Now there were only her parents' cars, the faded blue Volvo, the small pickup truck. As if the trooper had never come, as if it really had been a bad dream after all.

She opened the door to her room. The white ruffled curtains lifted, billowed in the breeze. Sunshine streamed through the ivy on the window screens, bathing the room in green, watery light. Ozymandias—no, *not* Ozymandias, she reminded herself—lay sleeping on the bed. When he heard her come in, he rolled over on his side and stretched, arched like a bow, his front paws reaching toward her. Before she could stop herself, she stroked his forehead. He purred beneath her hand.

Her old Raggedy Ann doll smiled at her from the rocking chair.

Stay, said the room. *Just a little while.*

She went over to her dresser, listening for the sounds of her father in his study. Through the bathroom that connected the two rooms came the quiet clicking of the computer's keyboard: a rush of typing, a pause, then another quick volley.

On the chest of drawers stood her china cat and a photo of the family, one of the few of all four of them, taken one winter's day after a snowstorm, when they had trooped into town for groceries because their road was too deep in snow to drive. They went to the little general store for milk and bread and then to the Rexall soda fountain for hot chocolate. On the way home Mother stopped a passing stranger and asked him to take their picture. They stood, red-nosed and breathless from the frosty air, her father's arms managing to embrace them all: Sarah, with her dutiful "picture smile"; Mother, looking like a happy schoolgirl; Sam, grinning goofily, holding a loaf of Wonder bread aloft like a trophy.

The days that are no more.

"Hang on, Sam," she said to the picture. "Just hang on. I'll come back."

She set down the photograph and opened the top drawer of her dresser: underwear, socks, a plump heart-shaped sachet she'd made at Brownie camp that had lost its scent long ago. The lower drawers held sweaters, nightgowns, shorts, her one pair of formal riding pants. She slipped her hand under them, ran it across the flowered paper lining the bottom. Nothing.

Between the mattresses? She knelt by the bed and lifted the blue and white quilt, reaching in as far as she could, then did the same thing on the other side of the bed. Ozymandias came to the edge of the bed and rubbed against her face. She drew back, and he looked at her reproachfully through half-closed eyes.

Where? She got to her feet, her knees sore from resting on the wooden floor, and turned around. She thought she saw someone move, over in the corner, but it was her own reflection in the oval cheval mirror. Or was it? She walked closer to it, fascinated, and the girl in the mirror stepped closer too. Sarah looked down at her clothes and back at the mirror. Both she and the girl were wearing the same white cotton blouse, with its wide, flat collar edged with a narrow ruffle, the same faded blue jeans, but while Sarah's clothes were stained and torn, the girl in the mirror's were spotless and freshly ironed. Her long hair, fastened at the side with a barrette like a crescent moon, fell in soft, shining waves on her shoulders; her skin glowed. But it was something else about her that drew Sarah closer to the mirror, something in her face, her eyes. *Nothing bad has ever happened to this girl,*

THE DREAM OF THE STONE

Sarah thought. *Nothing ever will. Her parents are alive, her brother is safe. She's happy. The way I was once. The way I could be again.*

"Stay," the girl whispered, and Sarah heard her own voice. *Stay,* the room echoed. A current seemed to swirl through the room, like an undertow.

Sarah snatched Raggedy Ann from the rocking chair and hurled her at the mirror. The doll fell spread-eagled on the braided rug, her shiny black eyes staring at the ceiling in astonishment. Sarah knelt to pick her up and held the doll to her chest. She felt the rough edge of the repair made in Raggedy Ann's chest so long ago, when a four-year-old Sarah had cut her with a pair of scissors, looking for the candy heart the storybook said was inside her, the heart with "I love you" written on it. She had poked her fingers in the hole made by the scissors, but there was nothing there, only pieces of cotton. Sam had thought it was funny and made jokes about "open-heart surgery." But when Sarah realized what she had done, she cried and cried, until the young Chinese woman who was taking care of them while their parents were in Shanghai for the day collected every bit of stuffing and mended the doll.

Sarah remembered Mai-Mai bending over Raggedy, her black hair a shining curtain, her lips pressed together in concentration. "Stop crying! I fix," she'd said, the tiny needle flashing in her fingers. "Why you cry so *much*? She only doll. Not like you."

Not with a heart like mine, Sarah thought now. She could feel her own heart, it was heavy in her chest, it hurt.

"Sarah?"

She hadn't heard her mother come up the stairs. Now she was halfway up, calling through the open door.

"Yes?" Sarah's heart beat wildly.

"I was just going to make a little lunch, lovey. What would you like? There's some nice leftover roast beef—"

"Thanks," Sarah answered, fighting to keep the quaver out of her voice. "But I'm not really hungry." *Please don't come in,* she prayed, *please, please don't come in.*

"Are you feeling all right?"

"I'm fine! Really! I'll be down later!"

Then her mother was there, in the doorway, looking slightly worried, wearing a wrinkled pair of khaki trousers with grass stains on the knees, her glasses resting on her head in a cloud of light brown hair. When she saw the doll in Sarah's hands she smiled and crossed the room to the rocking chair.

"Dear old Raggedy," she said, sitting down. "Remember when we left her behind on the boat in Athens, and Daddy ran all the way back to the harbor? By the time he found her, they were casting off again. He always said he nearly broke his neck leaping from the deck to the pier with Raggedy Ann in his teeth. All the Greek sailors were watching and laughing at him."

Sarah nodded, tracing a pattern in the braided rug with her fingertip, afraid to look up, afraid to speak.

"Is anything wrong, darling?" Her mother took Raggedy Ann from Sarah's hands and smoothed the yarn hair.

"I was just thinking," Sarah began, her voice sticking to her throat, "about the time I cut her open with the scissors."

"Oh, *sweetie!*" Her mother rubbed Sarah's shoulder. "You

aren't feeling bad about that after all these years?"

"Her heart . . ." Sarah choked back the tears.

"Darling, look at me. Look."

Sarah looked, thinking, *I don't care if she's just a memory, I don't care, it's her face and her eyes and her smell, it's her. . . .*

"Children do things like that, without thinking. You remember the story about the books. . . ."

"Tell me again," Sarah said.

Her mother smiled. "Well, once when I was four or five," she began, sitting the doll upright on her lap and settling back in the chair, "I found some little books inside a glass book-case at the aunts' house. I think I liked them because they were small and they had lovely leather covers—one was a deep ruby red, I remember, like the ruby port my grandfather used to let me sip—and I carried them all over to the desk and sat in the big chair, pretending to read. And then I noticed that at the front and the back of each book there were empty pages!" Her mother's eyes widened dramatically, as if she were telling the story to a small child. "I thought, 'They forgot to write on these pages, I shall help them finish!' and I sat at the big desk and took Aunt Daisy's fountain pen and went to work. I was nearly done when Aunt Elspeth walked in and let out the most horrifying shriek. It turned out they were first editions and quite valuable. Minor Victorian poets, I think. Perhaps that's why I've never developed a taste for them."

"Were you punished?"

"Oh, yes—everyone else ate high tea in the kitchen, and I was banished to my room in disgrace with a boiled egg and dry toast. Aunt Sophie did smuggle in a gooseberry tart later,

I remember. But I was terribly hurt because I hadn't known I was doing anything wrong and it seemed so unfair. Still, I felt ashamed because I knew that since everyone had made such a fuss, I must've done something dreadful, after all. But I simply didn't think a thing about it when I was doing it. And you didn't either when you cut Raggedy Ann."

"But what about when someone's older? When they do something wrong on purpose?"

She brushed the hair off Sarah's forehead and looked into her eyes. "What do you mean, darling?"

"I know I hurt you and Daddy. Not just accidentally. I meant to do it. I was selfish and mean sometimes and never even said I was sorry—and then I couldn't because . . . because . . ." A sob rose in her chest.

"Hush, darling—shhhh." Her mother stroked her hair.

"But I said I hated you that time," Sarah said, looking up at her, "when I wanted to buy the horse at the riding stable, and you and Daddy said no—I said I hated you, and I don't hate you, I never hated you, I love you. . . ."

"Oh, my poor Raggedy!" her mother cried, holding her close. "Poor heart!"

After a time Mother wiped away Sarah's tears with a wrinkled pink tissue. "Better?" she asked. Sarah nodded.

"I'll go make some lunch."

"Mother . . ."

She turned in the doorway.

"Do you believe in heaven?"

Her mother looked puzzled. It wasn't the question itself that puzzled her, Sarah knew. She was trying to understand why Sarah had asked it, what fear or hope might lay behind the words. Then Sarah saw that she did understand, and for a moment in her mother's gaze she discerned the warm, living reality that was far more than the sum of her memories, that lay beyond them, beyond the reach of the Umbra, beyond death and time.

"David Griffiths told me something once," her mother began, and Sarah thought, *David? Oh, she means Father Griffiths, from Saint Julian's.* "He said, 'Whatever we give into love's hands can never be lost.' I think he must be right about that, don't you?"

"Yes," Sarah answered. "Yes."

Her mother blew a kiss from the door and turned to go. Ozymandias leaped off the bed and shot past her down the stairs.

Sarah sat alone on the braided rug. The wind rustled the ivy at the windows, making patterns of light and shadow on the floor.

She took a deep breath and let it go.

"I'm ready now," she said aloud, and for a moment everything grew perfectly still. She looked at her hand lying on the braided rug. It seemed not part of her, but something with an independent existence. Almost on their own her fingers turned back the edge of the rug, uncovering the wooden floor. Years ago, playing jacks, she had discovered that one of the old oak floorboards, shorter than the others, could be lifted out of place. Underneath there was a dark, empty space between the floor of her room and the ceiling of the kitchen, where wires ran and where once she had discovered a field mouse nesting with her babies. Later it had become her secret hiding place, and she had kept her treasures there: a piece of green chalk that drew magic pictures, a swan's feather from Oxford, a purey marble she'd discovered in the woods.

She found the board and raised it. Her fingers searched the space, grazed something smooth, solid, cool. She curved her hand around it and lifted the Stone, holding it in the palm of her hand, gazing into its blue depths at the fields of stars, burning like a million tiny fires against the dark.

"Mine," said a voice from the corner of the room.

Sarah looked up. There was nothing there. From outside came the rumble of distant thunder.

No, not nothing. One of the shadows cast by the ivy grew denser, darker than the rest.

"Stay," the shadow whispered, sliding across the floor toward her. "Leave it in the mailbox and you can stay."

"No," Sarah said.

Two great wings stretched across the walls and ceiling. "You can never come back. They will be lost forever."

"No. I can never lose them. You don't know anything about love."

Thunder rumbled again, rolling across the hills, rattling the windowpanes. Sarah got up and put the Stone in her pocket.

"Good-bye," she said to the room, to the fireplace and the window seat, to her bed and her pictures and the white china cat and the girl in the mirror. Then the winged shadow spread and began to cover it all in darkness. She did not look back. She walked downstairs, slipped out the front door, and went up the walk, between the dogwood and the crab apple, across the grassy circle of the driveway, up to the mailbox. She went on a little way, farther up the lane, and turned around. Ragged gray clouds sped across the sky. Wind ruffled the surface of the pond in back of the house, and the towering sycamores, still bare, the last of the trees to get their leaves each spring, swayed and waved their long white arms. Someone—Daddy, she thought—had lit a fire in the dining room. A thin line of smoke rose from the chimney before the wind caught it.

A powerful gust whipped her hair in front of her face, nearly pushing her off her feet. And then, as though they were made of sand, the house, the barn, the woods, the mailbox— all of them began to crumble and blow away, vanishing in the wind.

twenty-five

Metamorphosis

Sarah slipped her hand into the pocket where she carried the Stone. She held it out in her palm, feeling its weight like an anchor as the world flew apart around her. "Is it time?" she called into the wind. She closed her eyes and concentrated all her attention on the Stone.

Once again she felt the odd lifting sensation in her middle, the shift beneath her feet. Then she heard the roar and hiss of waves and opened her eyes to a vast gray emptiness of sea and cloud. She was standing near the edge of a cliff. Black gulls wheeled and circled. Far below, against the rocks, dark water churned. At her back a slope rose steeply upward. She was back on the island of the Wrakir, outside the ring of mountains. If she could scale the slope, she might be able to get her bearings. She started up. The sharp, loose rocks hurt her bare feet, and the incline was so steep it seemed to push her backward, sending her sliding back down.

At last she reached the top of the ridge. The mountains stood around the crater like gigantic figures in peaked hoods, their faces hidden. Oily fumes hung in the heavy, humid air, and something worse, an odor she couldn't identify. Nothing moved. The rolling boil of the ooze had died away. Everything looked different, empty. Then she saw why. There were no Wrakir. Not a single one bathed in the ooze or sat perched on the rocks, licking itself. They all had vanished.

Except for one: the Wrakir that Zvalus had sacrificed. Far below, it lay on the crude stone altar, stiff limbed, its front legs curled toward its chest. Someone had tried to light a fire under the carcass. That was what she had smelled. But of course the Wrakir would not burn; the skin of a creature who could bathe in that lake of fire would never burn.

Get away! every cell in her body screamed. *Get out of here!*

But not without Sam. Where was he? And where were Zvalus and Oskar? She began to climb down toward an out-cropping of rocks nearer the clearing.

She had not gone far when she heard someone whistling. Sam? It had to be! She recognized the melody—it was the Major-General's song from *The Pirates of Penzance*. Now he was singing. The absurd, familiar words—she had been awakened by Sam's singing in the shower on countless mornings—drifted up to her:

I quote in elegiacs all the crimes of Heliogabalus,
In conics I can floor peculiarities parabolous, . . .

She nearly called out to him before she caught herself. *Think, Sarah!* She sat back, her heart pounding. If Zvalus and Oskar had heard her . . . She couldn't afford stupid mistakes.

The singing continued, lighthearted, out of place:

In short, in matters vegetable, animal, and mineral,
I am the very model of a modern Major-General. . . .

Keep singing, Sam. Once night fell, she would have only her ears to guide her. She glanced over her shoulder at the sun, blanketed by the overcast sky. Already it was low, sinking toward the sea. A dull red stain seeped into the haze. How long before dark?

She started down toward the open space again, every sound she made unbearably loud in her ears. With each one she braced herself, expecting to hear a cry of discovery from Oskar or Zvalus.

From the corner of her eye she saw something move. Too late. Someone behind her clamped a hand over her mouth. She fought to free herself, jabbing with her elbow, kicking, trying to bite.

"Sarah, stop! It's me! Don't scream!"

"Angel!" She whirled around. He looked like a wild thing, his eyes huge and black, shreds of dry grass tangled in his hair. She held him tightly, her face against his smooth, bare chest. He felt thinner, harder. "How did you get here?"

"The shortcuts. I stumbled across one and ended up in Miladras's garden. I told him you'd disappeared, that I thought a Wrakir must've taken you. He showed me a path to the island." He drew away. "Sarah, the Shadow's spreading! It's like a sickness. The flowers are all dying—the animals won't eat!"

"But we can stop it! I found the Stone! It was in my house, in my secret hiding place—look!"

The Stone gleamed in the twilight, casting a soft glow against the inside of her hand.

Angel took it from her, held it as he had done that rainy morning which now seemed years past. "Dear God," he breathed, then looked at her, puzzled. "You went back to Earth?"

"No, it wasn't Earth—it was the place Miladras told me about." She wanted to say more, to tell him about the illusion, but a faraway rumble came from the direction of the sea, and the ground beneath them rocked. Sarah grabbed Angel's arm to steady herself.

"Tremors," he said. "They've been coming off and on for hours." He took her hand, placed the Stone in it, and closed her fingers. "We've got to go, Sarah. To the Door."

"Not without Sam! He's down there somewhere—I heard him singing."

Angel went before her, creeping from one rock to the next. He stopped, beckoned her to look. Sarah peered over the top of a boulder. Sam sat with his back against one of the squat columns that supported the altar, his hands and feet bound with rope.

"Who tied him up?" Angel asked.

"Zvalus and Oskar."

"*They're* here?"

"The Looking Glass."

Angel stared grimly at the carcass on the altar. "Zvalus did that?"

"Yes. He'll kill us, too, if we're not careful." She scanned the edges of the open space. "They could be anywhere. They could be watching us right now. How are we going to get to Sam?"

Once again they heard the sound like faraway thunder,

and the ground shifted, shaking free a few loose rocks, which tumbled down into the ooze.

"I don't know," Angel said. "But whatever we do, we'd better do it quick."

As darkness fell, the wind began to blow, pushing the heavy clouds before it. The two moons rose over the edge of the ridge, the larger one glowing orange, like a jack-o'-lantern.

They used the last of the daylight trying without success to spot Zvalus and Oskar. The men might be in the cavern, but it was impossible to tell without climbing up and looking in, and that was too dangerous. So they decided on the simplest of plans: Sarah would go down and untie Sam, while Angel would keep watch and create a distraction if Zvalus or Oskar approached.

Sarah looked up at the moons sailing through flying clouds. As long as the moons remained visible, there would be just enough light to see by.

"Ready?" Angel asked. She nodded, afraid to trust her voice.

"Give me a minute or two," he said. They looked at each other. Angel leaned over, smoothed her straggly bangs from her eyes, and kissed her on the forehead. "See you later."

She watched him make for a hiding place farther down, then patted her pocket where the Stone lay. Her face itched from the sooty ashes she had rubbed into her skin to make herself less visible.

Suddenly a voice broke the silence. It was Sam.

"Zvalus!" he called loudly. "Are you listening? In case it escaped your notice, this is a volcanic island. The whole place is going to blow in a matter of hours."

Maybe Sam's spotted us, Sarah thought. *Maybe he's talking so loud to let us know he knows we're here.* Sam went on, "Why do you think all the Wrakir have flown away? Zvalus? Are you there?"

Okay, she thought, *let's go.* She threaded her way among the rocks, testing every step. *Don't make a sound, don't make a sound, don't make a sound.*

Beneath her feet the ground shook. With a groan that sounded almost human, the great slab on the altar tilted, and the body of the Wrakir slid off and hit the ground. Sam wriggled away from it.

Oh, God, she prayed, *don't let Sam get hurt! Don't let anything fall on him.*

She had to move faster. There was a shorter, steeper way down to the open space, through a narrow passage between two slabs of rock. She had to try it.

It was dark in the cleft. She took a first step. Something gave way beneath her foot, something soft. She swallowed a scream. Seconds passed before she could bring herself to look, and more while she waited for the moons to come out from the clouds.

Wedged between the rocks was a Wrakir. Or what was left of him. The creature's neck was twisted at an odd angle, as though he were trying to get a better look at the two moons.

Sarah backed out of the passage, afraid she was going to retch.

"Zva-*lus!*" Sam called. "Where are you?"

Silence. A chill raced up Sarah's backbone and tightened her scalp as if someone were pulling her hair.

He was there. Even before she heard the sibilant whisper, she knew it. She could feel him. He was reciting something, a jump rope rhyme:

> My mother said that I never should
> Play with the gypsies in the wood;
> The wood was dark, the grass was green,
> In came Sally with her tambourine.

He crouched on a rock just above her, his wings folded. His eyes, fixed on her, were mere slits in a mask that was part scabbed flesh, part glittering scales. He had shed his clothes, and in the darkness his white skin—where skin remained— stood out in pale, leprous patches.

Sarah froze. The Stone! She mustn't let him—

His hand shot toward her, no longer a hand but a claw, a claw with long, curving talons. One of them grazed her arm. A thin beaded line of blood appeared.

"It's almost time, little Sarah," he said in a raspy whisper. "The last tea party. I knew in the end it would be the two of us, face-to-face. From the moment I first saw you—on the library stairs, do you remember?—I knew that you were my real adversary."

Another tremor shook the island. Sarah covered her head with her arms as rocks broke loose and bounced past them.

"Doctor?" It was Oskar's voice. "Where are you? Answer me, please!"

"He's up here!" Sarah cried. Maybe Angel would hear, would realize she couldn't get to Sam. . . .

"He's up here," Zvalus mocked. "Poor, loutish Oskar. He doesn't understand. But you do, don't you, Sarah? You know the metamorphosis is incomplete. But soon I shall come into my glory. All the powers of darkness will be within my grasp." Suddenly he stood and spread his leathery wings.

> I went to the sea—no ship to get across;
> I paid ten shillings for a blind white horse;
> I up on his back and was off in a crack. . . .

He sprang nimbly to another rock and stood looking down at the lake, which once again had begun to seethe and bubble.

> Sally tell my mother I shall never come back!

Above the surface of the ooze, blue flames leaped, hovering like wraiths before they vanished and once more reappeared.

Sarah saw her chance and clambered down the rocks.

Oskar passed her, barely taking notice. "Doctor!" he panted, scrambling after Zvalus. "Where are you going?"

A crack shattered the air, so loud it sounded like a rifle going off next to her ear. The island groaned and heaved. Boulders broke away from the peaks and hurtled down, striking sparks and raising fine clouds of powder.

"Sam!" Sarah screamed. "Where are you?"

But it was Angel's voice that reached her through the din. "Down here! Hurry!"

She slipped and fell the last few yards down the incline, reaching them just as Angel flung aside the last rope and helped Sam to his feet.

"Are you okay?" Sam yelled at her. "Where were you? Where'd you go?"

Sarah waved off the question. "We've got to get out of here!" She grabbed his arm.

"Look!" Angel shouted. Zvalus was nearing the edge of the crater. A long finger of rock extended out into the lake. He stepped onto it.

"Doctor!" Oskar called from behind him. "Come back!"

A burst of blue fire from the lake lit up the scene like a stage set: the towering peaks in the background, the great pool of ooze, and the two lone figures on the promontory, feet from each other.

"Leave me!" Zvalus cried hoarsely as Oskar drew nearer.

"Come back! Sir, I beg you. . . ."

The two figures entwined, swaying back and forth. Then Zvalus broke Oskar's hold, lifted him off his feet, and flung him into the lake.

Sam drew a sharp breath. "Oh, God . . ."

Oskar's head bobbed above the surface. *"Why?"* he screamed. Then he sank into the ooze.

The lake bubbled furiously, hissing and spitting. Scalding drops stung Sarah's face and hands. A fireball exploded over the surface. In its light they saw Zvalus standing poised at the tip of the promontory, wings extended.

Sam's fingers pressed into her arm.

"Master!" Zvalus cried. "Lord of Shadows! Make me one with thee!"

Zvalus sprang from the rock, his wings supporting him for a moment before he veered to one side and plunged into the cauldron.

"He's gone!" Angel breathed.

Sarah stared at the spot where Zvalus had disappeared. Surely he *was* gone, and yet . . . A terrifying possibility took shape in her mind. *The metamorphosis is incomplete.* What if it had been Zvalus the Umbra wanted as a sacrifice all along, not the Wrakir?

The ground rose and dipped like a wave, so hot it burned the soles of her feet.

"We've got to make it to the water!" Sam yelled. "It's our only chance!"

"No! Hold on to me, both of you!" *Please,* Sarah prayed, gripping the Stone with all her strength. *Save us.* From miles beneath the crater came a roar that drowned out every other sound.

Her lungs burned. "Hold on!" she cried, but she couldn't even hear her own voice. Across the lake the peaks shuddered.

This is it, Sarah thought. The roar grew louder, and the whole island shook like an engine racing out of control. Nearly the last thing she saw was something rising from the lake, something with wings. Then a red flash lit the sky and the crater exploded.

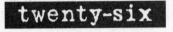

twenty-six

The Shadow in the Door

Sarah lay facedown, clutching the Stone. Beneath her the ground rolled, like a ball slowly coming to a stop. She took a deep, grateful breath of cool air and opened her eyes.

Sam and Angel lay sprawled nearby in the tall silvery grass. And there, towering above her, was the Door.

Sarah rose. She stood on a hilltop at the base of the great portal, overlooking a glittering sea. Framed by the arch, the sea and sky looked like a painting come to life. The arch itself seemed alive; the graceful limbs of the Dreaming Trees twined among creatures with wings and fins and horns to form intricate patterns. Carved in stone, even the ugly features of the Wrakir took on a homely dignity.

At the pinnacle of the arch the flower nestled among its leaves. The center of the flower lay empty, waiting like a setting for its jewel.

Waiting for the Stone.

But how was she ever going to reach the flower, so hopelessly far above her head? From behind her an eerie wailing rose: The Thealkir were leading a procession up the slope toward the Door in measured cadence, their branches sheltering a multitude of creatures. The mournful sound they made reverberated up through her feet, as though rising from deep underground.

They don't know I have the Stone, Sarah thought. *They wouldn't cry like that if they knew.*

Sam scrambled to his feet, cleaning his glasses on his shirttail.

The throng drew closer. Altair and Foxfire walked among the smaller animals, the stallion's white coat smudged with dirt, his proud head drooping with weariness. Flocks of birds circled and cried. In the distance Wrakir approached.

The multitude gathered in a half circle around the three humans. The eerie keening stopped. There was a restless settling of wings and leaves and hooves, and then silence.

One of the trees moved forward. For a moment Sarah failed to recognize Miladras. His leaves, his beautiful leaves! They were nearly gone, his branches stripped and bare.

"Miladras!" She ran to him, held out the Stone. "Look!"

But the tree made no reply.

"What's wrong? Why don't you say something?"

"It is the hour of the Shadow," the tree answered at last. "The Umbra comes to claim Oneiros."

"*No!*" Angel stepped up. "We can keep it out! Sarah will put the Stone back!"

A cold wind raced across the landscape, flattening the grass.

"I don't understand. . . ." Sarah faltered. "I thought . . ."

"The Umbra put you to the test in the realm of illusion. You might have relinquished the Stone and become nothing more than a shadow yourself, but you prevailed. Now it will summon all the powers of darkness to keep you from the Door. You have seen but a little of that power at work. . . ."

"In Zvalus," Sarah said.

"Zvalus is dead!" Angel cried. "We saw him die!"

But what had she seen rising from the lake just before the crater exploded?

The wind rose, filling the air with the smell of smoke. It was blowing in through the Door.

"Miladras!" Sarah clung to him, the great, slow drumbeat of his heart vibrating throughout her frame.

"Our foe is mightier than we," he said. "What we lack in strength we must have in courage."

On the horizon clouds gathered with astonishing speed. They writhed and swelled, turning inside out to reveal linings of lurid red and purple.

As if from miles away Sarah heard one of the Wrakir screaming and felt her spirit torn by dread.

"No!" she groaned. Suddenly she saw what she had not allowed herself to see until now: that it was her fault, that if she had listened to the Amarantha in the beginning, if she had returned the Stone to the Door instead of pulling back in fear and confusion, none of this would be happening.

It's true, she thought in despair. *It's true.* But no matter how sorry she was, no matter how much she wished she could erase her mistake, she could never undo the past. There was only this moment, now, with everything hanging in the balance. . . .

"Miladras," she said, her whisper so faint she was unsure he would hear. But of course he heard; he heard her very thoughts. "I will go to the Door."

"Will you do this for us, small one?" Something in his voice frightened her more than the wind. "Do you know what it may mean to bear the Stone to its place now?"

She drew away from him, slowly, until their gaze met. The moment prolonged itself, irreversible. In his silence she read the answer to her unspoken question. But she had no time to think about it, no time even to be afraid.

"I won't let you!" Sam grabbed her arm. "It's too dangerous! I took the Stone, I ought to be the one to put it back—"

"No!" Angel broke in. His eyes searched her face. And then, as if he had seen what he hoped to find, he said, "Sarah is the Stone-Bearer."

Sam quickly drew her close. "Are you sure?" he whispered into her hair.

Sarah nodded, not trusting herself to speak.

"Come, then," Miladras said, his voice like a river. "I shall lift you up and bear you to the Door."

High, then higher still, Miladras raised her, relaying her from one branch to the next until she reached his topmost branches and braced herself with outstretched arms. The tree straightened, took his first step.

A wave of force rolled over them. Miladras lurched and stumbled. Her hands slid along his branches as if they were glass. At the last second the tree caught her.

Angel and Sam called out to her, shouting over the roar of the wind. A moment later even the sound of their voices was lost. Once more Miladras moved forward.

At first it was no more than a black stain on the air, the Shadow in the Door: night black, black as the darkness she had seen when, lost in the city, she glimpsed what lay beneath the faces in the crowd. This was the darkness of utter despair, the darkness that swallowed up all meaning. Now it grew and spread and beat the air until a body took shape, a monstrous winged beast with the head of a man.

There was no need for it to speak. They both knew what it wanted.

Miladras took another step.

The beast opened its jaws, and smoke poured from its throat, and from the coiling smoke demonic figures took shape and flew at them. The figures groaned, spit, shrieked, filling the air with the hissing of gossips, the hoarse threats of torturers, the laughter of assassins.

Miladras dragged himself forward, but the Door seemed no nearer than before. Sarah's heart sank. Even if they managed to reach the Door, they would only come face-to-face with the thing waiting there.

The burning eyes of the beast fastened on Sarah. From the bedlam of voices a single voice rose. "You," it said. "I know who you are." After every syllable a thousand other voices trailed, echoing, beating against her eardrums:

"Stinking bag of blood and bones!"

"Mud and spit!"

"Bones and blood!"

The solitary voice spoke again, this time at her ear. "I know all your secrets," it said. And then, in poisonous whispers, the thousand voices named every action and thought of which she had ever felt ashamed, things she had long forgotten, things she had hidden even from herself. The voices grew louder, accusing, taunting, condemning.

"Stop it!" Sarah cried, but she was powerless to make

them stop. There was no longer any barrier between her and the thing in the Door, no protection. It had invaded her soul.

"We are the same," the single voice said. "You are no different from me. I am you. You are me."

No, Sarah screamed silently. *No!*

"The Stone is mine! Oneiros is mine!" shrieked the beast, and immediately the chorus joined in, howling, "Miiiiiinnnne!"

Sarah felt her will disintegrating. *Dear God—help me. . . .*

Miladras stumbled, lost his hold on her, caught her once more. He would not give up, she knew; he would fight to the end. . . .

A wave of love for the tree, for everything brave and good and lovely she had ever known, flooded her like light. She remembered the welcome in her mother's arms, laughter around the dinner table, fires in the fireplace, the sparkle of snow against dark windows. She thought of long blue twilights and wishing stars, and she thought at last of the kingfisher in the trees above the river, of the beauty that caught at her heart for an instant and stayed with her forever.

"I grind it to dust!" cried the Shadow in the Door. "All must come to nothing in the end!"

But Sarah knew a secret, and it sang in her. She offered the treasure of her life—blessing on blessing like an overflowing cup—to the One whose gift it had been. *Whatever we give into love's hands can never be lost.*

From deep within Miladras, Sarah felt a mighty joy rise. It carried them forward, step by deliberate step, a bright sword lifted against the dark.

Sarah's hands cradled the Stone for the last time, lifted it toward the gray heart of the waiting flower. For a span of time so brief it could scarcely be called time at all, she held it in trembling balance against the rim of the circle. Then, like the last piece of a puzzle, it slipped into place.

twenty-seven

Hail and Farewell

Sarah floated, like a balloon, beneath the great green dome of sky. Below her on the ground Sam and Angel huddled over a body. Her body. She looked so small! And her legs seemed ridiculously long. It occurred to her that she ought to be scared, but she felt only a vague connection to the body on the ground, as though the string of her balloon self were anchored there.

"Sarah, Sarah, wake up," Angel was pleading.

"She can't be dead, she can't be!" Sam cried. She saw him pressing his fingers against her neck, searching for a pulse.

It's all right, she sang out, *I'm here.* But the words melted away into nothingness. *Miladras,* she called. *Tell them I'm all right.*

Miladras? Where are you?

No answer came. Suddenly she *was* afraid. She grew heavy with fear, sinking down, down. Then, beneath her back, she felt the ground, the damp grass. She was in her body again. Everything hurt in the familiar places, as if she'd been running barefoot and now had to put on the same pinching, uncomfortable shoes.

"Sarah!" Angel was staring at her. "We thought . . ."

"You weren't breathing!"

With an effort she lifted her head. "Where is Miladras?" She caught the look that passed between Sam and Angel. "What is it?" Sarah asked. "What's happened?"

"Sarah," Sam began, but she wasn't listening. She braced herself on his shoulder, stood up on wobbly legs.

Fallen branches lay strewn all over the ground near the Door. All that remained standing was a blackened trunk.

For a moment she could not take it in. She staggered. Someone caught her elbow.

"No—" She pulled away, walked toward the tree, stepping over a broken bough. All his eyes were closed, sealed shut. From the corner of one of them ran a glistening line. She neared the trunk, held out her hand.

His skin was still warm.

Miladras! She fell against him, circled his trunk with her arms, her cheek pressed hard against the smooth bark. For an instant she thought she felt his heartbeat. But no. His great heart had fallen still. She would never hear his voice again, never rest beneath his golden shade.

He was gone, gone like Mother and Daddy. . . . She clung to him, her eyes squeezed shut, her heart a knot of pain in her chest, twisting tighter and tighter until she couldn't bear it a moment longer, and still it grew worse. She heard a thin, high wailing and realized it was her own voice, but she couldn't make it stop.

Miladras, Miladras!

She sank down among the ruined branches and held a sheaf of charred leaves to her chest, rocking back and forth. A hand touched her shoulder. Angel.

"Why did they have to die?" she sobbed, leaning against his leg. "Why?"

He stroked her hair but did not speak.

For a long time there was no sound but the sound of her crying, but then, one by one, the Thealkir began to sing, drawing her anguish up through their roots and branches and breathing it out again through the long, mournful syllables that hung vibrating in the air. On and on they sang, giving voice to her sorrow and theirs, making of it something haunting and beautiful and lasting. They sang of Miladras, of the garden he had created, of his great wisdom and his bravery when he had carried the Stone-Bearer to the Door. And as they sang, the clouds flew like gold and scarlet banners overhead.

When the last voice faded away, there was silence. Beneath the high arch of the Door a column of blinding white light began to glow. The air was filled with the scent of roses.

The Amarantha appeared, light cascading from her, spilling out onto the grass. Sarah heard Sam catch his breath. Angel knelt on one knee, like a knight, and bowed his head.

"Rise," the Amarantha said to him, her voice like water over stones. "Though I am a spirit and you a king, we are both servants."

King? Sarah looked at Angel, but he did not look back.

The Amarantha turned to Sarah. "You have done well, Stone-Bearer. Your work here is finished."

"But Miladras—," Sarah began.

"It was the destiny he chose, Sarah-kir. As you chose to bear the Stone, he chose to bear you."

"But I don't understand!"

"How shall I explain? The answers to your questions are written in a language you have not yet learned to speak."

"But will I? One day?" It seemed the most important question in the world.

"Remember the words of Miladras. Follow the path that leads to the Light." The Amarantha looked beyond Sarah at the creatures assembled on the hillside below. "Will you now do one last thing for these you have saved? Set aside your grief, that all may rejoice."

Sarah glanced over her shoulder at the crowd. She wasn't sure she could do what the Amarantha asked, but she would have to try. She nodded in answer.

The Amarantha spread her arms, scattering radiance. "Draw near, friends! Death has been turned from your Door! The Stone has returned to the Flower!"

A roar of gladness went up as the throng surged toward the Door. In moments Sarah, Sam, and Angel were surrounded.

The Amarantha looked over the three humans thoughtfully. "Perhaps you would like to make yourselves a bit more presentable before the celebration?"

They all glanced down. In the brilliant light cast by the Amarantha their clothes looked shabbier and dirtier than ever. Sarah's hands were stained with blood, her own and Sam's and the Wrakir's; the creases of her knuckles were black with grime.

"Yes," Sarah said. "Yes, *please.*" They followed the Amarantha down a winding stone staircase that ended at the edge of the sea. Angel and Sam, accompanied by a crowd of Wrakir, disappeared around the other side of some rocks.

"You may bathe here," the Amarantha said to Sarah. "The Loriakir will attend you."

"Who—," Sarah asked, but the Amarantha was already gliding up the staircase. Sarah took off her clothes and rolled them into a ball, then walked across the fine sand, straight into the water. It slid like silk against her skin. She could hear Sam and Angel on the other side of the cove as they waded in. Their voices were subdued, but there was a boyish happiness in them too, a delight in the water, the gift of it. As she listened, the heaviness in her heart lifted and floated away.

The setting sun turned the water into a sea of gold. Sarah lay back in it, letting it support her. High in the glowing green sky stars appeared, one by one, the same stars that had shone down on her that first night so long ago, when she had huddled fearfully in Miladras's garden. Now she found their names on her lips: the great blue star, Mirador, in the constellation of the Vine; Thira and Belwyn, the Eyes of Night; Archelon, Ozmir, and Dariel in the Crown of the Wayfaring King.

The Amarantha had called Angel a king. What could it mean? Sarah thought suddenly of the crown of leaves Angel had been wearing when she found him at the cove, his grief when she had told him of the prophecy of doom, and the way the Wrakir had flown away at his command, as if it somehow recognized his authority.

She didn't want it to be true. All along she had imagined that if they survived, the three of them would go back to Earth together. She hadn't thought much beyond that: where they would go, how they would live. She had thought only of going home.

But where was home? She and Sam couldn't go back to Sycamore Farm. Still, they had to return to Earth. They had to warn people—the government, someone in authority. CIPHER was still dangerous, even without Zvalus. Back on Earth the Umbra roamed at will—no, she wouldn't think about that now. There would be time enough.

The faraway sound of singing filled the air, and coming toward her across the water she saw what looked like a school of fish. But they were less like fish than women with greenish bronze skin and long, seaweedy hair, and less like women than sprays of sea foam, so lightly and quickly did they move through the water. The Loriakir swept around her, in and out of the water, scrubbing her skin with a sponge and washing her hair with a sweet-smelling cream they scooped from a shell. They combed and braided it in an elaborate arrangement. They even filed her jagged finger-nails with a pebbly stone. Finally they led her to the shallows, rubbed a perfumed ointment into her skin, and swam away, singing.

Sarah waded from the water and crossed the sand. In place of her dirty clothes lay a garment that looked as if it had been spun of spiderwebs and moonlight, and beside it, a wide belt set with opalescent stones. A small drawstring pouch hung from the belt. Someone had emptied the pockets of her jeans and tucked Angel's wooden comb and bandanna into the pouch. She picked up the gown—weightless as mist—and slipped it over her head. Then she fastened the belt around her waist and spun in a circle, the skirt floating out around her.

"Angel?" she called.

"I'm here." As though he had been waiting for a word from her, Angel stepped out from behind the rocks. He wore an emerald tunic and loose trousers. The cloth shimmered in the dusk. He walked toward her across the sand, a tall figure in flowing green, the breeze off the ocean tousling his hair, his face full of light.

Words formed in her mind: *Here is the one we have waited for.*

He reached her, clasped her hands. "How beautiful you look!"

"So do you."

They were scarcely aware of Sam's approach. He was walking along, fiddling with the belt around his ivory tunic, the Wrakir close behind, carrying a bundle of clothing. When Sam looked up and saw Sarah, he stopped in his tracks.

"What a transformation!" He looked from her face to Angel's and back again. "So, are we ready?"

"We'll be there in a little while," Angel said, never taking his eyes from Sarah's.

"You'll tell them, won't you, Sam?" she asked.

"Sure. Just don't be too long." He quickly kissed Sarah's cheek and, glancing at Angel, walked away toward the stone staircase, with the Wrakir lumbering after him.

Sarah turned to Angel. "You knew?" she asked. "All along?"

"Only that I belonged here."

He held her hands flat against his chest. "Stay with me, Sarah. I'll take care of you. I'll do anything to make this home for you, I promise."

"Angel . . ." She couldn't speak. Through the cloth of his tunic she felt his heart beating against her palms.

"It's all right. I know." He put his arms around her, and she breathed in the smell of him, the smell of wildness and summer and all she would leave behind. "You have to go back. I have to stay. But how can I say good-bye to you?"

She held him closer. He was crying, she knew, not even trying to hide it. For a moment he was simply her Angel again, the boy who had found her in her loneliness, her friend, her love, no one's king. "Don't," she said. "You'll make me cry too. . . ." But she was already crying.

"No, no more tears," Angel whispered brokenly. "No more." He wiped hers away with a fingertip, brushed away his own. "Listen," he said, "wherever you go, whatever happens, I'm with you. And you're with me."

He kissed her as he had done long ago in the stable, his lips against her temples, her closed eyes, her mouth. Then they walked, arms around each other's waists, beside the moonlit sea.

By the time they started back, night had truly fallen and the sky was thick with stars. Hand in hand they climbed the stairs to the Door and were greeted by cheering creatures who formed two circles around them, one inside the other.

Angel gave her a boost onto Altair's back and mounted Foxfire. The horses had been bathed too, brushed until their coats were glossy, flowers twined in their manes. Sam was claimed by a Wrakir, the homeliest of the bunch, but looking so austere and solemn as he carried Sam on his massive shoulders that Sarah didn't dare to laugh.

The two circles revolved in different directions around

her, dancing and chanting. In every face sweeping past she saw the same joy and relief and knew they all had shared what had seemed to her a solitary battle, all carried her to the Door by the momentum of their individual wills united against the dark.

The chanting grew louder as the creatures dipped and swayed according to some ancient pattern. The circles became two lines leading up to the Door. The Amarantha stood at one end, beneath the arch, Sarah and Angel at the other. The chanting died away.

"Come forward," the Amarantha said. They rode in silence up the long row and slid off the horses to stand before her. Next to them was Sam, hands clasped behind his back. He wore the same serious expression he did in church.

"Excuse me, Your . . . Your Ladyship," Sam said. "There's something I have to ask. It was you, wasn't it, who put the equations in the tree house?"

"It was."

"But why? Why did you make it possible for me to take the Stone?"

"I knew you would soon discover the equations on your own," the Amarantha explained. "Once you had done so, nothing would dissuade you from carrying out your experiments. And you had already begun your search for a living planet like your own."

"But it might have taken *generations* of human beings to find their way here using the Looking Glass! And they might never have stumbled across Oneiros!"

"And in the meantime, how many other worlds might have fallen under the Shadow, as CIPHER's power grew and spread?" the Amarantha asked. "There was danger in show-ing you the way here, in allowing you to take the Stone from the Door, but even greater danger in waiting. I left the equa-tions to hasten and guide you, trusting that in you Oneiros would have a friend."

"But Miladras's death," Sam began, his eyes stricken, "and Freeg's and the others'—none of that would have hap-pened if I hadn't taken the Stone."

"Victory comes only at a cost. But victory it is. Zvalus is dead. The Umbra has been dealt a great blow. And much other good has come to pass, which might have come by no other way. To bring light from deepest darkness, good from evil—this is the Great Magic, the work of the One Whose Name Cannot Be Spoken."

The Amarantha raised her eyes to the crowd. "For time beyond remembrance the Thealkir have dreamed of one who would save Oneiros from the Shadow. She stands before you now. She has overcome danger and fear and the craft of the Umbra, relinquishing much, that her hands might be free to carry the Stone. You, Samuel, opened the way for the Stone-Bearer.

"The Thealkir have dreamed of another as well, a king who would roam the planet until he knew every river and hill and branching path, who would guard and protect the crea-tures of Oneiros and be the keeper of the Door. You, Stone-Bearer, have brought us our Wayfaring King."

Sarah looked sidelong at Angel. His head was bowed, his hands at his sides.

"By what signs shall we know the destined one?" the Amarantha called out.

"By the golden ring he wears!" came the message from one of the Thealkir.

"By the name, his secret name!" sang another.

"And by the love he bears for the planet," Sarah said, recalling something Miladras had told her, "for all the creatures beneath the green sky."

Angel lifted his eyes and looked at Sarah. It was a look she knew she would carry in her heart for the rest of her life.

"Give me your ring," the Amarantha said, and Angel slipped it from his finger and handed it to her. "Within this ring are three words in an ancient tongue of Oneiros, long forgotten. There are yet a few of the Thealkir who will teach you it, if you are willing."

"The ring came from here? But how did it—"

"That is a tale for another long night. Give me your hand," she said.

"My lady . . ."

"Speak."

"A king should be good and wise, and I'm—"

"Only the one who knows himself to be neither wise nor good can begin to be either," the Amarantha said. "What is the secret name you bear?"

"My name is Jal."

A happy murmur ran through the crowd as they repeated the name.

"Jal, do you love Oneiros?"

Angel paused. "Yes. More than myself."

"Then you are the one we have awaited." One of the Thealkir moved forward slowly and held out a wreath of leaves. Sarah saw that some of them were scorched from the battle, their edges curled and blackened. Miladras's leaves.

The Amarantha placed the leafy crown on Angel's head and held high the ring. It glinted in the moonlight.

"Jal," she began, "hear the words written in the ring: 'Seek the Light.' May the Sower plant within your heart the seeds of wisdom, courage, and compassion. May your roots grow deep and your dreams great." She slipped the ring on his finger. "Reign in peace."

"Creatures of Oneiros!" she called. "The Stone-Bearer and King Jal!" Wild cheering broke out. Angel held Sarah's hand, and the two of them looked out over the crowd as once again the creatures began to dance.

A sensation of melting sweetness spread through Sarah, a longing so powerful it brought tears to her eyes, like homesickness, yet what she yearned for was a place she'd never been, her heart's home.

The scene before her shimmered like a reflection on water. She saw that everything—the dancing creatures, the Door, the Amarantha herself—was no more than a picture on the surface of a deeper, more solid reality, a changeless dimension.

Now she looked beyond the surface, into the clear depths beyond. And there, as if in a vision, the Dream of the Stone unfolded. Sarah saw, in every detail, all that had passed and the part she had played in it. Like a bright thread in a living tapestry, her own story was woven in, becoming part of the one great story, the story that had begun before time and would go on when time itself was no more.

She felt the grass beneath her feet. Angel was at her side,

his arms around her. Effortlessly, as though they had danced this way a hundred times, they fell into step, their feet flying over the ground. When at last they stopped, the horizon was glowing with a light that tinted the sea a deep rose. A feathered cloud, like the wing of a great sheltering bird, stretched across the sky.

They stood facing each other, holding hands. Angel brushed a strand of hair from her forehead. Sarah saw in his eyes what they both knew. In silence they walked to the Door, where Sam and the Amarantha waited.

She knelt beside the broken tree and placed one hand against his bark, still soft as living flesh. "I know you're not here anymore," she told Miladras silently, her tears falling among the leaves. "But this is all I have. Wherever you are, I'll never forget you."

Silently the answer came: *I will carry you in my heart as I bore you in my branches. You will dwell in our dreams forever.*

Something silver glinted among his leaves. For a moment she thought it was only her tears, but when she parted the leaves, she found an apple of the moon. She held it in both hands, her head bowed. "Thank you, my friend."

Sam helped her to her feet. Sarah faced the gathering, memorizing each face as her eyes passed over them. "I will carry all of you in my heart."

"May your roots grow deep and your dreams great!" called one of the Thealkir.

"May you seek the Light in every season!"

"Farewell, Stone-Bearer! Farewell, Brother!"

Sarah put the moon apple in the pouch on her belt. "You may need this," Angel said, taking his denim jacket from a

Wrakir who stood to one side, holding it in his claws. Angel slipped the jacket over her shoulders. Then he broke a leaf from his crown and placed it in her hand. "Remember me."

"As long as I live." She added the leaf to the small collection in the pouch and carefully tied the drawstring. "I have nothing to give you."

"Nothing?" He opened his arms as if to embrace the throng of creatures, the horses, the sea, the sky. "You've given me this. You've given me my dream."

The Amarantha raised her hand in blessing. "Dwell in peace! Blessed be the One Whose Name Cannot Be Spoken!"

"Blessed be He throughout all worlds!" came the response.

The Amarantha turned.

"Wait!" Sarah cried, dropping Sam's hand. "Ozymandias!"

"Here, cat!" Angel called. Ozzie dropped from a tree and trotted toward them, his tail a question mark. Sarah scooped him up.

"Ready?" Sam asked.

Sarah looked at Angel.

He touched her cheek, kissed her one last time. "Ja develesa."

"Go with God," she whispered. "Good-bye, my Angel."

Sam took her hand. The Amarantha turned, her long hair rippling behind her, sweeping around Sam and Sarah like a shining cloak. She lifted her cloudless eyes and looked through the Door at something visible only to her gaze.

"Come," she said, and they followed her through the Door.

twenty-eight

Almost Home

Sarah and Sam stood in a circle of light beneath an iron lamppost. All around them snowflakes whirled and spun away into the night. The Amarantha was nowhere in sight.

"Just like that," Sam said in amazement. Sarah clutched Ozzie to her chest. The damp air of the place smelled faintly familiar, a mixture of coal smoke and diesel fumes and wet greenery.

"Where are we?" She looked around, suddenly aware of the cold earth under her bare feet. Dark, billowing shapes of trees stood silhouetted against the dim glow of the night sky. In the distance rose spires, a tower. Ozzie squirmed. She was holding him too tightly. Not far away a bell began to ring. Another answered it, and then another from farther away.

"Bells," Sam said. "Wait a minute . . ." He turned in a circle, arms extended. "I know where we are! Come on!" Then he started down a wide path, his loose trousers flapping around his legs. Sarah hurried after him, between orderly rows of bushes, past a park bench and an enormous holly tree heavy with clusters of red berries. The drawstring pouch at her waist bounced against her hip.

They ran through tall iron gates and stood on a corner.

"That's the Banbury Road!" Sam said. "And look!" He pointed to a street sign on the low wall that bordered the sidewalk. "Norham Gardens! We're in Oxford, Sarah!"

"England?"

As if in answer, a red double-decker bus rumbled past beneath the streetlights on the Banbury Road. Ozzie stiffened and sank his claws into Sarah's arm. The bus stopped to pick up a very old lady standing under the bus shelter. As the old woman climbed onto the bus, Sarah thought she saw her turn and raise a hand in cheerful farewell.

"Sam—," Sarah began, but he was already running down the sidewalk in the falling snow, waving his arms as if he were about to take off. Oxford! It was almost home, Sarah thought, starting after him. On either side of the street called Norham Gardens stood the enormous Victorian houses she remembered, with turrets and leaded windows and small, scruffy front yards bordered by low brick walls. Only they weren't called front yards, Sarah reminded herself, they were called gardens. Near the end of the street they stopped in front of a house where the windows were brightly lit. In the big bay window on the first floor, through a lace curtain, they saw the twinkling colored lights of a tree.

"Christmas!" Sarah cried.

"That's why the bells were ringing! It's Christmas Eve!"

"But Sam, how can it be Christmas already? We've only been gone a little while, and it was October when—"

"I told you," Sam said, fiddling with the latch of the creaky iron gate, "the ratio between Earth time and Oneiros time is variable. We're lucky we didn't come back before we left!"

They hurried up the walk to the front door, where the bronze lion door knocker stared imperiously down at them, as if demanding to know why they were there. Sarah shifted Ozzie to one arm, lifted the ring in the lion's mouth, and knocked three times.

"Try again," Sam said. "They may not hear you."

But as she lifted the ring, there was the sound of a bolt being drawn on the other side.

The door opened. A tiny old woman in a red plaid bathrobe stood blinking at them. "Yes?"

Delicious smells floated out the door: nutmeg and roasting goose and freshly baked bread. Through an archway Sarah glimpsed a table set with china and silver, sparkling in candlelight.

"Great-aunt Sophie?" Sarah asked.

The old woman's face broke into a smile. "Sarah dear! And Samuel! In fancy dress, too! Lovely! Oh, what am I thinking of? Do come in, come in!" She beckoned impatiently with her small, gnarled hand, eyes bright as the Christmas tree lights.

The big door closed behind them, shutting out the cold. Great-aunt Sophie leaned forward with a conspiratorial air, patting Sarah's arm: "We've been *expecting* you!"

After taking hot baths and wrapping up in the aunts' soft woolen dressing gowns, Sam and Sarah ate Christmas dinner, and everyone sang carols around the old piano. It was very late by the time the two of them went upstairs and sat before the coal fire in Sarah's room.

Sam groaned, holding his stomach. "Nothing but liver

paste for days, and then *that*! I only ate a few mouthfuls, and I'm stuffed!"

"Me too. It's a good thing Great-aunt Elspeth warned us." Elspeth, who had been a nurse in refugee camps after the war, had taken one look at them, asked how long they'd been without real food, and forbidden them to eat more than one small plateful.

The other aunts had been crestfallen. "Are you quite sure, Elspeth?" Great-aunt Daisy had asked more than once.

"Absolutely," Elspeth replied. "Worst thing in the world. Saw more than one poor blighter kill himself eating. Couldn't stop them. Frightful way to go."

In the end Sarah had taken a tiny bite of everything, from Sophie's chestnut stuffing to Daisy's Christmas cake, just to please them.

Sarah rearranged herself in the big, cozy chair and tucked Great-aunt Daisy's robe around her legs. "I suppose we must look pretty scrawny to them," she said.

"They'll fatten us up in no time. Sophie's already talking about breakfast."

"I forgot to ask her how she knew we were coming."

"Can't you guess?" Sam asked. "Last week Elspeth was taking Jacko for a walk in the park and struck up a conversation with a visiting professor—'extraordinary woman, Latin scholar, too fascinating,'" Sam quoted Elspeth, and they laughed.

"The Amarantha and her disguises," Sarah said.

"They hit it off so well they went to a tea shop, and the lady offered to read Elspeth's tea leaves. Apparently, she had a knack for it, like Latin. She told Elspeth to expect two visitors whose names began with *S* on Christmas Eve."

"I wouldn't be surprised if that private detective the aunts hired knew Latin too."

Over dinner the aunts had told Sam and Sarah the story of their own "little adventure." Not long before the plane crash, Elspeth said, she'd had a conversation with Mother about the provisions in the will. If anything should happen, Mother told Elspeth, Sarah was to come and live with them, at least until Sam could make suitable arrangements.

When the aunts learned that after the funeral Sarah had gone instead to live with Helena and Bernard, they were thrown into confusion. They wrote Sam about their concerns, and he gave them the same answer he'd given Sarah when she objected to living with Bernard and Helena: "But it's in the will."

"Then we made a discovery," Daisy announced a little breathlessly, leaning across the table toward Sam and Sarah. "Our solicitors in London informed us that your parents had recently revised their will and sent them a copy—"

"It was the *real will*, of course," Sophie put in, sliding another sliver of cake onto Sarah's plate, "not the one that awful man fabricated."

"And Bernard must not have realized there *was* another copy of the real will," Sam said.

"Obviously not," Elspeth concluded. "Or I have no doubt he would've contrived to filch it somehow."

At the aunts' insistence their lawyers hired an investigator. The detective traced Helena and Bernard to a rooming house in New Jersey, where they had apparently been banished in disgrace by CIPHER. They admitted to falsifying the will and taking money from Sam and Sarah's trust fund. They would not say what they had done with the money, but Sarah felt sure they had handed it over to the Institute. Just before they were to be charged with the theft, the money was mysteriously returned. But Helena and Bernard had vanished.

"And good riddance, too," Great-aunt Sophie sniffed. "Dreadful people!"

Sarah and Sam were quiet now, watching the fire burn merrily in the grate. "Great-aunt Daisy kept calling me Margaret," Sarah said. "Did you notice?"

"You do look like Mother sometimes. When you smile."

The sound of singing drifted up from the street. "'To save us all from Satan's pow'r when we were gone astray . . .'"

Gradually the voices died away. Sarah rested her head against the wing of the chair and gazed at the fire. When she was little, she had sometimes seen faces in the flames. She didn't want to see any now. She turned to Sam. "It's not over, is it, Sam?"

"Not as long as CIPHER's in business. Losing Zvalus is a major setback, though. And they won't be able to use the Looking Glass."

"But Zvalus and Oskar did."

"By now the virus I introduced into the computer has had a chance to spread. They'll try a disinfectant, of course, but it won't do any good. The infection will have ravaged the whole works." He shook his head. "When I think of how I might have turned the whole thing over to them . . . if I hadn't had that dream about Dad—that's what made me suspicious enough to break into the files in the first place."

"The dream you mentioned in your letter . . ." Suddenly

Sarah was back on the playground bench in Central Park with a paper cone of green ice in one hand and Sam's letter in the other.

"I dreamed I was in Dad's office and he had a computer all in pieces on his desk. When I asked him why he'd taken it apart, he said he had to find out what was in there. And then he said, 'I'm surprised you haven't taken care of this already, Sam. These things can blow up in your face.' So I started to help him. That's when I saw the name of the machine was Decipher. And I knew what I had to do."

Sarah shook off a chill and pulled the bathrobe closer around her. "We have to stop them—we have to tell someone! But who can we trust? They've infiltrated everywhere."

"I've been trying to think about it. I will think about it. But right now there's only one thing on my mind."

Sarah closed her eyes and concentrated. "A hot-water bottle?"

"Hey!" Sam looked startled. "Mental radio! Great-aunt Daisy put hot-water bottles in our beds while you were brushing your teeth. And I was thinking that I'd better get in bed soon, or my sheets will be cold."

"Maybe we're finally getting the hang of mental radio," Sarah said. "We should try it again."

There was a scratching at the door. Neither one of them moved to open it.

"Let me guess," Sarah said, putting her hands to her temples. "Yes, I think I am getting the message. Even though you are closer to the door, you want me to get up and open it."

"He's your cat."

"Sam . . ."

Yawning, Sam got up and opened the door for Ozymandias, who sauntered in, explored the four corners of the room, and stretched out in front of the fire.

"I need sleep," Sam said, poking in desultory fashion at the coals. "Why aren't we going to bed?"

"In a minute."

He kissed the top of her head. "Merry Christmas."

"Merry Christmas." Sarah caught his hand. "I love you, Sammers."

"Love you, too, Sally Sue."

She looked up to find Sam gazing thoughtfully at her. "You know something?" he said. "You're a very brave person."

She held his hand against her cheek and looked into the fire. "I don't *feel* brave," she said after a moment. "There didn't seem to be anything else I could do."

"That's what real heroes always say." Sam whipped the trailing cord of his aunt's robe smartly around his waist and tied it. At the doorway he paused, turned, and saluted her.

When he had closed the door, Sarah sat gazing at the flames for a long time. Then she put on a pair of slippers and crept downstairs, through the sleeping house.

The library was dark except for the lights of the Christmas tree. The grandfather clock in the corner ticked comfortingly as Sarah crossed the room to scan the rows of books in the glass cases. Finally she found what she was looking for, tucked it in her pocket, and went back upstairs.

Ozzie sat on the windowsill, looking down at the garden behind the house. The snow had stopped falling. A dusting of white lay over everything, lining the top of the high brick wall, the stone angel in the corner, the bare limbs of the great copper beech. Through the tangle of branches she saw a handful of stars and the full moon.

"As long as one Gypsy is roaming," she whispered, "the end of the world won't come." Angel had told her that before their last good-bye, when they were walking by the sea. "Don't be afraid," he had said. "Not of CIPHER, not of anything. Fear belongs to the Umbra. We are all in God's hands."

Tomorrow, she thought, she would write to Mara and Mr. Muldoon, tell them Angel was all right.

She took the book from her pocket, hung the bathrobe on the bedpost, and quickly climbed into bed. The hot-water bottle was still warm.

The book's red leather cover glowed in the lamplight. Sarah opened it to the flyleaf. Childish writing, shaky but exuberant, marched across the page. Most of the letters were invented ones, squiggles and crosses and circles, but on the next page, in sturdy capitals, was written "MARGA."

That must have been when Elspeth came in the room, Sarah thought. *Mother never got to finish.*

Sarah opened the drawer of the bedside table and rummaged around among the spools of thread, scissors, and old-fashioned hairpins. She had almost given up when she spotted the fat black fountain pen. She uncapped it and drew the nib across a scrap of paper several times until the ink began to flow.

R . . . E . . . T.

Margaret.

Sarah blew softly on the ink until it dried, closed the book, and turned off the lamp. But she was not left in darkness.

Moonlight fell on sleeping streets and snow-covered meadows and poured through the high windows of Sarah's room. It gleamed in the eyes of Ozymandias, watching her from the foot of the bed, and in the buttons of Angel's jacket, hanging on the chair. On the table beside her bed the apple of the moon shone silver.

About the Author

Christina Askounis grew up in a military family and has lived in places as diverse as Okinawa, New Mexico, Oxford, and New York City. She attended Mary Washington College at the University of Virginia, and then earned an MFA in fiction and poetry from The Writing Seminars at Johns Hopkins University while working as a reporter for the *Baltimore News-American*. Following her stint on the city desk, she worked as a scriptwriter for Maryland Public Television and wrote a Peabody Award–winning series on the environment. Her short fiction has appeared in *Redbook*, *First*, and *Image: A Journal of the Arts and Religion*. Christina's feature-length screenplay, *Enchantment*, was a finalist in the 2000 Moondance Film Festival. She now lives in Durham, North Carolina, where she teaches writing at Duke University and recently received a Distinguished Teaching Award.

WITHDRAWN